———————————— ★ ————————————

The killing floor was the first floor: in a room on the first floor—specifically the front room; a huge room with a cavernous ceiling; the room that would have been the master bedroom. There were specks of dried blood on the wall, on the floor, in a corner farthest from the door and the window. Some months old, by all appearances, but blood nonetheless. There were bin-liner bags, later totaled to number nineteen by the scene of crimes officer, a carpenter's trestle, and, much used, a hacksaw, blood bespattered, and spare hacksaw blades, new and unused.

———————————— ★ ————————————

Also available from Worldwide Mystery by
PETER TURNBULL

LONG DAY MONDAY

PETER TURNBULL

THE KILLING FLOOR

WORLDWIDE.®

TORONTO • NEW YORK • LONDON
AMSTERDAM • PARIS • SYDNEY • HAMBURG
STOCKHOLM • ATHENS • TOKYO • MILAN
MADRID • WARSAW • BUDAPEST • AUCKLAND

THE KILLING FLOOR

A Worldwide Mystery/October 1996

First published by St. Martin's Press, Incorporated.

ISBN 0-373-26215-9

Printed in U.S.A.

THE KILLING FLOOR

ONE

Wednesday, 02.20-09.27 hours

THE MAN LOOKED about him. He saw blue flashing lights sweeping the roadway, and brief glimpses of the houses and the trees brilliantly piercing the night and the rain which fell vertically and relentlessly. The man saw the pillars and garrets of the prestigious Pollokshields houses, each set squarely and solidly and confidently and uncompromisingly in its own grounds. Many of the houses burned the lights as the occupants were roused by the police activity in the street. Above the blue flashing lapping lights were the soft yellow sodium streetlights. The man looked up at them briefly. He shut his eyes and opened them again and looked at the car, front end damaged, wheels damaged on impact with the kerb, and now resting half on and half off the roadway. Beyond the car was a gaping hole, a gap, in a wooden fence. Beyond the fence was shrubbery; in the shrubbery was yet another light, white this time, fixed to a metal pole at shoulder height and under the white light was a mound covered by a black plastic sheet, shiny in the rain.

The man's feet were cold; his shoes were old, they leaked and even when new were more suited to dry summer weather. The rain trickled off the brim of his fedora and down his neck, seeped in through his coat which, like his shoes, was also old and designed for use in mild weather. He glanced at his watch, 02.20 by the illuminated digital display. Yet he thought it warm, warm for January, but oh, so wet, as only it can be in the west of Scotland. Not cold, bitingly numbingly cold, not this winter; this winter the fuel won't freeze in the feed pipes of the buses and bring them to a halt as it has done in winters well within living memory, nor would it be snowbound as is the popular myth of Scotland's winters, but it was warm, warm for January, ten degrees above freezing perhaps, and that meant rain. Not fierce, briefly lasting, driving down in stair rods, causing actual discernible weight to fall on heads and shoulders, but relentless, incessant precipitation which had started some twenty-four hours earlier and still showed no sign of abating. But abate it would, for an hour, or a few hours and then it would start again and rain for two days and stop again, briefly. That had been the pattern since, well, the man pondered, well, since November, and by Christmas weather observers were predicting the wettest winter for the west of Scotland since records began.

The man turned and his eye was caught by the most recently arrived vehicle, a black van, two men inside, one irreverently smoking, and the other irreverently reading the morning edition of the *Daily Record* which had been available since before midnight. The two men had parked their vehicle in an interesting way or so the man observed: not so near as to get in the way, not so near as to be ordered to move back, but close enough to announce to any onlookers that they were part of the action. The man turned away and pondered the mound underneath the shiny plastic sheet and moved his feet and toes in the sock of water which his shoes had become, and he felt his hat tighten on his head as the rain shrank the leather band which ran around the inside. He didn't need this, he didn't need this at all, not at sixty years of age; he'd had it all before, more than thirty years of it, and he couldn't use it any more, not in the rain, causing dull aches in his fingers and knees; he couldn't use it at 02.20 on a January morning. The man's name was Sussock, he was a cop, and he felt he'd been too long at the job and he really couldn't use it any more.

And it had all started because a man driving a bronze-coloured BMW had broken a golden rule of the road: he'd swerved to avoid an animal. Swerve to avoid humans, but never swerve to avoid running over an animal.

'I knew I shouldn't have done it.' The man had chatted, nervously, excitedly. The first cop on the scene took the cigarettes from the fumbling fingers of the man, lit one and pushed the smouldering nail between the man's lips. It would have to be extinguished before he got in the ambulance, but that vehicle was then still to arrive and so the man leaned against the traffic car and said, 'But I did. That's it.'

The driver later gave a statement. He was driving down Sherbrooke Avenue, Pollokshields, fast, he conceded, but it was past midnight. He was in a hurry. He was sober. But all right, it was fast, fast, fast—I mean it is a BMW—kicking up spray like a speedboat. A fox ran into his path. He swerved, lost control, lost it completely; foot crushed the brake pedal but the car was travelling. And it was wet. Then it all seemed to happen in slow motion, the wooden fence, the shrubs, the silence. A routine job for the traffic police and the ambulance crew.

Sussock's eye was caught by a pair of headlights slowly probing the gloom, turning into the avenue from

Nithsdale Road, moving at walking pace and then increasing speed slightly as the driver saw the blue flashing lights and began to close in on the locus with confidence. Eventually as the car entered the spill of the streetlamp the headlights revealed themselves as belonging to a silver Volvo estate car. Sussock smiled. Things, he thought, would start to move now. He slopped in wet shoes towards the Volvo, and reached the vehicle just as the driver stepped out into the rain, wearing a deerstalker hat and an Australian 'drizabone' stockman's coat.

'Good morning, sir.' Sussock spoke with a forced cheerfulness.

'Good morning, Sergeant.' Reynolds smiled and nodded and the two men fell into step walking towards the blue and white police tape which had been strung over the BMW-sized gap in the wooden fencing. 'What do you have for me this fine morning?'

'A corpse, sir,' he said. He pondered an immediate afterthought: Why on earth else would the police summon a pathologist from his bed at 2.00 a.m.? 'I mean a much decomposed one and one without head or hands.'

'Intriguing.' Reynolds ducked under the police tape. Sussock followed and was dismayed to discover that the simple act of bending down and then up again caused the same hollow feeling in his stomach that it had once, in his youth, taken the exertion of a cross-country run to induce. 'It's a case of serendipity,' he said. 'Isn't that the word for "useful discovery"?'

'Or some such. You mean it was found by accident?'

'Yes, sir. Quite literally. A motorist, now in hospital with shock, swerved to avoid a fox which ran into his path, lost control, and you see the result. Traffic attended and called the duty garage and asked them for a tow truck. As the garage crew were winching the car out of the shrubs they came across the body, the car had landed squarely on top of it, and one of the crew who was following the vehicle out of the shrubs actually tripped over the corpse. Fortunately the traffic cops had hung around rather than just leaving the garage crew at it. Traffic called in requesting CID attendance. I came out, being on the graveyard shift, and I took one look and requested your attendance. I am sorry to have called you from your bed at this hour...'

'That's what I'm here for. It happens from time to time. At such times I try to slip away from my wife without waking her. She's a light sleeper to say the least. Gustav enjoys it though.'

'Gustav?'

'Our St Bernard. I never leave the house without something in my stomach, Sergeant, because you never know how long you'll be working and in what weather conditions; you never know what a call-out will lead to. I didn't want to keep you waiting, but I had a coffee and a bacon sandwich before I left the house. That meant Gustav got a bit of grilled bacon and a romp in the garden. I live in this area, just round the corner, and I know what you mean by the foxes. In recent years the fox has moved down from the hills and into the city. Apparently there are still foxes in the hills who live as predators, but the fox that has really multiplied is the fox that's moved into the city and who lives as a scavenger. They enjoy the mature gardens in this part of Glasgow, and the endless supply of dustbins to turn over. Anyway Gustav likes to get out at night, prowl round his territory, remind the fox of his presence. So he, at least, got rewarded for my being disturbed.'

'I had an arc light set up, sir, as you see. But nothing has been touched or disturbed, over and above the incident where the mechanic tripped over it.'

Reynolds crouched to examine putrefaction with professional interest. He looked about it, sampled the soil and brushed his fingers clean. He turned his attention once more to the corpse, raised his deerstalker— replaced it. 'Aye...' he said. 'Well, as you say, she's been here a good long time. This house, this house here, it's obviously empty, that is to say unoccupied?'

'It appears so. We've knocked fit to raise the dead...'

'Didn't raise this one anyway.' Reynolds stood and grinned at Sussock.

Sussock smiled. 'Wasn't the wisest expression to use, was it?'

'No matter.'

'Couldn't raise anybody. Shone our torches through the windows. It's just a shell, no furniture, nothing. A neighbour, he'd been disturbed by the commotion, he was able to tell us that the house has been unoccupied since last spring, nearly twelve months.'

Reynolds nodded. 'That would be my guess. There's nearly a season's growth in the shrubs and in the garden so far as I can tell in this light. I would think that the corpse was deposited here at about the time the house was vacated.'

'Oh?'

'Yes. I don't want to encroach on your territory, but I don't think that the outgoing occupier had anything to do with the death in question—but like I said, I don't want to encroach.'

'Oh, encroach all you like, sir. I'm clutching at straws and all ears.'

'Well.' Reynolds thrust his hands into the pockets of his 'drizabone'. 'It would seem to me, you see, that if anybody was going to vacate a house knowing that they would be leaving a corpse behind them, they'd bury it or burn it. On the other hand, if somebody wanted to get shot of a corpse they might dump it in the garden of an unoccupied house, especially if they thought that they only needed a few days in which to cover their tracks. In this case they were fortunate that the house remained empty for many, many months, allowing the corpse to assume a state of advanced decomposition, as you see. And as you point out it is sans head and hands, and as you further point out it may well have lain undiscovered for many more months had not a motorist swerved to avoid an urban fox, or if the fox had crossed the road ten feet from where it did cross. I don't suppose there're any more corpses in the shrubbery... just as an afterthought...?'

'We'll be doing a thorough search of the house and grounds in the daylight, sir... I take your point about the outgoing owners not being likely to be involved in this, but I dare say it's a stone that Inspector Donoghue will want to turn over, as he would say.'

'Donoghue,' said Reynolds. 'Yes, good man, Donoghue. Thorough. But there's nothing I can do here. Given this evident stage of decomposition it would be useless to take soil samples, air and body temperature. I'll take samples of vegetation growth from under the corpse; that will help us pin down the time that she was left here because the state of the vegetation will be "trapped" under the body: spring blossom, for example, will be able to be identified as such and would indicate that the body had been deposited here in the springtime. That sort of thing. I'll be able to remove insect life from the corpse at the laboratory, they're always a good clue as to the time of death. Will you be at the PM, Sergeant?'

'I'd like to be there. I'll be able to give Inspector Donoghue verbal feedback when he comes on duty, if I attend the PM, that is.'

'Well, as always, you're more than welcome. Constable.'

'Sir,' snapped a young ashen-faced constable.

'Signal the mortuary van to come up please. I'm ready for them now.'

And at the signal two men, who had parked their van not so close to the locus as to be asked to move back, but close enough to be seen to be part of the action, stirred: one dogged his nail and the other folded up his copy of the *Daily Record*.

IT WAS, mused the man, a strange contrast. Outside it was cold, dark and wet. Inside, in here, it was like this all the year round, night and day; in here the temperature was constant, a little below normal room temperature, or what on cheap gimmicky decorative thermometers would be called the 'comfort zone', and the room was continually illuminated by a series of filament bulbs hidden behind opaque perspex covers.

The room in question was the post-mortem suite, in the mortuary, in the bowels of the Glasgow Royal Infirmary, and the man who pondered as he stood in the room was Detective Sergeant Raymond Sussock. He had left his damp fedora and raincoat in an anteroom and stood, in shabby sports jacket and baggy trousers, reverently in the corner of the room. Dr Reynolds, tall in a crisp starched white coat, adjusted the microphone on his lapel which was attached to a small tape recorder he carried in the pocket of his coat.

Absent on this occasion, and from Sussock's point of view most pleasingly absent, was the mortuary attendant whose eyes glazed as they beheld whichever corpse happened to be on the dissecting table and did so in a manner Sussock, even with his years and his experience, had always found unsettling and endlessly unnerving. Sussock wondered briefly what the mortuary attendant would make of this particular form now lying on the stainless-steel lipped table, without head or hands, departed this life some six or eight months previously, her soul now in a far, far better place, and her earthly remains rotting peacefully, undisturbed in a shrubbery, throughout a damp summer and an even damper winter. And did so not more than three feet from a pavement, hidden from view by a wooden fence and a thick stand of rhododendrons. It was a wonder, he thought, that no one had reported or investigated the inevitable odour. But then the locus was Pollokshields, where people kept to themselves and only the postmen used the pavement. All others drove cars. Now the earthly remains lay here, in a state of advanced decomposition, barely recognizable as one having had human form. Surely, hoped Sussock, even the mortuary attendant would not cast a gleaming eye over such a mound of putrefaction. Or would he? In a sense Sussock wished the man had been there, just so that he could observe his reaction: the plain truth being that there are simply some corpses that are more easily washed down with industrial alcohol than others, and here the man with the gleaming eyes and slicked down hair might have met his match.

'If you'd help me?' Reynolds smiled across the bleach-sealed linoleum towards Sussock.

'Sir?' Sussock returned his undivided attention to the job in hand.

'Could you help me flip her over please, Sergeant.'

'No problem, sir.' Sussock smiled but his gut rose and fell. He walked towards the table.

'All her clothing has been sent to Dr Kay at the forensic science laboratory; she'll be getting on it first thing I'm sure. I've sent samples of plants under the corpse to the Department of Botanical Sciences at the university, to see if they can pin down the last date of growth. Ought to help you, though they'll feed back to myself in the first instance.'

'Of course.'

'Which leaves us with our friend here.' Reynolds drummed his fingers on the lip of the dissecting table. 'Dead men, or as in this case, women, tell us many tales, Sergeant, but the solemn fact is that the longer they are deceased before being found, the less they can tell us. Even despite the fact that American medical students once dissected a 2000-year-old mummified corpse and were able to identify its diet, it remains true that the number of tales a corpse can tell reduces in direct proportion to the time that has elapsed since life became extinct.'

Sussock said 'Uh huh' for the sake of saying something.

'So we have here the anterior of a human female, a white European adult but not aged. Anything between twenty-five years and fifty years, maybe even sixty. Can't be closer than that, yet. But I'll get there. There are no obvious marks of injury on the anterior of the

corpse'—Reynolds spoke for the benefit of his microphone—'and no evident cause of death.'

Sussock glanced at Reynolds.

'Well,' Reynolds replied, noticing Sussock's questioning glance, 'there isn't any evident cause of death.
She may well have lost her head, but that does not tell
us what brought about her death.'

'Of course,' said Sussock again. He looked beyond
Reynolds feeling embarrassed at his question; he looked
at the filament bulbs, at the row of seats inclined on a
steep plane, behind a sheet of glass. He wondered what
the occupants of those seats had witnessed over the
years.

'If you could help me, Sergeant.' Reynolds's gentle
request brought Sussock back to reality, back to the
time and the place. 'Grab a pair of surgical gloves, there
on the trolley, bottom shelf . . . good . . . If you hold the
ankles, as firm as you like; the flesh will be a bit mushy
but the bone structure is intact.'

Sussock did as he was asked and gripped the ankles,
feeling the unpleasant softness of the skin through the
thin membrane of the surgical gloves.

'Clockwise from your end,' said Reynolds, as he
gripped the shoulder. 'Three, two . . . now . . .' and the two
men regarded the posterior view of the much decayed
headless corpse. 'Well,' said Reynolds after a pause, 'I
know that she was found face downwards, or front
downwards, that's how you showed her to me. But I can
tell that she wasn't left face down.'

'No?'

'Not at all. She was moved after death, maybe as
much as a week after death. She was laid on her back,
then flipped over about a week later. The posterior is
much better preserved than the anterior. It indicates that

she lay frontways down and the decay became more advanced where the flesh was in contact with the soil and the flesh-eating insects that live in the soil. The covering of the rhododendrons meanwhile would have impeded the rate of decomposition of the posterior. In fact...' Reynolds took a scalpel and made a short incision in the lumbar region and prised the flesh apart. 'Yes, in fact, there you have hypostasis...'

'I'm sorry?'

'Deposits of blood, which really answers your question of a moment ago, the decapitation didn't cause her death. She was decapitated after death. If she had been decapitated whilst alive her blood would have largely evacuated her body, it would have flowed from the neck in quite a surge. If however the heart stops beating, the blood does not remain stationary in the veins and arteries as it congeals, it settles under the force of gravity, so that a corpse left hanging by the neck will have hypostatic depositioning in the feet and ankles, for example. Here we have deposition of dried blood in the lumbar region which, while it proves beyond doubt that following her death she was laid on her back and allowed to remain in that position for a period measured in hours, it also shows, as I said, that the head, and indeed the hands, were removed after death. If hacking off the hands and head was done in life, then this blood here, this hypostasis, would not be in evidence.'

'Because she'd have lost most of her blood when the head and hands were amputated?'

'Exactly.'

'And she was moved after death, you say?'

'Yes.' Reynolds nodded. 'At least forty-eight hours after she was laid face upwards, or front part upwards, she was turned over, but by that time the blood in her lumbar region, shoulders and buttocks had settled and solidified.' He paused. 'No, longer than forty-eight hours if she was murdered in the summer months. I would guess that she was moved about four, five days after she was murdered. I can't say whether the turning over of the corpse indicates that she was moved from one locus to another, or whether she remained in the same locus and somebody, person or persons, returned to where they had left her, turned her over as if looking for something they had forgotten, and went away again. That's really your department. Again, there's no apparent injury on the posterior and nothing to indicate cause of death, no knife or gunshot wounds, for example. I'll trawl for poison as a matter of course, but in my experience poisoning and a dumping of the body of the victim just don't go hand in hand. They don't make easy bedfellows. I would guess that the head or the hands would be the location of the fatal wound. Probably the head.'

'The hands?'

'I was thinking of severed wrists, but of course there would be little blood remaining had that been the case. I'm sorry, Sergeant, just thinking aloud.' Reynolds peered closely at the neck wound and then at the wrists. 'Both the head and the hands had been neatly severed, they've been sawn by a fine-bladed instrument of the sort a surgeon would use, rather than a cumbersome heavy-bladed saw. Mind you, such a fine-bladed saw is not at all difficult to get hold of—an ordinary woodworker's fretsaw would produce the same sort of striations and would be well up to the job.'

'She still doesn't appear to be telling us very much, sir.'

'All in good time, Sergeant.' Reynolds smiled, a calming authoritative smile. He saw the bags under Sussock's eyes and a dull pallor. Sussock's remark was, he felt, prompted by fatigue. 'Certainly we'd be able to do a lot more towards determining her identity with the head and the hands . . . they may still be at the locus, of course.'

'We'll be doing a thorough search of the house and the grounds at first light, sir.'

'Of course, but you know I can't help feeling that the head and hands have been removed solely to hinder identification and so if they are at the locus they'll be buried, or burnt to ashes. That means that any identification by personal possessions, rings, bracelets, wallet, etc., will also be impossible: everything like that will have been destroyed or disposed of.'

'You mean if somebody is going to go to the bother of chopping off her head and hands, they're not going to leave her handbag most conveniently behind?'

'Aye.' Reynolds nodded. 'That's the gist of what I mean. I confess that I'm beginning to feel a little frustrated, Sergeant. I have two jobs here. I have to determine the likely cause of death, and assist with the determining of the identity of the deceased. With what I've got, I feel I can't do the former, I can't make a certain determination of the cause of death. As you see, there's nothing as convenient as a gunshot or knife wound. All I can say is that I think we can safely rule out death by natural causes; that's fairly obvious but it's one of those things that has to be stated.'

'Of course.'

'Death occurred some months ago and the body was moved a few days after death. I'll test for poison as I said, but also as I said, it will be a formality, for rea-

sons that I have stated. Let us turn her over again.'
Reynolds gripped the shoulders and Sussock the ankles. 'As before, three, two, now... Thank you. You
know it's not a comforting thought to know that this is
what will probably happen to you should there be anything suspicious about your death, when it comes. Or
indeed about mine, for that matter.'

It was a comment which reached Sussock. He had a
tale to tell in reply to Reynolds's light-hearted observation, but this he felt was not the appropriate time, nor
did he really enjoy telling the tale, evoking as it did
memories of happier times, times when he knew bliss,
and the telling of it left him with a sense of loss which
he had always found dreadful in its depth of feeling. It
was a tale of a sensitive man in the wrong job, who had
developed a terror of death by anything other than natural causes. The man had been a mortuary assistant but
unlike the mortuary assistant with the gleam in his eyes
and slicked down hair, and whose presence Sussock always found unsettling, this man, a gentleman in Sussock's eyes, had no love for his work. The man was
trapped in the wrong job at the end of his working life
and had no means of escape. Because of his job and
only because of his job, he feared death by accident or
foul play. He knew that, if he met his end by anything
other than a heart attack, or a massive stroke, or because of a long-recognized and long-treated internal
growth, to which room in which building his corpse
would be taken. He knew which hands would divest him
of his clothing, and would rinse his body with alcohol,
and on which trolley his corpse would be laid, and
which second pair of hands would take which knife, at
which point on his corpse the first incision would com-
mence. So this man, this gentle gentleman, would not

leave his home alone, unless it was to go to work. When he did leave his home, his wife would have to guide him down the close step by step by step, and this man would wait for ten minutes, for fifteen minutes, before he considered it safe to cross the road. The couple had lived in the room and kitchen above Sussock when he and his wife were first married and when he had known bliss. Sussock and his wife, by then pregnant, had moved out to their bungalow in Rutherglen and he never did find out what had happened to the gentle mortuary attendant; he never found out whether the man's life drew peacefully to a close while the man slumbered or whether a careless moment had brought on a fatal accident and the man's last moments of consciousness were moments when he knew his worst fear would be realized. But this was not the time to tell that tale.

'But the law dictates that a Fatal Accident Inquiry be held in all cases on non-natural death, so go out with a bang, fatal heart attack, instantaneous and no need for me or someone like me to carve up your earthly remains.' Reynolds took the scalpel and made a long and deep incision into the stomach. The rotten flesh gave easily to the cutting edge.

Sussock stepped backwards.

'Don't worry, Sergeant. All the gases escaped long ago... Well, I can tell you that she met her death shortly after eating a meal, about one hour after eating it. The meal itself is decomposed beyond recognition but I think... I think... this...' Reynolds lifted out a short grey sliver on the top of the scalpel. 'This is a fish bone, evidently inadvertently swallowed and which would not decompose with the rest of the flesh which surrounded it, just as human bones in fact. She ate a fish supper about an hour before she died and may have choked on the mouthful that contained this bone. So she did not die in the morning. I mean who has fish and chips for breakfast?'

'Point taken.'

'Let's have a look at her liver, just behind the stomach, still identifiable despite the decomposition: more than a trace of scarring; the beginning of cirrhosis.'

'She was a bevy merchant?'

'Uh huh, she liked a wee refreshment.'

'Could you pin down her age, sir?'

Reynolds pursed his lips. 'Not easy, Sergeant. I know that I've given you a wide bracket, but the damage to the liver is unlikely to be sustained by anyone in their twenties, so a woman in her thirties, but probably not much older because the cirrhosis is not so advanced.'

'It would certainly accord with the statistical probability,' said Sussock. 'Murders and victims of murders tend to be in the mid-twenties to late-thirties age range.'

'Her teeth would have helped us but in the absence, I'll have a look at her bones.' He scraped flesh from the thigh and revealed a dull white length of bone. 'I'll take a cross-section and have a look at it under the microscope and determine the degree of ossification. Bone structure deteriorates with age, the bones become brittle and break more easily, but by the naked eye I would say this is the bone of a woman well under forty years of age. Still more ahead of her than behind her.'

'Or so she thought,' said Sussock.

Reynolds nodded: he enjoyed Sussock's dryness. 'Aye, or so she thought, or so she thought. So let's get some measure of her appearance in life.' He placed the scalpel in a tray of antiseptic liquid and took a metal tape measure from the lower level of the trolley. 'The length of leg from hip to ankle is normally equal to length of the spine from first to bottom vertebrae. If we then add another twelve inches for the head and neck we will have an indication of her height as given on her passport.' He paused and stepped backwards from the table. 'Sergeant, would you say that her legs appear longer than her spine?'

'Yes...' Sussock nodded. 'Just a little...an inch perhaps...difficult to say.'

'More, I'd say. I think I'll measure all of her rather than place faith in calculations and formulae.' He stretched the tape measure the full length of the corpse. 'Well, allowing for the head and neck, I'd say that she was five ten in height, give or take an inch, and her legs, look, are a full three inches longer than her spine and so she would have delighted in a natural "leggy" appearance and I dare say she'd have enjoyed the envy of other women. Her build was slim and slender and she was a redhead.'

'She was?'

Reynolds nodded. 'Look at her pubic hair. Dull brown now, it would have been lighter in life, nearer a ginger, carroty colour. Her scalp hair would have been the same: a natural redhead. The sort of girl who'd cut quite a dash if she carried herself well and dressed well.'

DONOGHUE REACHED forwards and tapped his pipe bowl in the huge ashtray which sat on the right-hand side of his desk, beside the blotting paper pad. Both items amused Sussock who sat in the chair in front of Donoghue. Sussock was present when a police cadet who was, at the time, still not fully acquainted with 'his place' had quipped 'all you need now is a couple of goldfish, sir' and it seemed to Sussock had been instantly turned to stone by a glare from the definitely not amused DI Donoghue. And the pad of blotting paper: a relic of the nineteenth century, Sussock held, not at all needed in the days of ballpoints, word processors, and desktop publishing, yet without which, he thought, no desk looks complete. That morning neither item caused its usual degree of amusement; that morning he was tired, he felt a sharp pain running across his eyes. He had given, he felt, as full as possible a verbal feedback to his senior and had hoped, vainly, that now his senior, youthful in his early forties, still thrusting onwards and upwards, would allow a little latitude towards him, the older man, tired, at the dog-end of a graveyard shift. Sussock wanted to sign off, he wanted to be home more or less on time. But Donoghue seemed to Sussock, as he watched him relight his pipe and lean back into his chair, to be a man settling into a 'kicking it about a bit' mode. Donoghue began to suck and blow on his pipe and Sussock knew he would continue to do so for the rest of the working day, at the conclusion of which the fug in his office would be as thick as a Lanarkshire fog. Sussock too settled back in his chair, resigned to the fact that the man in the university tie and grey three-piece suit was beginning to ruminate, and after the fire in the bowl of his pipe was blowing to his satisfaction he would then say: 'Let's kick it about a bit, Ray.' Sussock sat in the chair, running his fingers around the rim of his still damp fedora.

'So.' Donoghue cradled his pipe in the palms of cupped hands. 'Let's kick it about a bit, Ray.'

Sussock's heart hit the floor.

'First let me summarize and then tell me if I have the story so far. Courtesy of an urban fox, doubtless of the type that turn over my dustbins at night, and courtesy of a motorist's monumental error, we have encountered a badly decomposed corpse of an adult female, the corpse being found in the shrubbery of a house which we believe to have been unoccupied for some time. The corpse has been mutilated, that is to say, head and hands cut off.'

Sussock nodded wearily.

'Are we talking about murder, Ray?'

'I would think so, sir.'

'It's not given, Ray.' Donoghue smiled. 'There is the possibility of natural causes, a brain haemorrhage, or the ever-mysterious sudden death syndrome, and later someone cut off her head and hands and in the process he, or she, rolled the body over. It's a possibility but so unlikely a probability that I think we can discount it. Sorry, Ray, it's just the way my mind works.'

'Dr Reynolds pondered on similar lines, sir.'

'I'm sure he did. He's a professional. A very thorough man. So I think that we proceed on that assumption. One assumption that I am not prepared to accept is the one proposed by Dr Reynolds, just offering his opinion, that the body was dumped in the shrubs of a house known to be empty so as to provide time for the killer or killers to cover their tracks. We are the police not Dr Reynolds. I want to know the identity of the last occupants of the house and when they vacated the property. It seems to me from what you said about the degree of decomposition that the time of death would equate with the time that the house was vacated. It may well be a coincidence but it's a stone worth turning over.' Donoghue scribbled on his pad under a heading which Sussock, reading upside down, saw read 'For Action'. 'Who's on the day shift this week, Ray?'

'King and Abernethy,' said Sussock. 'Montgomerie is on the back shift.'

'And you're on nights, evidently.'

'Aye.' Sussock forced a smile.

'Right, that's something one or both of them can address. We'll also have to sweep the locus, but you've put that in hand, you say?'

'Certainly have. Ten constables and three dogs, waiting for the word.'

Donoghue looked at Sussock and held eye contact. 'I'm going to look inside that house, Ray.'

'You'll need a warrant, sir.'

'I'll argue about that later. But I want in that house and I want in today, this afternoon. You know, part of the skill of observing rules is knowing when to break them.'

'Damn right, if only by committing an offence you prevent the commission of a higher offence.'

'That's the basic philosophy, Ray. I'll attend the sweep of the locus because I want to carry the can if there's any flak to be taken about unlawful entry. So the next question is, why were the head and hands severed?'

'To hinder identification.'

'Has to be.' Donoghue replaced his pipe in his mouth but the smoke began to attack Sussock's chest. 'Why the hands as well as the head?'

'We must have her prints on file.'

Donoghue nodded. 'And her killer or killers knew that we had her prints.'

'Or maybe he or she or they were being cautious, or thorough, depending on how you look at it.'

'Point taken. We don't want too many assumptions. You know I find myself more intrigued by the fish supper and the marks left by the hacksaw.'

'Oh?'

Donoghue nodded and indulged himself in a long and leisurely pull on his pipe before explaining himself. 'Yes, I do. Consider a fish supper eaten as either a lunch or as an evening meal, a mere half-hour prior to being murdered.'

Sussock shrugged his shoulders.

'Come on, Ray. I know you're tired but think. You can still do that. The fish supper meant that she did not know what was going to happen to her. Yet her murder has all the hallmarks of premeditation. She may have been held against her will for some time and kept alive on fish suppers, or she wandered into a fish and chip shop and bought the fish supper and wandered out again not knowing what was waiting for her. Had she known she wouldn't have eaten. She would have been terrified. I think that the fact that she ate just thirty minutes prior to being murdered with premeditation is significant.'

'There's still no indication of premeditation,' Sussock snapped with a sharpness born out of fatigue. 'An argument could have escalated and the other person panicked... it's happened before.' He glanced longingly out of the window of Donoghue's office, out along Sauchiehall Street, a canyon of angular buildings, traffic bumper to bumper, with liveries of different bus companies among the 'fast blacks' and the private cars, and all under a heavy, grey, low sky and a light, but incessant, rain. Glasgow, mid-January.

Donoghue placed his pipe in the ashtray. 'Let us consider why the body was moved from being face up to face down, or vice versa, I can't remember...'

'Face up to face down,' said Sussock. 'If she had had a face that is. She was found face down, but all her blood had fallen to the rear of her body'—he touched his own lumbar region—'and solidified there, so she was left face up immediately after her death.'

'On her back.'

'On her back.'

'It implies one of two things, Ray.'

'That she was killed elsewhere and her body dumped where it was found and a week or so had elapsed between the time of death and the time of dumping.'

'Or,' said Donoghue, 'that someone found the body, turned it over but didn't report it out of fear of being implicated, or because when he found it he found it because he was up to no good, casing the house before turning the windows for example. If he was a known felon with track for theft by OLP he'd know we'd do him for intent if he reported the body. In fact it implies three possibilities, Ray; your point hadn't occurred to me, it's valid, and so there are three possibilities, as I see it, why the body was moved. The two we've said, and the third which is that the murderer returned to the scene to retrieve something he had omitted to take with him, or her. Something which could identify him or her, or identify the victim. It took him the best part of a week to realize that it, whatever it was, was still on the body. In the process of retrieving it, the corpse was rolled over.'

'Sounds likely.'

'All three sound likely, Ray. She was a temperamental woman.'

'She was?'

Donoghue smiled. 'She was a redhead. I have both personal and professional experience of redheaded women. The reputation they have for flying off the handle is, in my experience, very solidly based.'

Sussock nodded, as if from similar experience.

'She was a drinker.'

'Apparently so.'

'And if she was at liberty up to the time that she was murdered and was not held against her will, then fish suppers evidently played a part in her diet. She was not a placid, non-drinking vegetarian; she was a hard-drinking, tantrum-throwing carnivore.'

'It shouldn't be too difficult to trace her through the missing persons files.'

Donoghue shook his head. 'No need, we know her.'

'We do?'

'Aye, we do. We know her more as a missing person than as a criminal but we know her. You see that's the beauty of kicking something about a bit, something will be said, some point, some observation will be thrown in which triggers a memory, or makes things clear. I'm sorry to have kept you from your rest, Ray, but we've just saved hours of work.'

Sussock looked at Donoghue, intrigued.

'Yes, yes, yes, six months ago.' Donoghue drummed his fingers on the rim of his desk. 'A missing person case, got a lot of publicity, tall girl with a striking head of red hair.'

'A social worker, I remember now.'

'A community worker, Ray, same sort of thing, a welfare type. Community workers are a bit more gung ho, tend to play the outfield of the welfare game, and a lot of them have track for civil disobedience crimes, such as being lifted for breach of the peace when taking part in protest marches against taxes they feel are unfair, or for chaining themselves to railings outside the nuclear submarine base.'

'Which is why her hands were removed. Her prints are on file.'

TWO

'I HAVE A FEELING, a strong and positive feeling, that we'll wrap this one up very quickly. Despite the six months or so that have elapsed between the commission of the offence and the discovery of the body.' Donoghue shuffled a few inches backwards, making much use of the canopy of the beech branches above him.

'Hope you're right, sir.' King stood rooted in a disadvantaged position; the canopy of the beech branches was narrow in the extreme, and rank held the occasional privilege. He stood fully in the drizzle, though barely two feet from Fabian Donoghue, and hunched his shoulders against the rain. 'Hope you're right.'

A line of uniformed officers in capes inched across the lawn at the rear of the house, and over which an Alsatian crisscrossed in single-minded determination. Other officers sifted through the shrubs at the front of the house and a second Alsatian moved lithely between the rhododendron bushes. A third dog remained with its handler at the top of the driveway.

Donoghue glanced up at the house, very Pollokshields, a rambling Victorian mansion, all turrets and gables. A basement, there would be a basement in a house of this design and period, and then three storeys above. Glancing through the curtainless windows he saw evidence of dreadful 'modernization' having been carried out. The sort of thing that had been in vogue some thirty years earlier when much of the wooden panelling, the waist-high door handles and the intricate cornicing, all the examples of Victorian attention to detail, had been removed or smoothed over in the name of fashion. Irretrievable destruction, in Donoghue's mind, he being an aficionado of the architecture of his native city, which, justifiably, he thought, prides itself on being Britain's most Victorian city. Though in many cases in the late twentieth century the only Victorian part of the building was the shell. Nonetheless, that alone Donoghue found more than pleasing. And he found it much more desirable than his own 'economy friendly', easy-to-manage bungalows in Edinburgh.

His own inclination would be to have moved into a large stone-built house in Glasgow's south side many years ago, but his wife had dug in her heels... 'And besides the children are settled in school and it would be wrong to disrupt them.' So he commuted, forty-five minutes each way, not at all an impossible journey, many hundreds of thousands of people do the same, shuttling between the two cities. It was a practice which had the welcome compensation of keeping him well away from work during the evenings and weekends.

The forty miles between Edinburgh and Glasgow represents a distance measured in more ways than a simple linear measurement: it represents a cultural gulf. Despite the short travelling time, Donoghue, and many like him, felt massively distanced from one when in the other. It had never failed to amaze, and to an extent amuse Donoghue that convicted murderers with enemies seeking cold revenge would, upon their discharge from prison on licence and too frightened of retribution to return to Glasgow, settle without fear in Edinburgh. And vice versa: even when a deeply felt old score could be paid off after a 45-minute journey on the M8. That was the compensation for Donoghue when he returned home at night: the sensation that Glasgow might as well be on another planet. but it was only a compensation, and a compensation is only a compensation; it is not a full redress of grievance; it does nothing but take the edge off the pain, taking the sting from an injury.

In the foreseeable future his children would be out of school and his wife would be deprived of the excuse she had always relied on to keep her and hers in her native Edinburgh. It was an excuse which in Donoghue's privately held view was more than a little transparent. Her reluctance, nay, her refusal, to settle in Glasgow was he felt more to do with her Edinbrovian distrust of Glasgow than it was to do with concern for the children's schooling; it was yet another expression of the culture which allowed Edinburgh folk to believe themselves 'better' than Glasgow folk. Or so Donoghue thought.

'Rear door could be forced without too much trouble, sir.' Donoghue's mind was brought sharply back to the matter in hand. He smiled at the speaker, an apparently passed-over-for-promotion constable, or a constable who did not want promotion, happy to serve usefully and valuably as a foot soldier.

'The front door isn't an option but the rear door will give. It's not a secure house at all, sir, in fact the only reason the windows have not been turned is that it's clearly empty, I would say anyway.'

'Doubtless you're right.' Donoghue nodded. 'Punt it in, please.'

The constable returned to the rear of the house, was lost from view. Donoghue delayed for a few seconds, not wanting to crowd the constable and then said, 'Right, Richard, let's see what we see.' And as he spoke there came the unmistakable sound of splintering wood.

'*He* hasn't found anything, sir.' King nodded to the Alsatian, still crisscrossing the lawn and herbaceous border. 'If any part of the McArthur woman had been buried in the garden he would have found it by now.' King walked half a step behind Donoghue as the two men strode across the gravel to the rear of the house.

'Maybe we'll be luckier, Richard. Like I said, I have a feeling that this one will fall into place very easily. We think we know who she is, that's the first obstacle all but cleared. We've got off to a strong start.'

'I remember her going missing but only because the surname McArthur has personal associations, best friend at school had that name, but the point being that the surname registered as it does in such instances.'

'When you know someone of the same name? Yes I know what you mean. Though we still don't have a positive ID so we'll have to temper our optimism with caution. We'll see what Abernethy comes back with.'

Cold.

Cold. Very, very cold. That was the first impression that Donoghue had of the inside of the house. And it was his impression throughout the investigation, and of all the memories, recollections, and observations of the inquiry into the slaying of the woman, and her beheading, it was the coldness of the huge house in Pollokshields, on Sherbrooke Avenue, which stayed with him and remained with him for many years. It was not simply a matter of temperature, it was a coldness mixed with a sense of oppression, a 'presence', a sensation of the building itself being hostile. It was strong, unmistakable; nonetheless as quickly as he had felt it, Donoghue was about to dismiss it equally quickly as being a figment of fanciful imagination and would have done so had not the chubby, bearded 25-year-old detective constable who followed him into the house stopped and stood still and said, 'Something has happened in this house.'

Donoghue turned and glanced at King and nodded.

'I'm not suggesting anything supernatural, or paranormal,' King explained hastily.

'No, no.'

'My feet are firmly planted when it comes to things like that, but I've attended sites of violence, meaning murder of violent accident, and very occasionally I've had the sense of "something happened here", long before I've known what "it" was. I walked into a close in Bridgeton once, a long time ago when I was a teenager, and I got that sensation, first time I had felt it. Turned out that a murder had been committed there some years before.'

'But it's here, don't worry, Richard, I felt it too. I think we'd better proceed with caution.'

'Announce ourselves too?'

Donoghue nodded. 'I think so. Carry on.'

'Hello!' King raised his voice. It echoed in the old, cold, empty house. 'Police!'

King's voice continued to echo until consumed by the silence. Still the house felt cold, oppressive, hostile. Not a happy house. Not even, thought Donoghue, a house that could ever be made happy. If he ever did get his stone-built house in the south side of the city, it would never be this one, not even if it was offered at a knockdown price. The house now stood as near empty as the day the builders had left it, down to the bare floor-boards and curtainless windows. Its age, a slight smell of damp and old wallpaper, were the only things which belied its vacated, rather than new, status. And the sense that it was a house with a history. Donoghue turned to the constable who had forced entry and said, 'If you'd wait here, please, no one to enter until myself and DC King return.'

'Very good, sir.'

'Very well, Richard.' Donoghue turned to King. 'Even if there appears to be little to disturb, we proceed with caution. We'll do the upper floors first, and the cellar last.'

The killing floor was the first floor: in a room on the first floor—specifically the front room; a huge room with a cavernous ceiling; the room that would have been the master bedroom. There were specks of dried blood on the wall, on the floor, in a corner furthest from the door and the window. Some months old, by all appearances, but blood nonetheless. There were bin-liner bags, later totalled to number nineteen by the scene of crimes officer, a carpenter's trestle, and, much used, a back-saw, blood bespattered, and spare hacksaw blades, new and unused. A bottle of Three Bells, still a quarter full of spirit, stood by the trestle, and cigarette butts were distributed liberally around the floorboards. Donoghue and King took it all in with a sweep of their eyes. Donoghue glanced out of the window: the rain ran down the panes of glass, beyond was a row of beech trees swaying in the breeze, and beyond the trees, through the naked winter branches, Donoghue observed the elegant, stately lines of the houses on the opposite side of Sherbrooke Avenue.

'The fish supper that the deceased ate as the last meal of her life was a fish lunch,' Donoghue said matter of factly.

'Excuse me, sir?'

'The pathologist, Dr Reynolds, found a fish bone in the stomach of the deceased, being the remains of a fish supper, eaten about thirty minutes before she died. It meant that it was a fish lunch, eaten at lunch time. You can tell by the room, this room.'

'You can?' King looked at him questioningly.

Donoghue made as if to speak but stopped himself. He had long recognized King's potential, long recognized a young officer well on his way to senior officer rank, and he had always believed in 'stretching' his staff to their maximum potential. So he smiled and raised an eyebrow in the manner he had and which King knew, always unnervingly, meant 'explain'.

'Ah...' King looked about the room, the patches of dried blood, the bin liners, the cigarette stubs, the bottle of Three Bells.

'The answer is outside.'

'Sir?' King felt himself to be struggling.

'The answer to the question is outside, Richard. Come on, observe, think, common sense will still get you further than high-tech gadgetry. Why is it certain that the murder took place here, and that it took place in the early afternoon?'

'Because he or they would have needed illumination to see what they were doing.'

'Good.'

'The stand of trees there, in the summer months they would be in full foliage and quite sufficient to prevent anybody in the opposite houses from viewing the goings-on in this room. But a light at night in a house probably known to be empty would have aroused suspicion.'

'That's it. What else would you think it safe to surmise?'

'That he, or they, found it hard to cut off her head. That is to say that he found it a difficult thing to do. They, or he, or whoever, needed a good drink before or during the process. The murderer sank a good bucket of whisky right enough and smoked a good few nails. He must have been really strung out.'

'He or they?'

King considered the locus. 'They.'

'Yes?'

'Well the amount of whisky—three quarters of a bottle; no evidence that it's been watered down; drinking neat from the bottle; too much for one man, if they were going to walk away and walk away after carrying the corpse downstairs into the shrubbery. But three quarters of a bottle between three or four, that's more like it, more feasible.'

'Yes?'

'Well, the number of cigarettes...' King knelt and looked at the filter-tipped butts. 'There's at least two different brands here.'

'That's what I thought.' Donoghue walked over to the workman's trestle. 'More than the whisky, some of which could have been spilled, or could have been a half-bottle to start with, it's the cigarettes which give an indication that this is the work of two or more persons.'

'Amateurs too, by the look of it.'

'Hired neds out of their depth, in too deep before they realized what they were into. I don't think that they took the job to its conclusion.'

'No?'

'No. The pile of bin liners, Richard. I think that they indicate what happened to the head and the hands and why we are not likely to find them after this length of time, but do you not think that it indicates what they had planned to do with the body?'

'Cut it up into lots of little bits.'

'Cut it up into lots of little bits and drop them in the council collecting points all around the city, or in skips at the roadside. So they eventually end up incinerated or in the Clyde with the rest of the city's refuse. I imagine that getting rid of a human body is not at all difficult—spend a little time thinking and planning, set your stall out.' Donoghue tapped the workman's trestle. 'Plan ahead, be thorough, don't panic and cut corners...'

'Hardly bears thinking about.'

'Yet that's exactly what someone, or some persons, did. Hired the wrong neds, left them at it and didn't hang around to supervise the job. They panicked, panicked after too much alcohol, and panic once it sets in spreads like wildfire. So once they had the head and the hands, they cut corners, hid the body in the shrubs, intended to return to clean up the mess, but once outside the house they were too frightened to return and so they fled, trusting to luck.'

'Which held until this morning when a motorist swerved to avoid a fox.'

'That's it. I dare say they told the man who hired them that they'd cleared up the mess and distributed the body here and there.'

'And he for some reason would not or could not return to check that the job had been done.'

'Good point, Richard. Either that happened or the whole thing was unplanned, a spontaneous outburst of violence among a small group of people. But whatever, we'll get the scene of crimes officer to photograph this room and get Bothwell to lift any latents. It's probably too much to hope that they didn't wear gloves, but they didn't steam the label off the whisky bottle so we'll do that for them and identify the retail outlet from the bar code...' Donoghue's voice broke off and he smiled. King followed his gaze. 'Not as much of a Christmas present as a set of latents left by a known felon but not bad, not bad at all.'

'Nicest footprint I've seen in a long time,' said King, looking at one of the smaller, not immediately noticed patches of dried blood.

IN A MODEST HOUSE, but yet a privately owned house, a young woman reached into a playpen and lifted her infant son and held him to her. She walked to the window of the room and looked out onto a small garden, green, and grey, and brown, barren shrubs, under a relentless rain which fell at forty-five degrees from a low, grey sky. She held the child. She didn't care for the winter, the winter was when what happened in the neat house had to be taken into the streets—not just the streets, but the streets of Bearsden. The reason she often had to cancel visits to her mother in Barrhead, or put off friends from calling, was the same reason that she had to wear sunglasses. In the summer she could get away with it, but not in January. She often wondered why she hid it; the world and its mother knows why a woman wears shades in the winter, that she knew, and she knew it fine well. Maybe the women in Barrhead have the right idea: in Barrhead they show them off like medals, to prove they have a man. She kissed the child. 'It'll be all right, Toby,' she said. 'Promise you, one day it'll be all right.'

ABERNETHY AND the man pondered each other. Both men reflected upon the youth of the other. Abernethy had expected an area officer of the Social Work Department to be a well-set man in his middle years, a man with a contented 'this will do us' look, a round face, a swelling stomach, a man strolling gently towards retirement. In fact Ralph Deakins, who was able to offer him ten minutes prior to a case conference, was a young man, hard packed and slender, in his early thirties, with a green blazer, 'loud' tie, neatly and closely cut hair, and well-manicured hands. Ralph Deakins wore a wide and a heavy gold wedding band and had a glint of gold in his teeth, clearly seen whenever he smiled.

This, Abernethy noted, was not often.

Deakins was evidently of the 'new breed' of social worker managers of which Abernethy had heard, thrusting, self-serving and either obsequious or truculent, depending upon the designation of the person to whom he was speaking. He had three phones on his desk, all in a line, three ballpoint pens neatly lined up on the left of his blotter, and a ruler above it. His office was small, if not cramped, and had nothing to soften it, no plant, no framed picture, not even, that Abernethy could see, a framed photograph of a wife or child. He was, thought Abernethy, the sort of man who would walk down the street holding the tips of each middle finger pressed against the tip of the thumbs, the sort of man who would polish his car fastidiously and fly into a rage at the slightest, most superficial scratch to the paintwork. Not a man bestowed with imagination or fair-mindedness, but petty, peevish and unforgiving. Dangerous when crossed. All this Abernethy decided within five seconds of sitting in the offered seat.

Deakins for his part viewed Abernethy with a mixture of surprise, embarrassment and a little anger that he had not been thought worthy enough to be visited by an older, more seasoned, more weighty police officer. Abernethy was young for a CID officer, he still held himself with the last traces of adolescent awkwardness. Good material, no doubt, Deakins pondered, but still a little lightweight. But affable, polite, pleasant, mild mannered, shaking hands firmly and not sitting until invited to do so.

'I'm afraid that I have to be in a child protection case conference in ten minutes, Mr...'

'Abernethy, DC Abernethy.'

'Of course, Abernethy.' Deakins consulted an elaborate digital watch which slid out of the white cuff of a gold-cufflinked silk shirt and then back again.

Abernethy responded by consulting the railwayman's watch his father had handed down to him when he joined the force. Wound once a day, it kept perfect time. 'Shouldn't keep you at all, Mr Deakins, just making some preliminary enquiries.' He took out a note pad and fumbled for his biro, first one pocket and then another. Eventually Deakins handed Abernethy one of his. Abernethy smiled an embarrassed 'thank you'. 'I'll take a few notes if you don't mind.'

Deakins waved a hand of imperious consent. One of the phones on his desk rang. He snatched it up, listened and then said, 'I'm busy, Hilda. Freeze all further calls.' He replaced the receiver with practised precision. 'How can I help the police?'

'It's about one of your staff.'

'Oh?' Deakins's brow furrowed with intimidating speed.

'Pam McArthur?'

'Deakins groaned. 'Oh, that woman. Not my favourite person. Don't tell me she's been found and she's coming back to make us all miserable again?'

'Yes and no. Yes, she's been found, and no, she won't be returning.'

'I don't follow.'

'A body has been found. We think that it may be that of Pam McArthur. The description seems to tally with the description on the m.p. posters . . .'

'MP?'

'Missing person. And the age of the body also coincides. Further the amount of decomposition is what would be expected had she died at about the time she was reported missing.'

'I see. So I ask you again, how may I help?'

'We suspect foul play and so were trying to build up a picture of Ms McArthur in life, as full a picture as possible.'

'I see.' Deakins leaned forward and pyramided his fingers beneath his chin.

Abernethy found himself fighting a growing dislike for Deakins. 'What sort of person was she? What enemies did she have, any feuds with anyone . . . ?'

'She was a community worker. It's a form of social work, organizing local people into pressure groups, helping them to fight their cases. It's dispiriting work because people in the housing schemes are often poorly motivated. McArthur was particularly venomous about the dampness issue; a lot of the housing stock in the east end of Glasgow is rotten with damp, black with it, so they tell me, mushrooms growing out of the living-room wall, that sort of thing. We have two high-rise blocks of flats in Easterhouse, just opposite the road. You will have noticed them, they are particularly bad.'

'McIntyre Heights?'

'Those are they, block one and block two, McIntyre Heights. Well, McArthur had a thing about those two towers. An obsession. She was a typical community worker, it's the aspect of social work which seems to attract the loony left. Thankfully there are exceptions creeping in, but generally your average community worker will still be in denim in their thirties, have a canvas knapsack with political badges stuck to it, will spend a working afternoon in the pub with "community leaders", or spend a working day visiting peace camps outside the submarine base. They're also very good at getting arrested; it's a particular skill they have. In fact, I think McArthur was arrested for cutting the razor wire at Faslane and spent a night in the cells before being fined a modest amount in the Dumbarton Sheriff Court. She returned to the office, and to the scheme, as a sort of local hero.' Deakins paused. 'Enemies, you say?'

'Any enemies?'

'Plenty.'

'Really?'

'Yes, really. You see I don't want to hang out my dirty washing, Mr A...'

'Abernethy.'

'Mr Abernethy. I don't want to hang it out, don't like washing my linen in public, nor do I wish to speak ill of the dead.'

'But?'

'But if I am to be of assistance to the police, if it is she whose body has been found, because you say that is still not certain, then I have to advise you that Pam Mc-Arthur had enemies without number. Myself included. If I were to tell you that a great sense of relief came over this workplace when it was announced that she was missing, you may perhaps understand how people felt about her. People started talking to each other more freely, the atmosphere became more relaxed. Nor was there any surprise—people actually voiced the opinion that it was only a matter of time before she got a kicking, a real kicking, sufficient to pay her off. I've come across such instances before. It's astounding what effect just one or two people can have on a workplace and they don't necessarily have to hold a key position.'

'I have had similar experiences,' Abernethy said, recalling one of many jobs he held before finding his feet in the police force. A woman, once, with a dominant streak, employed in the post room, but whose personality pervaded the entire building: her he recalled clearly.

'Pam McArthur, Mr Abernethy—and this is speaking for myself, you understand—had, in my view, no sense of friendship. Friendship is a concept that was alien to her. She kept slaves or had enemies, and if you were known to her you would fall into one of those two categories and it was safer to be an enemy. All you needed to do if you were an enemy was ensure that you never turned your back on her. Her slaves, well they had the dubious privilege of having McArthur link arms as they walked down the street, but they'd still be traded off when their usefulness expired.'

'You didn't like her.'

'Oh I make no secret of it. She didn't like me either which caused me great feelings of reassurance. I'd be really worried about myself if McArthur had ever come to like me. I dare say she'll be dancing round the fire, I mean where she's likely to have gone to. If the body is hers.'

'If it is hers.' Abernethy doodled on his pad.

'Her memory makes me shudder. In fact I go as far as to say, in my opinion, that she was, maybe still is, an evil person. She struck me as being without normal checks and balances that prevent most of us from doing wrong. My friends, and people that I respect, would do no wrong because of their integrity and sense of morality. McArthur's only restraint seemed to me to be the fear of consequences; she always seemed to me to be capable of great wrongdoing, whatever that might be, if she thought that she would get away with it. She would in fact hurt and damage here in the workplace for the sake of hurt and damage—use of gossip, spreading gossip, and actually starting it, were her favourite tricks.'

Abernethy drew breath between his teeth. Again he had crossed paths with similar people.

'Once I overheard her say to someone who wasn't particularly one of her associates: "He was wrong to have done that so I've started putting it about the office." That was Pam McArthur, and this being public service you can't get rid of people so easily. You have to be caught with your fingers in the till or convicted of committing a serious criminal act before you can be given your cards.'

'The breach of the peace convictions?' Abernethy raised his eyebrows questioningly. 'You'd be bounced out of the door for that in the police force.'

'I dare say, but the answer's "no". This isn't the police force. In fact the union would fight tooth and claw for her on that issue; technically it's a criminal act but it would be argued as being morally justified, and given the anti-nuclear policy of her employer...'

'I see. Did she have any particular enemy? Any enemy that stood head and shoulders above the common herd of enemies?'

'And who would want to do her in?' Deakins shook his head. 'Not that I am aware, Mr Abernethy. Not many will weep at her passing and few will attend her funeral, but if there is one person who would want to kill her then it's no one I could identify.'

'What was her home situation?'

'I shudder to think. Working with her was well-nigh impossible, living with er...ugh. She'd start a riot in an empty house. You know, it's strange but I don't think she had much of a separate life outside work, chose her "slaves" from her colleagues, even went on holiday with her "slaves"—well, a couple of them—so her home life and work life gelled into one. I got the impression that when she went out with her friends, whom I would call her slaves, they spent the night in a pub calling the register of all their colleagues and subjecting each to a character assassination as each name came up. And that would be considered a night well spent. My name would invariably be the first on the register and my assassination would have taken up the first two rounds of bevy and, as I said, that knowledge made me sleep easily at night. I keep my social life and my professional life well separate. I like it that way, it's neater, tidier. But like all people who seem to look to their colleagues to provide their social life, McArthur was deep down a very lonely woman. Whenever you saw her, she always seemed to be with someone, but the core of her life was loneliness. If she had a partner she would probably have been less malicious. But that's conjecture.'

'A lonely woman.'

'Plenty of human contact, but this constant wanting to be the hub of a social life woven amongst her colleagues, this constant gathering about her of all who could be manipulated, or who were too naive to see the dreadful look that flashed across her eyes from time to time, well, it always spoke to me of a soulless personality.'

'Good at her job?'

Deakins shook his head. 'Frankly, no, Mr Abernethy. She held it down but that's not difficult. I mean, community work? Difficult to do? She'd work away at something if she felt driven but her motivation was worrying.'

'Oh?'

'At least I felt it to be. She came from a rough scheme, as in fact many of us in the social services do. We're motivated to right wrong, right social injustice, champion the cause of the individual, those are the motivations of most entrants to this type of work, that's the sort of thing that makes most people gravitate to social work. But McArthur to a large extent keeps her roots alive; she had a rough way of talking, real Bridgeton street-speak, a classic inverted snob, and carried that as her badge of office as it were.' Deakins paused and glanced at his watch. 'I'm beginning to run over time but we'll continue, get this out of the way. She didn't do a good job for the sake of doing a good job. She'd sit in the canteen for days on end leafing through old copies of *Socialist Worker* defying me to say something, and then she'd come across an issue here in Easterhouse that she could get her teeth into and she'd worry away at it like a terrier. Here again there was some cause for concern, because her motivation wasn't to improve the lot of the people, it was to bring something, or somebody, down. It is not an appropriate response for a member of the department to adopt.'

'I'll say.' Abernethy scribbled on his note pad. 'Could we return to Pam McArthur's home life. I presume that she lived alone?'

'Lived alone.' Deakins stroked an eyebrow with the delicately manicured little finger of his right hand. 'I'm led to believe that she had many and varied lovers of either sex. No children. She has at least one sibling, a sister. I know that because when she didn't turn up for work for two days and hadn't phoned in sick, two of her colleagues went to her flat in Denniston, hammered on the door, didn't get a reply, made two more visits and eventually I alerted our personnel section who contacted the person named as her next of kin. This person then made attempts to contact Pam and eventually reported her missing to you gentlemen. Her sister was courteous enough to phone me, advising me what she'd done and thanking me for alerting the personnel section. She seemed a very pleasant lady, lived out in Cumbernauld, where I stay in fact, and I recall wondering how could it be that two women could come from presumably the same background and both turn out so different? Like chalk and cheese. She never spoke of her parents and you know I could never picture her with them, she just seems always to have been around, a ready-made adult as it were.'

Deakins leaned to one side and opened a drawer of his desk, extracted a framed photograph and handed it to Abernethy. 'Some of the staff thought it would be a good idea to have a photograph of us taken. I went along with it, and that's her, centre of the front row. It says everything that when the team was positioning itself she should fight herself to the centre of the group, and that smile, frozen on her face, not at all spontaneous, not at all natural.'

Abernethy tapped the photograph with the top of the ballpoint. 'Hard to miss her, isn't it? Tall, all that red hair tumbling onto her shoulders.'

'That's an opportune photograph, Mr Abernethy, puzzling too.'

'Oh.'

'Yes, it was taken the day before she didn't turn up for work. Can't get more recent than that. The police have a copy of it. It was taken on the 6th June, last year.'

'You're certain of the date.'

'Very. I'm a bit of an amateur military historian, not been doing it for very long, but as I peel off the day on my desk calendar, I keep coming across anniversaries of battles—21st October is Trafalgar, 1st July is the Somme—and when that was being taken I remember thinking that it was the anniversary of D-Day, the invasion of Normandy. That photograph was taken on the 6th June.'

'Do you recall what time of day it was taken?' Abernethy looked at the photograph, two lines of people, mostly under thirty-five, it seemed, and a striking redhead at the centre, who reminded him of Edward Lear's poem about the crocodile and its 'gently smiling jaws': her hard face with the false smile. The group were dressed in summer clothing, the building behind them, now dripping with rain, was then basking in sunshine.

'In the forenoon,' Deakins said.

'Certain?'

'Positive.' He reached behind him for his previous year's diary and turned to the 6th June. 'Yes, I had no appointments that morning, but I had a lunch date in the town and spent the afternoon in a meeting between department managers and elected representatives. I remember the meeting well. I'm in the photograph so that photograph must have been taken before lunch on the 6th June.'

'What do people do for lunch around here?' Abernethy grasped at straws.

'Grab a fish supper,' said Deakins. 'Little alternative in Easterhouse.'

'Even on a hot day in June?'

'Even on a hot day in June.'

'Why do you think it's a puzzling picture?'

'Well look at her. A woman without a care. Nothing troubling her. She was the sort of person who'd let everybody know if she had received a red gas bill. If she was concerned for her safety I tell you the world and its mother would have known about it. But that's more your province.'

'But a noteworthy point,' Abernethy agreed and duly noted it. 'Did Pam McArthur have any identifiable item of jewellery or other possession?' Abernethy listed the clothing that McArthur wore when the photograph was taken, the very day she may well have died: jeans, with a large, clearly identifiable patch on the right knee, moccasin-type shoes, white blouse, light brown leather jacket. A determinedly rebellious dresser at the age of twenty-nine. He looked at the photograph, the low-rise, flat-roofed, pebble-dashed scheme stretched to the skyline. The roads were narrow and pasty grey in colour, an orange double-decker bus edged into the photograph on the left-hand side, and in the centre, always drawing the viewer's eye to her, was the woman who was probably dead, horribly murdered, within hours of the photograph being taken.

'Well, she wasn't a jewellery person, but she had a distinctive watch.'

'Oh?'

'It had no intrinsic value as such, but it was special. The story is that she went on holiday to the Soviet Union, when it was the Soviet Union, with the Scottish Trades Union Council. She brought the watch back with her; it had a red hammer and sickle in a white face and CCCP in red letters under the hammer and sickle. I confess I thought it was a bit crass, something of an affectation, but she was pleased with it, showed it off like a wean with a new toy. She said she bought it from a disaffected soldier in Red Square. Apparently this poor guy was standing there selling off his uniform and other bits and pieces; he kept his shirt, trousers and boots but all else was exchanged for western currency. Anyway in time the strap broke, and she didn't replace it or have it repaired but took to carrying it round in her jeans pocket—you know, her rear pocket—and fished it out whenever she wanted to clock the time. I haven't seen a watch like it before or since. I dare say there are others in the west but I have not seen another.'

'Watch, CCCP, hammer and sickle, red on a white face,' Abernethy scribbled, 'and a broken strap.'

'Without a strap.'

'Sorry.'

'I've just thought—shortly before she disappeared the strap broke off completely, or she took it off, one or the other, because I noticed that she had taken to carrying the watch itself but without the broken strap.'

'No strap.'

'Why, is it important?'

'Could well be,' said Abernethy writing on his pad. 'You see the body was moved after it had been dumped, as if somebody had returned to look for something. It's a possibility that that something could have identified her or her assailant. If the watch isn't in the manifest of effects then it is probable that the person removed it from her body when he or she, or they, returned.'

'I thought that dental records helped identify people in a situation like this, or even fingerprints—she's got a criminal record for breach of the peace.'

'Oh, we don't have those bits of her.' Abernethy enjoyed watching Deakins's polished composure falter before his eyes. 'I'll see myself out. Thank you for your assistance.'

Abernethy stepped out of the cramped room and out of the cramped office building which had grills over the windows. The grills were there, he knew, to keep out the neds who would turn the windows for the hell of it because there is nothing of value in a Glasgow Social Work area office, nonetheless the grills were there and posed a dreadful fire risk to the employees. Just one entrance and grills on the windows. It's what, reflected Abernethy as he turned his coat collar up against the rain, is known as trusting to luck. He walked down the narrow path leading from the building, the fire station on his right, and then paused at the gap in the low fence where almost eight months earlier Pam McArthur and her colleagues had posed on a bright summer's day. Across the street, greasy with rain, on an expanse of green stood the Health Centre, a squat brick-built building, and beyond that the twin towers of McIntyre Heights rising up to meet the sky at about the twelfth floor, but rising another ten floors beyond that. And they were by no means the tallest high-rises in the city. Not by any means.

Abernethy drove back to the city centre on the M8. The police heap was old, battered, on its last legs and the wipers did little more than smear the moisture across the windscreen—the moisture, and also the muck thrown up by passing lorries and buses, all of which seemed to be making better speed than he was making. But he made it to Charing Cross, to the awkward right-hand exit, turned off the road by the roundabout and arched footbridge and drove into the yard behind P Division police station. He parked the car in a vacant slot and entered the building by the 'staff only' entrance, signed in, checked his pigeonhole—two messages, neither urgent—and took the stairs two at a time up to the CID corridor. He tapped on Donoghue's door. he waited. He knew Donoghue's code: door shut—engaged; door open—out.

Eventually Donoghue called, 'Come in,' and Abernethy entered. Donoghue was sitting with the phone pressed to his ear, listening and occasionally responding with a grunt. He motioned to Abernethy to sit in one of the chairs in front of his desk. It was an indication of being in favour that was not lost on the young detective constable. He sat and waited while Donoghue held the phone trapped between his ear and shoulder, scribbled notes and occasionally said 'Uh huh'. Finally he said, 'Thank you very much. Goodbye.' He replaced the handset, looked at Abernethy and raised an eyebrow.

'Well, sir, I've just spoken with Pam McArthur's manager at her place of work and was shown a photograph of her taken just before she disappeared—apparently the same photograph is in the m.p. file. We ought to be able to make a positive ID. The woman was of a striking appearance.'

Donoghue continued to look at Abernethy, holding eye contact.

'I noted the clothing that she was wearing in the photograph, particularly moccasin-type shoes, and jeans with a distinctive patch here.' Abernethy tapped his left knee.

Donoghue slid a sheet of paper across the desk towards Abernethy. 'Notes from a phone call I just took from Dr Kay at the Forensic Science Laboratory at Pitt Street. She's sending a typed report by courier; we'll get it later today.'

'Bloodstained blouse,' Abernethy read aloud.

'After that.'

'Leather jacket.' Abernethy looked up. 'Yes, she was wearing a soft leather jacket.'

'Below that.'

'Ah . . . jeans with a patch on left knee.' Abernethy smiled. 'Has to be her.'

'It's looking like it. Dr Kay also points out that her jeans were clumsily fastened. She had jeans of a button type rather than a zip. They were held together by only two buttons, not the full six, and those two were buttoned in the wrong buttonholes.'

'Oh . . . sexual assault?'

'That's a reasonable implication,' Donoghue agreed. 'In fact it's the only implication. Exactly what happened is as yet unclear. There's no reference to semen deposits in Dr Reynolds's report and they would still be identifiable after this length of time.' He shrugged his shoulders. 'But it's early days. So, I am confident that you will produce a report with your usual thoroughness, though remember, avoid flowery language, I've spoken to you about that.'

'Yes, sir.'

'Simple plain English and facts in a logical order.'

'Very good, sir.'

'But anything I should know now, any verbal feedback you feel to be necessary?'

'Well, yes, the first thing is that the deceased is or was a lady who had many enemies, many people disliked her. Just to add to that, her manager described her as a keeper of slaves and a maker of enemies.'

'I see. I've met such types before.'

'And I may, I think, have found the reason why the body was flipped over. The deceased, if it was Pam McArthur, was in the habit of carrying a distinctive watch in her jeans pocket. A Soviet military watch, and no strap which is why she carried it in her pocket.'

'I see.' Donoghue reached for his pipe.

'I don't know if it's listed among her possessions...'

'It's not.' A flash of flame from a gold-plated lighter.

'Oh well. I thought that it might have been removed to hinder her identification.'

'Good man. So somebody did not want her to be identified, at least for a while. I would say that that means her identity could be a direct link to her killer or killers. What do we know about her private life? What lovers did she have?'

'A number of either sex over the years, but having said that Mr Deakins couldn't say if she had a particular friend at the time of her disappearance.'

'She wouldn't. Nothing is ever so simple.' He took his pipe from his mouth. 'I'd like you to go and see Pam McArthur's sister. She's the next of kin. You can tell her all that we know. Better take WPC Willems with you.

Ask her for a key to Pam McArthur's flat, the m.p. file has her down as the key holder.'

'Very good, sir.' Abernethy stood. 'Be all right if I grab some lunch first?'

Donoghue took his hunter out of his waistcoat pocket: 12.20. My God, it really was that time already.

THREE

'MR KING.' The woman stood and extended her arm, confidently, professionally, somewhat, thought King, imperiously, and with the smile manufactured to greet money-spending clients. King accepted her hand, briefly, gently and then separated again. As a cop on duty he always felt uncomfortable about shaking hands, even with people who are merely suppliers of information: there was, he felt, a danger of suggesting a relationship, an alliance, which does not necessarily exist. A police officer must see himself as standing outside society, or so Richard King believed, and practised. 'May I offer you tea? Or would you prefer coffee?'

'Tea, please.' King slid into the chair and felt ill at ease in his dripping three-quarter-length waterproof, especially in a warm, everything-in-its-place office. He glanced around him, taking in his surroundings: succulent plants in terracotta pots softened a room already soft in pastel shades which instantly reminded him of his wife and her preference for similar shades. There, he thought, the resemblance between Rosemary King and Sara Sinclair ended. King knew that his wife's Quaker values would not make Sara Sinclair's dress sense in any way appealing to her. Somewhere, thought King, somewhere underneath or behind all that, minerals and metal and make-up, and lacquered, dyed hair, a crisp white blouse, must be the woman called Sara

Sinclair. Nor would Rosemary King's reading extend to *Vogue, Elle, Cosmopolitan,* and the Central Belt's own glossy magazine *M8,* which lay on the glass-topped coffee table to the left of Sara Sinclair's desk.

'A tray of tea for Mr King and myself please, Margaret.' Sara Sinclair pressed a button on a piece of plastic which stood on the corner of her desk. And the piece of plastic answered in a metallic voice: 'Right away, Miss Sinclair.' Sara Sinclair beamed at King with heavily rouged lips and eyelashes so falsely long they looked ridiculous to him. 'How may we help the police? I confess that in five years of operation I can't recall a visit from the police, on official business that is, although we have sold houses to police officers from time to time. One just last week in fact.'

'Well it's in connection with a property on Sherbrooke Avenue.' King shuffled in the chair. 'We had occasion to attend the house this morning on a serious matter and inside the house— '

'Inside?' Sara Sinclair attempted a tone of indignation. It didn't quite work and King was unimpressed.

'Inside,' King continued, 'we—'

A tap on the door.

Sara Sinclair waited for a moment and then said, 'Come in.' The door was opened by Margaret, King presumed the bumbling, middle-aged lady who had greeted him as he had stepped in from Byres Road, sweeping a soaking hood off his head, and who now carried a tray of tea for two, and biscuits, was Margaret. Margaret placed the tray on the edge of Sara Sinclair's desk, Sara Sinclair smiled a silent thanks and Margaret withdrew with a shuffling subservience and humility.

'We were obliged to force entry,' said King. 'We entered by the rear door, caused minimal damage. We are still at the house and will have a joiner secure the premises prior to leaving.'

'I see. Thank you.'

'In one of the downstairs rooms on the floor, we found one of your posters. It seems to have fallen from the window. So first question is, are you the estate agent for the property in question, 1273 Sherbrooke Avenue?'

Sara Sinclair nodded. 'We are.' She extended two heavily clawed hands and began to pour the tea.

'Can you tell me who is the owner of the property?' King took his notebook from his pocket and then fished for his ballpoint.

'It's a finance company.' She placed a cup of tea in front of King with delicate movements, a little too forcibly feminine for King's taste—'twee', in a word. 'I'll get the file.' She stood, pleased with her slim figure, and walked high-heeled across the carpet to a lilac green filing cabinet and opened the top drawer. 'It's a top-drawer property,' she said and King was about to respond with a slight tension-easing laugh when he suddenly realized the woman was being serious, completely so. 'That's the way we file, by value, the higher the drawer, the higher the value. This particular property is top drawer, near the front in fact.'

King watched as the scarlet claws spidered across the spines of the files then stopped, seized one, and withdrew it. Sara Sinclair slid the drawer shut with a gentle click and returned to her desk with dainty steps.

'Yes,' she said, opening the file, 'the property is owned by Dalmuir Finance Ltd.'

'I've never heard of them.'

'They're new. Quite sound despite their name. I mean Dalmuir—you'd have thought they'd choose something a little less . . . modest.'

'And they own the property?' King let the reference to Dalmuir ride, that game wasn't worth the candle.

'They do. You see the property was the home of an elderly gentleman who never married, and his housekeeper. The gentleman came to an agreement with Dalmuir Finance Ltd of a nature which is not uncommon these days, what with Britain's ageing population. What's that terrible statistic, more pensioners than people in employment in less than ten years' time?'

'Yes, I heard that too.'

'Hardly bears thinking about, since it's our taxes which will have to support that army of old biddies. But anyway . . . the elderly gentleman, Colonel Headly by name, retired, came to an agreement with Dalmuir Finance to the effect that he sold his property to them, thus realizing the cash he had in the stones. The agreement being that he remained in residence until obliged to give up residence because of infirmity or upon his eventual death. The gentleman, Colonel Headly, died in the summer of last year, and the finance company engaged ourselves as the selling agents on, let me see . . . May 10th.'

'May 10th,' King scribbled.

'The colonel left a will: all the cash in his bank account went to his housekeeper, and the relatives got the contents of the house. The next of kin cleared the property with a vengeance because the colonel had not told them what he'd done. They spent the last few years waiting for the old boy to curl up his toes thinking they were going to inherit a very nice property, only to be told that a finance company now owned it and all the money in his account had gone to his housekeeper. They were not best pleased.'

'I imagine.'

'So they fell on the property and removed everything. Carpets, curtains, everything, in an attempt to deprive the finance company of as much as possible, but in fact much of it was not worth a great deal. Despite his title, the colonel was not a wealthy man. I visited the house before we marketed it, to take measurements and so on, and I met the housekeeper and saw the possessions.' She shook her head. 'Not much to boast about really. In fact, until he sold the house, he had to keep having his television repaired because he couldn't replace it, hadn't the money, you see.' She sipped her tea. 'The colonel spent much of the money that he received from the sale on himself, so the housekeeper said. Apparently the colonel was fond of the expression "there's no pockets in a shroud" and spent his declining years travelling, first-class air tickets, top hotels, cruises, just seeing the world, travelling globally. When he died there was sufficient left to see the housekeeper comfortable in her declining years. I was pleased about that, having met her, a solid, salt of the earth Glasgow woman, gave the colonel thirty years' service and was just grateful to have a job, a wee room at the top of the house to call her own and all found. I was happy for her and she wasn't unhappy to leave the house. She liked the colonel but she never felt comfortable in the house.'

'Oh.'

'There was an atmosphere that wouldn't be got rid of she said. She could never heat the place, even in the summer it had a chill about it. I visited in the summer, and it was cold then. I thought it was the product of a cold day for May and no source of heat in the old house, but apparently it had always been like that. Not haunted or anything paranormal, but eerie. Anyway the Housing Department gave the housekeeper a high amenity apartment in a good scheme and the relatives cleared the property. We advertised in the *Herald*, quite pleased to do so; it's good to be seen with a prestigious property in Tuesday's *Herald*. We had the normal flurry of interest, particularly from the vultures during their wee nosey...'

'The vultures?'

'Vultures. It's an occupational headache. Every time we advertise a house there are always one or two who will ask to view the property just to have a look around, they have no intention of buying. It's always the same people. There are two middle-aged sisters, live just around the corner in Mansfield Street, whenever a property in Partick comes on the market they're round here like a flash feigning interest and asking to be shown round. But only if all the owners' possessions and furnishings are there. They just want to look in their neighbours' houses; it's their hobby, and we have to go along with them, escort them there and back. So when the property in Sherbrooke Avenue came on the market one or two people asked to view the property. I had the impression that they wanted to view the inside of a late-nineteenth-century mansion, and I may have been right because no one took it as far as a survey. No bites at all. Part of the problem is that the price is too high for the present market, but Dalmuir Finance won't consider lowering it.'

'I dare say that they can hold out for the price they want.'

'That's it exactly, Mr King. They are not like a private seller who might have committed himself to another property and absolutely must sell and so will lower the asking price. Dalmuir can hang on until the market picks up as one day it will, meanwhile the house isn't going anywhere.'

'Certainly isn't. Do you have a note of the next of kin, please?'

'They are a Mr and Mrs Headly of Lowerkirk Wynd, Dunoon. I believe they keep a guesthouse.'

'And a list of people who did view the house. I don't suppose anybody viewed it after about the 6th June last year?'

'No.' Sara Sinclair consulted the file, shook her head. 'No, in fact nobody has visited it since just before that date. What's going on?'

'Can't tell you, sorry.'

'Well, nobody viewed the house after 4th June last year.'

'Who did you show the house to on that date?'

'No one.'

'Excuse me?'

'No one, we showed the house to no one. The house being empty of all possessions we did as we always do in such circumstances which is to hand over the keys to the property. Once we have verified the identity of the interested party of course.'

'Of course.'

'Estate agents, particularly lady agents, are always vulnerable when showing strangers around the houses and so whenever we can we arrange for the owner to be present or we hand over the keys.'

'Sensible, so who did you hand the keys to on the 4th June?'

'Gentleman called Marjerison, Toby Marjerison.'

'Address?'

'It's a business address, care of Littlejohn, Houston Ltd.'

'What are they, a firm of solicitors?'

'Civil engineers, address in Blythswood Square as I recall. It'll be in the Yellow Pages.' Sara Sinclair paused. 'I hadn't realized that.'

'What?'

'Mr Marjerison viewed twice. He viewed on the 12th May, one of the first to view, and then came back for a second look on the 4th June. I remember him now, he kept the keys overnight which isn't unusual, and dropped them off again at lunch time the following day. He made some comment about the house being over-priced and I remember agreeing with him and mentioning that there was little interest in the property and he seemed to be pleased about that.'

'He did?'

'Yes. I wasn't surprised because I interpreted it as a sign that he was interested, and I expected him to go ahead with a survey and follow it up with an offer which would be in keeping with the tenor of the market. I would have told him that the price was non-negotiable before he paid for a survey of course, but we never heard from him again. He was quite young to be looking at such property, in his mid-thirties, but he was monied by his bearing, either that or a good con-man. That's another headache we have, the con-men who string us along pretending to be an interested party because they like being fêted and cultivated as a valued customer and take it as far as they can before running for the hills. But Mr Marjerison, he seemed to be the genuine article, he gave the impression that his interest in the house was sincere.'

'I think it may well have been.' King stood and thanked Sara Sinclair for her time.

King left the offices of Sinclair and Reid and turned right down Byres Road, towards Partick Cross and the Kelvinhall tube station. The rain fell vertically, the cloud was low and dark. It was still only mid-afternoon but the streetlights were switched on and the traffic hissed and splashed across the surface of the road; most had headlamps burning. King bought a ticket from the vending machine in the tube station and pondered upon the age of Sara Sinclair: not a day over twenty-six, he decided.

ABERNETHY AND Elka Willems drove along Royston Road, out to Cumbernauld, half an hour's drive from central Glasgow. Cumbernauld, the new town: squat, concrete blocks; grey flat roofs; wooden fencing squaring off small gardens; down in a hollow in the landscape to the northeast of Glasgow. They took Thomasina McArthur by surprise.

'Our parents always wanted boys'—Thomasina McArthur shrugged—'and Pam was the nearest they got, in terms of her attitude; couldn't control her. Me, they christened me before I was born and when I came out wrong they just stuck a few letters on the end of the name. It's not an uncommon practice on the Western Isle, where my dad came from; all the lassies up there are Thomasinas, Edwinas, Paulas. With me they were doubly disappointed because I gave them a granddaughter. They made me less popular, but they're both dead. God rest them. So Pam, she's dead, aye?'

'I'm afraid that we have reason to believe so.' Abernethy spoke softly but firmly.

'I thought it might be like this.' Thomasina McArthur glanced down at her kitchen floor. Behind her the window was steamed up with condensation and beyond the window clothes flapped on a line. She had evidently snatched a brief rain-free spell to dry her daughter's clothing. A pile of still damp clothing lay in a red plastic bin on the work surface beside the stainless-steel sink. 'And when I saw you, I knew. It's not a surprise; it's good to know at last. You see when the police came the first time in the summer, when Pam had disappeared, it was a WPC like this lady here...'

Elka Willems smiled.

'She told me that if two cops call then it's likely to be bad news. She said that one police officer might call to check a detail or some such, but if two call, one a woman, and they look solemn... I watched you leave your motor in the parking bays and start to look for an address... See Cumbernauld, it takes a Philadelphia lawyer to sort these streets, even the postie gets lost. There's no logic in the numbering and the streets don't look like streets... anyway, I ken how you looked and I knew, like you do, you ken, I just knew you were looking for me.' She leaned back against the breakfast bar and behind her a small portable colour television flicked and flashed; the volume had been turned down but Elka Willems recognized scenes from a brainnumbing Australian soap opera which she occasionally exposed herself to in her more exhausted, less guarded moments. 'I'm trying to be upset but I just feel relieved.'

'That's all right.' Elka Willems smiled. 'I think I know what you mean. A sense of relief that you don't have to worry and fret any more seems to dominate all emotions…I think you'll find other emotions come out in time.'

Thomasina McArthur nodded and fumbled a Benson and Hedges from a battered packet and lit it with a match held in trembling fingers.

Abernethy thought that the woman did not look like her sister, not according to the photograph, but he was acutely aware of just how misleading photographs can be. But even allowing for that, Thomasina was dark, she had a rounder, fuller face, she appeared to be shorter and childbirth had ensured she had a fuller figure than her child-free sister. She appeared to be temperamentally different too. Thomasina seemed calm, at least calmer than her sister reportedly had been, and capable of being receptive, unlike the constantly warring and manipulative Pam.

'It's the funeral I'll be dreading.' Thomasina drew on the nail and exhaled through her nose, two plumes of smoke diverging downwards from a round, flat face. 'See, there'll be two of us. I can see it now. There'll be me and there'll be the priest and that's all. Can you imagine the atmosphere in the chapel, the pure embarrassment with a turnout like that?'

'No other family?'

She shook her head. 'Like I said, parents died, me on my own with the wean. I'll not be taking her. Don't get me wrong, I don't think children should be shielded from death, but she's not one year old yet… Sorry, can I make you a coffee, aye?'

'No thanks,' said Abernethy. Elka Willems shook her head. Thomasina McArthur smiled at Abernethy. She liked him, gentle, quiet, nervous still, but time, she knew, would take care of that.

'No friends?' Elka Willems asked.

'Who, me or Pam?'

'Pam.'

'No.' Thomasina shook her head. 'Never did have, not that I knew, no social life at all to speak of. Went out with her mates from work, but nothing outside work. She was a strange girl, she was my sister but she was strange—loopy, but unpleasant with it, flying off the handle, always looking for some insult coming her way, looking for a fight all the time. Ever tried to walk on glass? That's what it's like spending any amount of time with Pam. No, she didn't have a lot of friends, didn't Pam. See, to let you understand, two Christmases ago you remember that bad flu epidemic, a really vicious virus going round. She took it, laid up ill but phoned me to go into Glasgow to get some messages for her, plenty of fruit and some tins she wanted to see her for three or four days. I got the messages all right and took them to her flat—I have a key. Christmas Eve, not one Christmas card, not one in the mail that she hadn't opened—that was all bills and junk mail—and not one on display except the one I had brought with me. So no, hen, there's no friends, and no family. Just me. Me and the priest at the funeral.'

Thomasina McArthur paused. 'I don't know if it's important, maybe it's not but I'll tell you anyway, I'll tell you because I want to tell somebody.' She dragged on the nail. 'See there's a good ten years between me and Pam, nearer eleven, so we didn't really grow up together, we were always in different stages of growth, and there was always this, this... atmosphere in the home, just a damp council semi in Blackhill—Drumpellier Street, Blackhill—as though something big was going on but unsaid, something between my dad and Pam.

It's only when you're an adult and you know of such things that you can tally it all up, like the times I'd get home from school and Pam and Dad would come downstairs together. I mean I was wee, about four or five and so Pam was fourteen or fifteen. My mum worked and my dad didnae, so he was in all the time and she was out. And I remember Pam stopping going to school and so with me at primary one and two, my mum at the tobacco factory, Pam and my dad were at home alone all the day. Then I ken lying in bed one evening and this awful row going on below between they three. Then my mum gave up her work and stayed at home. Then there was no conversation in the house at all, for years, I mean years. Then when I was fifteen my dad took a stroke and didn't recover. Pam wouldn't go to the funeral. See it all adds up but only when you can look back. I never did find out what had gone on, me and Pam we were not so close. I hoped we'd talk to each other one day but…well I'll never find out now, will I? But if something had gone on it explains why Pam turned out the way she did, all anger and bitter and looking for fights, really hating authority, any form of authority, and no friends because she seemed to run away from any sort of permanent thing, just lots of lovers, men and women—aye, women, may as well know that.'

'It had been mentioned,' said Abernethy.

'Aye, imagine it had. So, are you going to tell me how she died?'

'We believe that she may have been murdered.'

Thomasina McArthur's jaw set firm and then relaxed. She nodded her head slowly. 'Murdered,' she said. 'You know, I can see that, I can really see it. I can really see someone wanting to fill Pam in. I mean I don't like violence, I took a good few doings off my man before we split but I'd think: "Well, hen, you're on a two-way street, if you bring on violence by goading your man and provoking him and nipping his head when he wants to eat his supper, you can't complain too much if he lets fly," so I stuck it until I was convinced I wasn't doing any nippin' or provoking and I was giving him peace, and all the rest of it. I stayed until I was convinced he'd do it anyway. Then I picked up the wean and left, ran out into the rain. I remember it well, it was a day like this.' She tossed her head towards the window. She dogged the nail in an ashtray evidently lifted from a Tennants pub at some point in the past. 'But Pam, if she saw a sleeping tiger she'd shove a stick in its ear. It had to happen, she spent her time poking tigers with sticks, so one turned on her.' She fought to extract another nail from the packet.

'You know of no one in particular who'd want to harm your sister?'

'Harm! I know a good few who'd want to roast her on a slow spit.'

'If we were to tell you that some considerable effort had been put in to attempt to conceal your sister's identity, so as to hinder our inquiries, would that mean anything to you? Any one enemy spring to mind, anybody stand out from the rest?'

Thomasina McArthur studied Abernethy with steadily cooling eyes. 'You're saying it was premeditated. I can see somebody paying her off in a fit of temper but, well, I just can't see Pam ever being so powerful that somebody would want to put thought into planning to kill her. I always had the impression that Pam was annoying but not dangerous. Not the sort of woman to be worth doing a life stretch for. She's the sort of person who'd laugh at you from the grave saying "look what you made me do to you".'

'You didn't like your sister?'

Thomasina McArthur shook her head. 'No. I spent a lot of time trying to like her, but I couldn't find anything to like about her. I had little to do with her so I don't know of any one person who'd want to murder her.'

'Well in the first place we don't know whether or not it was premeditated. It could be the result of a rammy that got out of hand, but the indications point to premeditation.'

'You know I once said to our Pam, I once said, "You know, hen, before you're thirty you'll either be very famous or murdered." You see she had this ability to get under your skin very quickly, but she also had this selfish determination to succeed. If she got the bit between her teeth she'd be away and nobody could stop her. So I thought that before she's thirty, she'll be murdered or famous. Or maybe infamous, because if she did get the bit between her teeth it wasn't so much to build or create, or to do something for others, it was to drive to the complete destruction of her enemies.'

'Whoever they might be.' Abernethy stood. Elka Willems did likewise. 'Could we borrow the key to her flat?'

'Aye.' Thomasina McArthur reached for her purse, red plastic, torn near the hinge. 'Her enemies, you ask about her enemies, apart from individuals—the wealthy were her enemies, the employers, anybody who had got what she hadn't got. That was her reasoning: if she couldn't have it, then no one else could have it either.' She handed Abernethy a bunch of keys, two mortices and a Yale. 'You'll need all three.'

'Thank you. But you don't know if she had her sights on any organization in particular, or any individual?'

Thomasina McArthur shook her head. 'Nothing that she discussed with me. I don't even understand the job she did, some fancy name, community worker. See me, I'm a single parent on Income Support and my man, my ex-man, he's a welder. I can understand titles like that. Do you know how she died?'

'Not yet.' Abernethy shook his head.

'Where was her body found?'

'Pollokshields.'

'Pollok— What on earth was she doing there?'

It was Wednesday, 15.10.

WEDNESDAY, 15.10. Elliot Bothwell checked the time, noted it on his pad, to be incorporated in his report— place, date and time of examination. He moved clumsily in awkward uncoordinated movements, blinking behind thick-lensed spectacles as he padded around the room keeping out of the camera angle as the scene of crimes officer recorded the scene. Having taken two spools of still film, one colour, one black and white, still preferred by the police because of its 3-D effect, he now panned slowly around the room with a camcorder, shooting a thirty-minute footage of the locus. There were, Bothwell pondered, aspects of his job that he found somewhat routine; there were aspects which he found difficult to stomach, like lifting fingerprints from corpses, or even from a hand amputated from a corpse for his convenience. But it was a job which was never dull, nor were two jobs ever the same. For most of his working life Bothwell had been employed in a secondary school as a chemistry assistant, mixing the same calm chemicals to be used as teaching aids for uninterested adolescents, and all the while watching the hair of the chemistry teacher turn grey. Then he had noticed the post of Forensic Chemist with Strathclyde Police advertised in the regional council internal vacancy bulletin. He applied, he was offered the job and he had never looked back. The money was the same, the hours were irregular and the work itself he had found to be eye opening. He told his friends at the Queen's Park Bowling Club, as he had overheard the cops say as they joked with each other in the canteen, 'the pay's lousy but we see life'. The job of forensic chemist, Elliot Bothwell had found, was essentially a slow and a methodical plod: it suited his temperament entirely. He was thirty-seven years old, overweight, gauche in speech and movement and still lived with his mother in the three-roomed apartment in Queen's Park in which he had been born.

He knelt by the side of the pool of seven-month-old dried blood and scraped a small quantity of it into a self-sealing cellophane sachet to be dispatched to Dr Kay at the Forensic Science Laboratory 'forthwith,' he was told, 'for DNA matching'.

'Just to make certain beyond all doubt that the blood came from the corpse we found in the shrubbery,' Donoghue had said to him upon Bothwell's arrival, and prior to Donoghue's departure. 'Then pay close attention to the whisky bottle, there.'

'Very good, Mr Donoghue,' said the heavy-jowled Bothwell.

'And after that, anything you can lift, from anywhere in the house, but from this room, stairs and back door particularly.'

'Understood.'

'Respectfully draw your attention to the hoof print.' Donoghue nodded to the trainer print in the dried blood. 'Don't disturb it until scene of crimes has captured it on celluloid.' Bothwell smiled at the scene of crimes officer who at that moment was setting up his equipment.

'Again, fully understood.'

Bothwell now placed the sachet containing the scrapings of blood into his briefcase and snapped the penknife shut. Camcorders and identikits made up by computer graphics, rather than multiple layers of cellophane with parts of faces printed on them, may be all very well, he thought, but the forensic chemist still needs his pocket knife, and his iron filings and squirrel hairbrush to lift latents. He placed his ballpoint pen in the mouth of the whisky bottle and, tilting it, lifted it and placed it in a large cellophane bag. That item he could dust for prints in the ease and comfort of the laboratory.

The scene of crimes officer packed his equipment and left Bothwell at it. It was now all down to slow, meticulous plodding—spreading iron filings and dusting them away gently, so that only the filings which adhered to the ridges left by a fingerprint would remain. He then laid clear adhesive tape over the fingerprint, peeled it back and the latent was 'lifted'. Or he would have done had there been any prints to lift. He dusted the windowsills, the hearth, the mantelpiece, the door handle, the carpenter's bench and came up with many smudges of gloved hands but no prints. He fared better in the hallway, in the kitchen, in the downstairs rooms, but his trained and experienced eye told him that he was lifting prints made earlier than the gloved smudges in the front bedroom. These were the prints of the previous owner and his family or of the estate agent when he or she looked around the property. Bothwell knew that he was on a hiding to nothing, but he was nothing if not thorough, and continued to spread and dust, and lift, and spread and dust.

'I CAN SEE WHAT her sister meant.' Donoghue pushed the door of the flat open.

'I'm sorry?' King stood behind him.

'Abernethy told me that her sister had called on her one Christmas Eve and found that Pam hadn't received a single card.'

'Not even from her so-called "slaves"?'

'Apparently not.' Donoghue stepped into the flat. 'See, hardly any post at all, assuming of course that we two are the first over the threshold since she closed the door behind her to start her last day at work.'

'The first since the cops who would have checked the premises as part of the missing persons procedure, at least,' said King, but Donoghue's words struck a chord as it occurred to him in an instant that only those fortunate ones who reach retirement really know which is going to be their last day at work. Many people have lost their lives travelling to or from their employment, others have died at their work, still others have been 'laid off' in recession-hit late twentieth-century Britain and have lived in ever fading hope of re-employment. But only those who calmly pack up their tools, or switch off the engine for the last time, or clear their desk on the last afternoon, know which is their last working day.

'Indeed,' said Donoghue. 'Indeed. But if somebody called between now and the time of her disappearance, then they called soon after her disappearance. Just look at that pile of junk mail, and we appear to be the first to disturb it. Have a sift through it, Richard, look for any personal mail.' Donoghue walked down the short, narrow hallway. His eyes and his keen interest in Glaswegian architecture told him that Pam McArthur's flat was a refurbished, three-room-and-kitchen, two up in dim Finlay Drive, Denniston.

He went into the living room and switched on the light. A red bulb in the ceiling glowed and showed an odd assortment of furniture, ill at ease with itself; bought, it seemed, from charity shops with little thought about mixing, matching and colour scheming, much like a student's flat, or indeed his own first just-starting-out flat. The curtains were of a pattern very common in the households of the east end of the city, or so he had found, grey with diagonal red stripes, much like many of her neighbours' curtains would be, and Donoghue fancied that it would probably have been Pam McArthur's one concession to conformity with those about her. It's difficult to be different in the east end. The room he felt had a solid, down-to-earth, practical feel to it. The light coloured wallpaper and the high ceiling of the old tenement gave a sense of space.

The books on the shelf in the alcove seemed to be of a political nature—books about Marx and Engels, books by them, political pamphlets about issues current to Scotland and issues currently 'live' in Britain. A small television was sensitive to the surroundings; it gelled with the room and didn't dominate it unlike many homes in the city.

King joined him. 'Junk mail,' he said. 'Bills and promotions and the like. Not a personal letter, postcard or note shoved through the letter box amongst it all. And that's after six months.'

'Nearer eight. If she was murdered on or about June 6th last year, the beginning of June, it's now mid-January... nearer eight months.'

'Aye, it is, isn't it? Eight months and not a single item of personal mail.'

'I'm beginning to get a feel of this lady,' Donoghue mused. 'She was angry about something, some injustice; burning up with it and directing it all into her work, manipulating those that she didn't go to war with.'

'She seemed to live comfortably enough.' King surveyed the room and glanced out of the window at the tenements across the street, glistening with rain. They were just above the level of the streetlamp and King wondered if the constant glow had been a source of annoyance for her. Or perhaps not, he thought, instantly recalling pleasant nights spent in the company of a lady, some time before he met Rosemary, and how they used to leave the curtains of her bedroom open, enjoying the soft glow from the streetlamp, bolted to the wall just below the window.

'It's the sort of standard of living that we'd expect of her in her position. We won't find that she was blackmailing anybody. No sign of anything here but the paltry salary of a lowly public servant. Anything strike you as being out of place, or of interest to ourselves in the capacity of police officers?'

King looked carefully, feeling that the question implied he ought to notice something. Eventually he said, 'Frankly no.'

Donoghue shook his head. 'Me neither and that in itself is significant. Let's see where she took her rest.'

Pam McArthur had slept on a double mattress on the floor. It had a blue fitted sheet and a matching blue duvet over the sheet. Both heavily crumpled but the single pillow still had the indentation of a single head. A rug lay over bare floorboards; two old wardrobes— Oxfam castoffs, thought Donoghue. Clothing lay strewn about the floor—much denim, winter boots and summer sandals. The room had a musty smell which Donoghue felt in fairness was only to be expected, given that the windows had been closed for nearly eight months. 'Nothing here for us,' he said. 'One more room.'

King turned and led the way to the third room, the room closest to the front door, what would have been the second bedroom of the flat, being noticeably smaller than the room Pam McArthur used as her sleeping quarters. It had been turned into a study. The curtains were closed. King strode across the floor and opened them; grey afternoon light flooded in. 'I think she was a night hawk,' he said. 'Study curtains closed like this.'

'Probably,' Donoghue conceded as he surveyed the study. Loudly on the wall were two posters, side by side, hugely disproportionate to the size of the room: one, in grey, was of Karl Marx and the other, in blood red, of Joseph Stalin. Donoghue looked at the posters. 'You know I can sympathize a little bit with that one.' He indicated Karl Marx. 'I don't wholly agree, but his heart was in the right place. But him, him, for heaven's sake, he was responsible for the deaths of more human beings than Adolf Hitler. The anger of socialists and their indignation about our unjust society is all very well but I do wish they'd read their history books before choosing their icons.'

'Maybe she did,' said King quietly. 'She's not coming across as having been a particularly pleasant young woman. Maybe she knew fine well what Stalin did, and saw him as a hero.'

Donoghue caught his breath. King had a point. Full knowledge of the activities of Joseph Stalin would be more in keeping with Pam McArthur as she was becoming known than would political naivety. Yes, King had a point.

A small table stood by the window. An Amstrad personal computer stood on the table and beside the computer were files labelled 'Dampness Campaign', 'Welfare Benefits Take-up Campaign' and 'Youth Unemployment'.

'All very predictable,' said Donoghue. 'Old-fashioned computer—second-hand, I'd say; files on community work issues.'

'Just what you'd expect really.' King looked around the room. 'The lady took her work home with her.'

'Or worked at home. I believe the job of community worker has that degree of latitude...'

There was a sharp, insistent rap on the front door. Donoghue and King glanced at each other and then stepped into the hallway.

'Yes, hen?' King addressed the woman who stood on the threshold: late middle-aged, short grey hair, eyes with a piercing expression. A nail smouldered between nicotine-stained fingers and a black poodle stood behind her, attached to her hand by a slender yellow lead. The dog looked tired, cold, dejected and dispirited. King firmly believed in the saying that if you want to know a man look at his dog. Or her dog in this case and indeed the woman looked cold, tired, dejected and dispirited, yet there was a hunger in her eyes.

'Just watching the house.' Her voice was high pitched, a note of urgency stopped just short of a whine, and both cops saw then that the piercing hunger of the eyes was nothing more nor less than burning curiosity.

'Can I ask your name, hen?' King said.

'Mrs Sloan. Only my man's been away these fifteen years.'

'Sorry, hen.'

'But I keep my eye on her house. I live across the landing. I've got the single end,' She deeply inhaled.

'The single end,' said King. The woman had put the lead on the poodle to walk three feet from one door to another.

'I didnae like the woman, ken, but you have to be neighbourly, but that woman would start a fight in an empty house, so she would. But you've got to be neighbourly, so you have. Who are you, sir?'

'Police.' Donoghue was amused at Mrs Sloan's concept of neighbourliness.

'Oh, again? I wondered—'

'Again?'

'Aye, again. You've been twice already.'

'Twice?'

'Aye, twice.' She nipped the nail between two blunt fingers and tossed the dog-end on the stair. The section that she didn't have to clean—or so Donoghue assumed, if the rule was as normal and the residents cleaned from their own door down to the next landing. 'See the first time they came, they were two uniformed polis, just after the woman disappeared. They came to check that she wasn't lying dead in the house—they had a spare set of keys taken from somewhere. They locked up behind them and then left. A few weeks later it was, a man in plain clothes, as you are, came and took a bag of something away with him.'

'He did?'

'Aye.'

'You wouldn't have any idea what was in the bag?'

Mrs Sloan shook her head. 'Just a plastic carrier bag—the sort you get from supermarkets—and it wasn't full. It looked as though something was in the bottom. He held it screwed together halfway up.'

'You're certain he was the police?'

'That's what he said when I asked him. He looked the part, tall, smart, and had her keys, so I thought they'd found her.'

'He had her keys?'

Mrs Sloan nodded. 'It was her key ring that he had. That's why I heard him at her door. He was trying the locks, and the chain and the cross were banging on the door. She never went in for dainty feminine things. The key chain was a loop of thin chain fastened with a padlock, then a length of heavier chain attached to a metal Celtic cross. Couldn't mistake it. I just assumed that you'd found her, or at least her bag—huge leather satchel, she carried, no handbag for her. Slung it over her shoulder and held the strap, like my man used to sling his rifle. She was too masculine for my taste but really slim, like a stick insect. Mind you, it's a pity she disappeared when she did, she seemed to have a change of attitude.'

'Oh?'

'Aye, like someone had given her her raw meat and she was satisfied. See, she came home with a good drink in her one day. I found her fumbling with her keys and she said to me—oh, breath like a flamethrower, she'd been on the heavy bevy—she said to me: "Something big went down in this town thirty years ago, something big." Then she found the right key and collapsed into her flat. It was a week or two after that that she went missing.'

Donoghue asked: 'This man, the second man, the one who had obtained her keys, you'd recognize him again, aye?'

'Oh aye.' Mrs Sloan nodded. 'Tall, good-looking, posh.'

'Posh?'

'Aye, posh, upper class. I used to be in service before I was married and when you've been with that sort you can tell 'em. I don't know how, can't put my finger on it, but you can tell, you just can.'

'I wonder if you have time to come to the police station, Mrs Sloan?'

'Now?'

'If you wouldn't mind.'

'I suppose—'

Her attempt to sound unenthusiastic was transparent to both cops and Donoghue cut her off. 'Thanks,' he said. He turned to King. 'Richard, nip back into the study, will you, please? Address your attention to the computer; see if there are any computer discs about.' King did so. He returned a few moments later. 'No discs, sir,' he said.

'You know'—Donoghue tapped his pipe stem against his teeth—'you know, I didn't think there would be. They're just the sort of thing you'd carry off in a plastic supermarket bag.'

DONOGHUE DROVE TO Edinburgh and home. He left P Division shortly after 5.00 p.m. and eased his Rover gently into the traffic at Charing Cross as it inched its way north and east. He drove out of Glasgow, gradually picking up speed as the traffic congestion eased.

Out past the sprawling east end schemes, glowing with lights in early evening darkness, straddling the M8. He settled behind a lorry moving at a moderate speed, just beyond the reach of the spray from its rear wheels; it was always the safest place while driving on a motorway. Find a heavy vehicle that's moving at the speed you want to move at, tuck yourself in behind it and stay there. He relaxed to Radio 4: '*PM* at 5.00 p.m.'. He drove past the Kirk O'Shotts, always eerie to his eyes, a huge building standing isolated on a hillside, black studs of gravestones in the land around, always with lights burning, but never had he seen a living human being in its vicinity. He switched off the car radio at the approach to Edinburgh, as the stock market closing prices began to be announced, and placed his pipe in his mouth. It helped him think.

A young woman had been murdered. She had by all accounts been a very unpleasant character, just the sort who would get under the skin of all but 'her slaves' of whom she had, again by all accounts, not a few, though none had thought her deserving of a Christmas card. Had she been found with a smashed skull or with a knife in her ribs, the police inquiry would have been concluded very quickly or not at all; so many people could have been pushed far enough to murder her. Such things happen with alarming frequency, and in fact is the most common form of murder: a husband kills his wife or vice versa in a fit of rage. It is that which makes the ordinary five-inch bladed kitchen knife Scotland's number one murder weapon.

But not in this case.

In this case there was a story.

In this case there appeared to be clear premeditation.

In this case there had been a distinct, though clumsy, attempt to conceal the identity of the deceased.

In this case somebody had visited her flat shortly after the murder and had removed the discs from her computer.

That, Donoghue felt as he drove past Edinburgh Airport, was the crux. Find the discs, or at least the contents, the information they contained, and the case would crack open.

He also felt that Mrs Sloan, whose vigilance was born out of curiosity, had pointed the police in the right direction with her recollection of a drunken Pam McArthur tripping into her flat with the words 'something big went down in this town thirty years ago'.

Pam McArthur was a woman adept at treading on toes and she had trodden on the toes of a beast who was not at all intimidated by her, but was sufficiently terrified of what she could do to him that he had turned on her. Murdered her. Severed the head and hands from her body to hinder the identification of her, so as to give himself a few days to cover his tracks perhaps, but in the event had been allowed a full eight months. The murderer, or murderers, had returned a few days after the event and had removed her watch.

There was a story here, he thought, and was convinced that information about the big thing that had gone down 'in this town' had been stored on the computer discs which had been removed by a tall, good-looking, 'classy' male.

At his home, while his wife sat with Louisa in her room reading her a story before switching out the light, he sat in the living room with Timothy, amused by his son's ploy of delaying bed time by engaging him in a sensible conversation. He listened patiently as Timothy explained the dire consequences of global warming—how the lowering of the water table had decimated the frog and toad population in Europe and so allowed insects to flourish, how the sea levels were rising and the average wind speed increasing. Not bad for an eight-year-old, thought Donoghue. Not only did Timothy grasp the concept of global warming but he was also clearly intelligent enough to see that a delay of bed time was more likely to be earned than fought for. Indeed it was only when the conversation began to get frivolous—about the possibility of flying kites in hurricancs—that Donoghue felt that it really was time for bed. The inevitable protest was instantly devastated by the raising of an eyebrow.

He reached for the much crumpled copy of the *Scotsman* and settled into his chair. 'The discs,' he said aloud. 'Find them, or what they contain, and you'll wrap this one up.'

FOUR

MONTGOMERIE STROKED his down-turned moustache, leaned back in his chair and pondered the photofit. Without taking his eyes from the computer image print he extended his right hand and curled his fingers around a mug of coffee. He brought the coffee up to his lips and continued to study the image. A common face, seen often. Not a criminal, more of the ilk of a male model. Montgomerie nodded, yes, yes, that was it, that's where the familiarity lay; he'd seen this face often, usually while leafing through magazines in dentists' waiting rooms: clean cut, a little fleshier than his own chiselled features; thick head of hair, longer than his own, curly, whereas his hair was straight. He held the photofit at arm's length. Me, he thought. That's me in about ten years' time.

'They said I'd be home before this,' said Mrs Sloan, sitting upright in a chair, having declined a coffee and, thought Montgomerie, missing the attention now that the image had been created.

Montgomerie lowered the photofit and beamed at her. 'Aye,' he said.

'Aye,' groaned Mrs Sloan.

Behind the screen of the print-out Montgomerie allowed himself a brief smile, short, but it was there. It was his distinct impression that despite her protests, Mrs

Sloan would far rather be sitting in a police station, assisting with enquiries, than at home.

'Soon have you back, madam. You know this is quite a detailed impression that you've created.'

'Took me long enough. Mind you, that's how I recollect him, good-looking, very distinct, lush brown hair, curly, and like I told the other gents, he had style, class; he was a Scot right enough, but definitely Hyndland, not Easterhouse. He had yon softer accent.'

'So you said.'

'A bit like yours in fact.'

Montgomerie glanced at her. 'Like me?'

'Like your voice, the voice of an educated man. You have an education, I think?'

'I went to Edinburgh University to study law.' He shrugged his shoulders. 'I didn't finish the course. It's another story.'

'But you've been at uni even if you didn't come away with a bit of paper. You're a young man with that stamp about you.' She pointed to the photofit. 'Well, he had the same.'

'That's a good point. We'll take a note of it. I'd like you to look at some photographs, if you would?'

'I've been here for two hours already.'

'More.' Montgomerie smiled. 'Nearer three.'

Mrs Sloan shuffled in her seat and lit a cigarette. 'Do I wait here?'

'If you would. I'll nip downstairs and get a couple of photograph albums.'

Malcolm Montgomerie left the interview room and walked down the CID corridor with long, effortless strides. He had started his shift late, having been delayed a little by a diversion at his flat. He had not found it easy to leave the flat, feeling that he had to wait until she was slumbering as soundly as might be expected of a healthy young woman at one o'clock in the afternoon. Eventually he decided he could wait no longer and had slipped out from under the duvet, washed, dressed, written a hasty note which he pinned to the cork notice board above the fridge, and eased out of the flat, but not before he heard a plaintive 'Malcolm...' come from the bedroom.

He walked down the scrubbed stairs of his close and stepped into Hyndland Street, just opposite the swing park. He had driven to P Division, at Charing Cross, arriving at ten minutes past two in the afternoon, signed in, checked his pigeonhole—nothing—and had run upstairs to the CID corridor, preparing an apology to pant to a doubtless irate Richard King who would be anxious to hand over the shift and return home. But he found the CID room empty. He found Sussock's office empty, but he expected that—Sussock had drawn the graveyard shift that week. What did surprise him was that DI Donoghue's office was empty. 'Something,' he said to himself, strolling down the corridor, the feeling of guilt at being late lifting sweetly from his shoulders, 'cooks.'

He had returned to the CID room and fixed a coffee using powdered milk because that day the 'everybody thought somebody else would do it' number had applied and the fresh milk had been exhausted. Montgomerie walked across the floor to his desk sweeping the much battered copy of that day's *Glasgow Herald* from Abernethy's desk top as he passed it. He had a mountain of paperwork to move, to file, to process, to pass on to the next box in the system, but he couldn't, as always seemed to be the case, address his tasks in hand until he had devoured the newspaper and attempted what might remain of the crossword. He sank in his chair, feet on his desk, mug of coffee in hand and opened the newspaper.

The newspaper, the crossword it contained, and further mugs of coffee at frequent intervals occupied him for the following two hours.

Finally, without further distractions at his disposal, he had tossed the newspaper aside and without taking his feet off the desk managed a sufficiently long arm to reach the in-tray on the corner of his desk. He picked up a case that had been allocated to him as being the 'interested officer'. He began to read: two families had lived in the same close for upwards of thirty years, in and out of each other's houses, had children who'd attended the same schools and who'd played together, had grown up together, had gone out drinking together. Two of the boys, one from each family, too much lager, an argument, a shove, a knife... One dead and the other standing over him disbelievingly and looking at a mandatory life sentence, presently in the slammer, in the basement of P Division, checked every fifteen minutes being deemed a suicide risk. And the two families, according to initial reports, were still living in and out of each other's houses, not knowing whether to blame, or comfort, or commiserate. Both families still too shocked to take it in; both families losing sons to each other. Montgomerie would visit the families, talk to the bar staff, take witness statements, speak to the youth in the cells, and prepare a report to send to the Office of the Procurator Fiscal.

There was nothing extraordinary about the case, it was a typical Glasgow murder: alcohol related, impetuous, victim and assailant known to each other, cheap, grubby, futile. He thought that in this case the two families might well continue to coexist while they both had suffered a loss. But if the High Court accepted a plea of guilty to manslaughter on the grounds of absence of malicious aforethought and perhaps a plea of mitigation due to provocation, then the youth now being checked every fifteen minutes could walk in five years. Could return home in five years and make one of the families complete again. At that point, a look of smugness, an insensitive remark, would cause the families to begin to drift apart and the seeds of retribution would be planted in the minds of the family whose son did not return. Such things take years to become resolved, if ever.

There had been a shuffle of feet in the corridor. Montgomerie had swung his brogues onto the linoleum and glanced up as Donoghue and a tired-looking King entered the room.

'There's a lady downstairs, Montgomerie.' Donoghue had sat at Abernethy's desk. 'She's come here to draw up a photofit. If you'd take her to one of the computer terminals and remain there with the operator...'

'Very good, sir.' Montgomerie stood.

'She's likely to be anxious to get home to feed her poodle.' King walked to the kettle and the mugs and powdered milk. 'Coffee, sir?'

'Please. Milk, no sugar. After that, if you'd go through the mug shots with her. She might ID someone. It's a murder inquiry. Richard will give you the nuts and bolts. File's on my desk if you need to consult it or add anything. Hand the whole thing over to Ray Sussock when he comes on at 22.00. I want to keep the momentum up on this one.'

'Very good, sir.'

Richard King fought off fatigue with a coffee, strong, black, and had given Montgomerie the nuts and bolts of the investigation into the non-natural death of Pam McArthur.

'Not a pleasant lady.' Montgomerie drained his cup. 'That poster of Stalin . . . I mean, says it all.'

'Not pleasant at all by each and every account. You'll be reading the file but we have not yet met anybody who has had a good word for her. But Fabian is right . . .'

'As he tends to be.'

King had smiled. 'There is more to this than somebody filling her in on impulse. She was cooled after a period of premeditation and planning. She was lured to that empty house, which somebody knew to be empty. The estate agent fed us a name and a business address which we'll visit tomorrow. A lot of trouble was taken to hinder her identification, even to the point of going back a few days later and disturbing the corpse, possibly in order to remove a distinctive watch she possessed.'

'Disturbing what remained of the corpse.'

'Aye, the head and hands will likely have been taken away in the sludge boat.'

'Or in a weighted sack in the Forth and Clyde Canal, or burnt on a bonfire which in fact is about what a bonfire is. In the good old days when felons were hung, drawn and quartered, their remains were put on a bone fire. Over time it has contracted to bonfire.'

'I didn't know that.' King had continued to sip his coffee.

'That's me, fund of useless information, makes me a star player at Trivial Pursuit.'

'Well, anyway, our friend downstairs, Mrs Sloan, a neighbour of the deceased, across the landing on her stair, she reckons she saw a guy leave her flat, one guy in particular, a guy with class, plenty of style. Had a plastic carrier with him when he left her flat. Fabian clocked the computer and asked me to look for the discs.'

'None?'

'Right first time. Apparently, according to Mrs Sloan, she had come home one night smashed out of her skull, all arms and legs, and had said, or slurred, something about something big going down in the city about thirty years ago.'

'Oh...'

'Yes, so it's all down to the photofit and mug shots. The key to this is the information contained on the discs, so Fabian believes, and I think, again, he's right.'

'No files, handwritten notes, newspaper clippings?'

King had shaken his head. 'Files about things like benefit take-up, dampness, but that appeared to be connected to her employment as a community worker.'

'A what?'

'It's a form of social worker—tend to work with groups rather than individuals.'

'I see.'

'Elliot Bothwell's been at the locus with the scene of crimes officer. I don't suppose...?'

'Not since I've been here.'

'Well, there was a hoof print in the blood and a whisky bottle—dare say they needed a stiffener as they sawed her up. Bothwell will lift any prints off the bottle and steam off the label so we can trace the retail outlet from the bar code. I reckon that's for the day shift as well; that's for me to come into tomorrow.'

'So I'm down to the photofit and a trawl through the albums.'

King stood. 'That's about the size of it, pal.'

Malcolm Montgomerie collected the photo files of men in the age range of the man described by Mrs Sloan. 'About thirty-two I'd say, son.'

'About,' had echoed Montgomerie.

And Mrs Sloan had replied in all seriousness: 'Aye, about.' Mrs Sloan had impressed Montgomerie as being a very exact woman, who had already that afternoon placed the computer operator in a state of near exasperation as she had taken close to three hours to produce an enhanced image of the man she had glimpsed leaving Pam McArthur's flat which was to her satisfaction. Three hours to produce an image of the man she had seen for a few seconds, eight months previously. Montgomerie had shared the computer operator's exasperation which was made more annoying because he sensed Mrs Sloan was clearly enjoying herself.

Richard King drove to his home in Bishopbriggs. He was tired, he was hungry, he was four hours late and he knew that Rosemary would have begun to worry. But being late was nothing new, and he'd warned her when they were talking of marriage. 'You're not just marrying a man, you're marrying a job. That's what it means to be a cop's wife.' His eyelids felt like lead, but they had felt like lead before and doubtless they'd feel like lead again, and do so in the immediate future. That he knew, but the sense of unfairness, of resentment about compulsory overtime, never left him and he doubted that it ever would. Even oft repeated comments, such as 'If you wanted to punch a time card you shouldn't have joined the police,' or observations along the lines of 'It comes with the job', 'It's part of the territory', didn't dull the cutting edge of his irritation at his em-

ployer's intrusion into his free time. He had a home to
go to, a modest semi-detached, with good neighbours.
It was a home unique, unlike any other. It was his
home. It was good to be there: difficult to leave.

He parked his car in the street. He felt it could stay
there until the morning, no point in garaging it, can't be
fussed, just want to rest. He walked up the path to his
front door and was met by Rosemary dressed as most
often in a dress of pastel shades with her hair tied in a
bun. She embraced him and held him and helped him
peel off his damp coat. She took it from him and hung
it up on the peg, allowing it to drip onto the hall carpet. She followed him to the kitchen in which he sat, at
the breakfast bar, beside planks of wood which he had
brought home the previous November to fulfil Rosemary's repeated request for shelves in the kitchen. He
had brought them home from the DIY store, propped
them against the wall; had turned his undivided attention to Iain and had helped him build a tower of
brightly coloured plastic bricks. The planks of wood
had not been moved since then, not from that day to
this. And Rosemary never complained, never nagged
him, never even mentioned them, but occasionally,
when she thought it fair, when she knew he was rested
and refreshed and when she knew he had time to spare,
and when she knew he was looking at her, she would
throw a glance at the wood in her silent Quaker way.
But this was not one of those times. On this occasion
Rosemary King knew her husband to be an exhausted
man and she pressed a mug of steaming tea into his
hand and left him in the kitchen, left him to 'come
down' in his own time. Leaving him alone with the
Evening Times. Later she returned to the kitchen with

Iain in her arms who wanted to say 'good night' to 'Daddy'.

'SEE THESE, they are bandits, son.' Mrs Sloan exhaled as she spoke but kept her eyes glued to the photographs. 'No, I don't like the look of him neither I do, nor him either.'

'If you'd just look to see if you recognize the man you saw leaving the McArthur household.' Malcolm Montgomerie waved his hand to clear the cigarette smoke. He recollected clearly the information he'd read in an article about passive smoking.

'Oh, I am, son, I am.' Mrs Sloan drew on the nail, hissing slightly as she did so. She studied each photograph carefully, one by one, before slowly turning the page, working her way from cover to cover of each book and upon reaching the end, would place it on the pile and reach for the next book. Occasionally she would shake her head and remark, 'Never knew there were so many bandits,' or, 'See all these bandits, son,' or, 'See these, they all bandits, son?'

'Only the ones we catch, hen.' Montgomerie clasped his hands behind his head. 'They're only the ones we catch.'

'You don't say, son. See, I wonder if my man's in here. He could sink a good bucket so he could and see him, he was lifted so often it's a wonder he didn't recognize the inside of the pokey more than his own house.'

'Could? Liked?'

'Aw, son, he's been dead these fifteen years so he has.'

'Well, he'll not be in there, Mrs Sloan. If you could keep looking please, and if you wouldn't browse—really look hard at each photograph.'

'Aye. He was a shipyard worker.'

'Who?'

'My man.'

Montgomerie sighed and wiped his face with his hands. But it reminded him of an obligation to visit a relative by marriage who had also been a shipyard worker. An obligation deferred until the man's wife, and Montgomerie's aunt, had returned from Winnipeg, having just 'popped over' to Canada to visit her sister: as was the whim of Montgomerie's aunt.

'Aye, son...the photos...' Mrs Sloan turned a page.

There was a sudden polite yet insistent tapping on the door. Montgomerie made a long arm and turned the handle.

'Phone call, Mr Montgomerie.' Phil Hamilton stood on the threshold.

'Didn't know you'd drawn a back shift, Phil.'

Hamilton shrugged. 'It's Dr Reynolds. He'd like to speak to any CID officer involved in the...' Hamilton looked at Mrs Sloan.

'Don't mind me, son,' said Mrs Sloan. 'Just pretend I'm not here.' Hamilton and Montgomerie glanced at each other and smiled.

'Very well.' Montgomerie stood. 'Could you remain here with Mrs Sloan? As you see, she's looking at our...our snapshots.'

'Certainly.'

Montgomerie walked briskly to the stairs and took them two at a time. He went to his desk in the CID room and snatched up the phone and dialled a two-figure internal number. The line burred and cracked at

Montgomerie. 'Switchboard? You have a Dr Reynolds holding, I believe? Put him through here, please.' The line cracked once. Montgomerie had a sense of listening to a void, a huge hollow empty silence. He said, 'Dr Reynolds?'

'Ah, hello, knew I'd get through to someone eventually.'

'DC Montgomerie.' Montgomerie reached for pen and note pad.

'I've just completed the postmortem on the deceased lady, the girl who was found in shrubbery in Pollokshields this morning.'

'Pam McArthur.'

'You've already identified her? Good. I'll be sending the report over to you by courier once it's been typed up. Won't be until tomorrow now. Our typist comes in at about 8.30 and needs a few pints of black coffee before she sobers up, but once she gets into her stride she's a good worker. But anyway, I thought you'd like to know the gist of it.'

'Certainly would.' Montgomerie trapped the handset between his ear and shoulder and held the note pad and ballpoint with his hands.

'She had,' began a voice in his ear, 'engaged in sexual activity, or maybe was engaged against her will in sexual activity, shortly before her death.'

'Oh?'

'There are semen traces in the vagina.'

'I didn't know semen could survive that length of time.'

'It didn't survive in the sense that it's able to fertilize; it dies, as the host dies, but it remains resistant to decomposition. I once did a PM on a rape/murder victim whose body had lain in a remote part of the countryside for a number of years. The flesh had all but decayed but the semen was visible to the naked eye—a trained naked eye, but visible nonetheless. And what's more the blood group of the donor and his DNA signature will be able to be extracted. So I've sent a sample off for DNA profiling. That result will take a few days. I've marked it for priority, but we're still talking days, at least.'

'How close to the actual death would that have been? The sexual activity, I mean?'

'Virtually simultaneously. The semen wouldn't be identifiable if the host had lived for even an hour after intercourse. Also some of the semen is close to the opening of the vagina. Semen is a wiry, tough character and can make its own way to where nature intended it to go if it's deposited in close enough proximity. In this case it's been deposited both in and on the lips of the vagina. It hadn't travelled from the lips and so death followed immediately upon it being deposited. Or had occurred before it was deposited—a stomach-wrenching possibility but not without precedent.'

'It certainly isn't. Two semen deposits?'

'Yes. It could mean two men. It could mean a generous deposit from one man. We'll know when the results come back. I took samples from both locations.'

'You're not suggesting rape?'

'I'm not suggesting anything. I am a humble reporter of facts. Besides which rape is a legal definition, not a medical diagnosis. Mind you, off the record, it's likely to have been forcible, the degree of mutilation, the murder; this is your territory but I for one find it inconceivable that an act of love should be followed by an act of butchery. What is conceivable is that an act of

rape would be followed immediately by dismemberment.'

'Certainly adds up better. The house itself is not the
sort of place a couple would go to for an act of passion. Bare floorboards, so I believe; no curtains.'

'Putrefaction was rapid because the deceased was
slim. Vulva was swollen and discoloured, that's wholly
because of putrefaction...' Reynolds mumbled over his
notes. 'Adipocere.'

'Adi...?'

'Adipocere...it's not uncommon; it tends to be found
on bodies that have been deposited or buried shallowly
in moist soil. As in this case. It's a transformation of the
fatty tissues of the body into a greasy, waxy substance,
being adipocere; it's pale yellow in colour and gives off
a stale odour. It's useful because its presence means that
the corpse spent its entire time from death to discovery
on wet or damp soil. It would confirm that the body
was left where it was found, although it was moved
once, about a week after death, but it wasn't brought
there from another, drier locus shortly before it was
found. Its development also suggests that the corpse is
six to ten months old, earlier than I had first thought.'

'Our enquiries indicate that the murder may have
been committed about eight months ago, sir.'

'Well, that dovetails quite neatly. Now, of possible
interest is that her attacker wore a beard.'

'He did?'

'Probably. Won't stick my neck out and make a def-
inite statement, but I think it highly probable that he
was bearded. You see, there was a single hair on her
chest, by which I mean it was lodged there as opposed
to growing. I had a close look at it, black in colour, so
it didn't come from her scalp and it was triangular in

cross-section. It was hair from a beard. Scalp hair is circular in cross-section, pubic hair is oval in cross-section. I've sent it off for DNA examination too, but it would not surprise me if it proves to belong to the gentleman who deposited the semen inside her.'

'For DNA examination...' Montgomerie repeated as he scribbled notes on his pad, more to reassure Dr Reynolds that he was taking full and accurate note of the information being relayed. It was one of the skills of telephone work: give as well as receive.

'I've done what tests I can for poison,' Reynolds continued, 'but the results are negative, which doesn't surprise me.'

'Not poisoned?'

'Well, no trace of poison. Some poisons—arsenic, and strychnine, for example—will have left traces identifiable after this length of time. Others—coniine, or gelsemium, for example—will have left no trace after the time period in question. Though again, this is where your remit and mine merge, Mr Montgomerie. I can only report observed facts, but if I am allowed to opine...?'

'All you like, sir.'

'Well, I hardly think that poison goes with dismemberment, doesn't fit; as I said to Mr Sussock this morning they are uneasy bedfellows. One is neat and the other violent and messy. But that's really for you gentlemen to ponder.'

'Thanks very much.' Montgomerie smiled, knowing that a smile can be heard. 'But I take your point and I think Inspector Donoghue will be happy to eliminate poisoning as a cause of death.'

'Keep an open mind, be prepared to look beyond first appearances, but never ignore the obvious—I think we can say we've done that in this case. Death, I would think, will have been due to a blow on the head, or suffocation, or strangulation. The head being missing and the neck damaged and decomposed to the extent it has been, I'm afraid that we'll never be able to obtain forensic proof of the cause of death.'

'We can live with that, or without it, as the case may be. Thanks. I'll make sure DI Donoghue has this information a.s.a.p.'

'Advise him, please, that a full report, plus the DNA results, will be with him shortly.'

RAY SUSSOCK WOKE. He glanced at his watch: Wed 22 Jan 19.37 by the digital display. He closed his eyes again. Still Wednesday, still the same day on which he was called out to the corpse found in a shrubbery. There seemed to him to be no let up. He closed his eyes, hunting the elusive escape of sleep. Minutes later he opened them again, kept them open, but also kept his head turned to the wall. Eventually he conceded that resistance was futile, he could run away no more, and he turned to face his world. His world.

His world at his age was a dim bedsit, once diplomatically described as 'cosy' by Elka Willems shortly after he had moved in. That, he recalled, was in the middle of the Glasgow knife murder case, in a January which was, unlike the present January, the coldest in living memory. My God, had he been here all this time, having taken the room for a few weeks, which had run into months and now into years? He looked about him: the single chair, the narrow wardrobe, the small writing desk, and the ludicrously tight floor space in which he could turn around and walk the length of his bed to the door. And that was it. He turned and looked at the ceiling. Had it come to this? he wondered. Was this all he had to show for in excess of thirty years' service? A modest rank and a bedsit, and a battered old Ford in the gutter? But still, he felt, this accommodation was preferable to exposing his desperation for a bed, and a failed marriage, by asking for a place in police quarters. He wanted to 'keep the lid on', keep 'it' low profile. Sort it out neatly and quietly and without gossip. He didn't want gossip. So he stayed.

He stayed with a shared toilet.

He stayed with shared cooking facilities.

He stayed in a room within a huge old house in Kelvinside. His neighbours, in the other rooms, were strange people, like the young man who occupied the box room at the turn of the stair and who, it seemed to Sussock, had been in and out of psychiatric hospitals since his adolescence and was convinced that Martians were coming for him. He would, Sussock had observed, sit on the edge of his bed with the door open and a water pistol in his hands waiting to defend himself, sometimes remaining awake for thirty-six hours before collapsing from sheer sleep deprivation, at which point the first passing resident would enter the room, throw a blanket over him and turn out his naked light bulb.

Sussock levered himself out of his bed. Outside dusk had fallen, it was already dark and that was the way of it: night shifts in Scotland in the winter mean that daylight is seldom seen. His bed was difficult for him to leave. Rain pattered depressingly on his window. He shook himself awake and glanced again at his watch which stood on the cabinet beside his bed; now it was Wed 22 Jan 19.45.

The house, as most often at this hour, was quiet. It was the time of the day when the office workers who lived in the room above him were still in the bar, still throwing alcohol down their necks. They would return at about 9.00 or 10.00 p.m. at which point their hi-fi would boom, boom, boom, down into Sussock's room. And it was the time when the two boys who slept together on the other side of the plywood partition would also be out socializing with kindred male spirits. When at home they would make noises which Sussock found more disquieting than the screams of a more mainstream sexual nature which came from the room of another couple, also upstairs. But at present, all was quiet, save for the rain on the window. A lull before noisy returns from the pubs and the clubs, after which was silence, broken in the dead hours by soft, menacing sounds: the hushed conversations of people padding softly upstairs and then creeping away again, the front door quietly clicking open and shut.

He left his room and walked to the bathroom, squeezing the last remnant of sleep from his eyes and as he did so the linoleum chilled his naked feet. He ran the hot tap but the water was cold, which did not surprise him. The parsimony of his Polish landlord meant that the water for the house was heated for an hour in the morning and one hour in the evening; at all other times it was unheated. If necessary, he was told, shortly after moving in, go downstairs to the kitchen and boil water in the kettle. Not so easy when you are chilled to the bone and just want to climb into clean clothing. Sussock rested his hands on either side of the basin and studied his face in the mirror; antique, he thought, both himself and the mirror. He saw a lean, thin face, craggy, weather beaten, a tired pallor, grey hair and whiskers, and he pondered the image while he decided whether to boil water or steel himself for a wash with cold water.

He decided on the latter and washed his upper body briskly, making only the occasional hiss and gasp of discomfort. In his room he towelled off and ran the Remington around his jaw and throat and upper lip.

He left his room, turning the heavy key in the lock behind him, left the house and walked down to Byres Road in a mood of grim determination. He turned his collar up and pulled down his hat against the rain which fell relentlessly. It caused car headlights and street-lamps to dazzle him. He didn't see puddles of water. It was Glasgow and it rained as only it can in Scotland's principal city.

He felt cold and he felt damp, but above all Sussock felt the thin air of January. Each breath chilled his lungs, as it had each winter, but it seemed, as it also did each winter, that somehow this winter he was worse than in the last winter. His bronchitis was to him a lit-tle like being on a roller coaster ride, going up in the respite of the summer, and down in the winter, but each time he went up he didn't seem to go up as high as he had done the previous summer, and each time he went down, he went a little lower than the previous winter. There was little he could do but live with it, it being the legacy of years of cigarette sucking: full strength, no filter.

He crossed Victoria Crescent Road, glancing at the impressive curve of the buildings, a graceful terrace in a crescent shape, leading down towards Byres Road. Lights burned in a soft, enviable, homely way in all the buildings. They were prestigious owner-occupied buildings of the type that Sussock knew rarely enter-tained the presence of the police except perhaps to in-vestigate a break-in. Once, in the nineteenth century, in their heyday, they were the houses of merchants and their families, and enjoyed single family occupation. Now, in the late twentieth century, they were broken up into flats, still owner-occupied, still prestigious and very 'West End', with polished floorboards, and rubber plants in the window. They all had iron bars over the basement windows, retained these days to keep the burglars out, but originally, so Fabian Donoghue had told him, put in place to oblige the servants to leave and return by the front door.

He reached Byres Road and turned left, entered McDonald's and broke his fast with a quarter-pounder with cheese and a large coffee. It was a meal, he knew it well, of dubious food value pound for pound, but it was a meal, and it was tasty. He felt better for it. He returned to his flat, walking slowly, easing the pain in his lungs by breathing through his nose.

Sussock climbed into his car. He turned the key and to his delight the engine fired first time. Then died. He groaned. He knew his old Ford, a trusty beast but a dog to start. Especially in the wet. He knew that he'd have to coax the engine into life, pausing to allow the flooded carburetor to clear, but the battery was tired and it would be touch and go as to whether the engine fired before the battery died. In the interim he could only sit, turning the key, and cringe with embarrassment at the sound of the empty grating sound, echoing along and inside the old houses. But eventually the engine fired, spluttered, and fired again. Sussock toyed with the choke and then gunned the throttle.

He drove south of the water, to Rutherglen, but he did so with no great enthusiasm. He pulled up outside a bungalow of modest proportions and switching off the engine found himself pondering the building. Any sense of regret, of stricken conscience, had long since left him. These days, in fact, the regret, guilt, and emotional torment had been replaced by a sense of freedom; the sense of responsibility, once unfairly placed, now slid from his shoulders, like snow sometimes slides from a roof in winters colder and deeper than the present winter. The garden first: the garden, he saw, with the aid of a soft yellow sodium streetlamp glow, was unkempt, a full season's growth, now staggering and bending in the rain, like the gardens of the frail and elderly. The house second: the paint was peeling from the window frames, slates were missing from the roof and rain would be dripping into the main bedroom. 'Tough,' he said softly to himself. 'That's tough.' Then, after a car or two had swished past, he added: 'Needs a man; that house needs a man.' He pulled back the door handle and stepped out into the drizzle and strode purposefully up the overgrown path to the side door of the house. He banged on it with the palm of his hand.

It was instantly flung open.

'We saw you coming, Daddy.' The young man with slicked back hair and rings in the lobes of his ears sneered at Sussock, looking down at him from the vantage point of the top step. He wore a skin-hugging black jersey tucked into his equally skin-hugging black trousers. He was barefoot. 'Why do you wait so long before getting out of your little car? Plucking up courage?' He had removed the hair from the back of his hands with his mother's lotion and stood, one hand up to his mouth, as if attempting to hide further sneers.

'Courage is the last thing I need to come here.' Sussock strode up the stairs and pushed the young man aside. 'I come and go as I please.'

'Not for long.' The young man made a show of being pushed back against the cooker and grasping the kitchen sink for support.

A woman wailed from deep within the bungalow—from a soft chair, no doubt, thought Sussock—from behind a closed door: 'Is he in, Samuel?'

'Yes, Mummy.' Samuel stepped behind Sussock as he stamped down the corridor.

'Get him out, get him out.' The woman's voice rose in pitch, approaching hysteria. 'Tell him to catch robbers. Get him out...'

'Mummy says...'

'I heard what Mummy says.' Sussock wrenched open the door of the small storage room at the end of the short corridor. He reached for a black refuse bin liner and rummaged through it, extracting a pair of brogues, a heavy winter coat, and two thick winter shirts.

'Cold out there is it, Daddy? And wet?' The young man flicked the collar of the raincoat.

'Not as cold as you'll be pretty soon.' Sussock turned on the youth. 'Just as soon as the divorce comes through, and we can sell the house, pay off what we owe, split the remainder; then you and Mummy are on your own.'

'And very happy we will be too, Daddy.'

'You think so, you really think so?'

'Oh yes, I think so.'

'Isn't there just a wee bit of fun in living here, knowing I'm in a bedsit? Don't you think you'll miss that, that driving me onto the streets to make my own arrangements? I mean, don't you think you'll miss that number? A little bit of power will be taken from you when I've got my own room and kitchen, a place that's mine, bought and paid for, that no one can throw me out of. Don't you think you'll miss a bit of fun then?'

'We can only see, can't we, Daddy?'

'I've failed with you, so I have. Is it my fault or is it . . . that, that . . . ?'

'I've Mummy to thank for everything, Daddy. I know who I owe and who I don't owe.'

Sussock and the young man held eye contact. Sussock's eyes were filled with despair. The eyes of the young man smiled, contemptuously. Sussock spoke: 'You know the frightening thing about you is that you genuinely believe that the world is smaller than you.'

'Isn't it?'

'GOLD DUST.' Montgomerie swung his feet off his desk and reached for his pen and note pad.

'Would have got to you sooner,' said the collator, his voice soft with a natural telephone manner, 'but the computer's been down for two hours, as normal, for updating. Taking felons off and putting new ones on, mostly new ones on.'

'No matter.'

'But like I said the latent on the whisky bottle of the locus in Sherbrooke Avenue has been identified.'

'Uh huh.'

'Belongs, or so the flickering screen tells me, to a felon yclept Petty.'

'Petty?'

'In fact you could say a petty ned called Petty.'

'Can't forget that.'

'Scanning his track: breach of the peace, reset, that sort of thing. Sums him up until now, I suppose. Murder's a different league.'

'I'll say.' Montgomerie scribbled on his pad. 'I wouldn't call murder and mutilation petty.'

'His name is Wayne Petty. Twenty years of age, track for breach, reset, like I said . . . nothing indicating violence . . . one theft by o.l.p.'

'Address?'

'Boghall Street, Ruchazie.'

'Magic.' Montgomerie stabbed the note pad with the tip of his ballpoint. 'That's pure magic. I'll take a trip out there. See what we see. You'll be sending the file up?'

'Directly.'

Montgomerie replaced the handset, drummed his fingers on it, glanced at the clock and then picked it up again. He dialled a two-figure internal number.

'Uniform bar,' snapped a crisp voice on the phone.

'DC Montgomerie here. How are we fixed for uniforms?'

'Thin on the ground as always. Two officers phoned in sick and we couldn't get cover for them.'

'I see. I want to make an arrest in Ruchazie. Boghall Street, Ruchazie.'

'You'll be going?'

'Aye. I need at least two constables.'

'We have Sergeant Piper and PC Wanless due back from their refreshment in thirty minutes.'

Montgomerie glanced at his watch. Thirty minutes, plus forty-five minutes' refreshment, would bring him up to 21.30.

'Right, I'll take you up on that. Give me time to read over the file. Ideally I'd like to bring him in for questioning, but might come to an arrest.'

SUSSOCK WALKED OUT of the bungalow. He stood on the pathway as the door was slammed shut behind him and breathed deeply, relishing the odour of the plants as it was released by the rain. Outside it was growth and health and even the rain was welcome. Inside the low bungalow was corruption and stress, causing his forehead to tighten and inducing an overall sense of nausea and a loosening of his bowels. When he went there, he went reluctantly, and when he left, he left thankfully.

He returned to his car, lingered for a minute or two before starting the engine and driving away: just to make the point that he came on his terms and left on his terms, in his own time. Yet, he felt a sense of sadness that it had all come to this, to playing games in order to transmit messages to one's wife and to one's child.

Sussock drove away slowly, still transmitting the same message, turned the corner and stopped. He glanced at his watch: 21.00 hours. Still an hour to go before starting the graveyard shift. To go to Langside or not to go to Langside?

He decided against it as the rain pitter-pattered on the roof of his car. It would be a gauche thing to do. To knock on her door, grab a coffee and leave again. No, it would look too bad, she was on the day shift, 06.00 start; she'd be turning in right now, maybe after washing her golden hair and twisting a towel into a turban about her head. Carrying a mug of cocoa into the sitting room, to read a little before switching off the light. How could he tumble into that bliss with a dripping gabardine, shouting for a coffee? He drove back to his flat, changed into the brogues and newly rescued coat, and then to Charing Cross, signing in for the night shift at 21.50.

'I'M NOT arresting you as such—' Montgomerie spoke to the youth '—but if necessary I will.'

'You're not leaving him much choice.' Petty's father stood behind him. Petty the elder had two or three days' growth on his chin and held a screwed-up copy of the *Daily Record* in his hand. He had a resigned attitude. The police at the door was, it seemed, a scene he'd seen and played in many times before, a 'you can do sixty days on your back' merchant. Montgomerie had met men like him before. Behind the man a television played loudly, and a voice announced 'the best of Sky sports'. The house smelled strongly of damp.

'Maybe it's not much of a choice,' Montgomerie conceded, 'but it is a choice. I want to ask him a few questions. If he cooperates, I won't forget it. So how about it, Wayne? Are you coming or are you coming?'

'So what's it about?' Wayne Petty's voice had a nervous edge.

'The murder of Pam McArthur.'

The youth's face drained of colour.

'It wisnae me,' said Wayne Petty.

'You wee ejit,' snarled Petty the elder. 'See what you've gone and done, you've gone and hung yourself by saying that.'

'So what do you know about it, Mr Petty?' Montgomerie addressed the elder of the two.

'See me, I know nothing, I always did and I always will.'

Wayne Petty glanced over his shoulder. Anxiously.

'No back doors in a tenement, son,' said Montgomerie. 'And this is the third floor.'

'Dad...'

The older man shrugged. 'You're on your own, pal. I'm just glad your mother's not here to see this, God rest her. Look, they don't want to arrest you because if they do they've got to charge you within twelve hours or let you walk. But they know you'll fly the coop and tip the wink to your mates on the way. That's right, aye?'

'I'm saying nothing,' said Montgomerie. 'But I'm not waiting here all night.' His voice hardened as he detected the elder man wishing to provoke a conflict with the police. Something that Montgomerie wanted to avoid.

'All right, hen, nothing to worry about.' Wanless addressed a middle-aged woman who was peering from her door across the landing. Now a crowd was gathering.

'Make a decision, Wayne.' Montgomerie looked him square in the eye. 'Or I'll make it for you.'

'Dad...'

'You're twenty. You're your own man.' Petty the elder turned and padded back into the dampness and satellite TV.

'It wasn't me...'

Montgomerie stepped forward and grabbed Wayne Petty by the shoulder. Behind him he sensed Sergeant Piper and Wanless stiffen. 'Wayne Petty,' he said, 'I arrest you in connection with the murder of Pam McArthur. You are not obliged to say anything, but anything you do say will be taken down and may be given in evidence.' He pulled Petty away from the threshold of the door and passed him to Hamilton who snapped handcuffs on Petty's left wrist, and the other cuff onto his own right wrist.

FIVE

MONTGOMERIE TOOK two audio cassettes, broke the seals, snapped them both into the recorder and switched the machine to 'tape'. The spools turned slowly and a small red light glowed in the centre of the control panel.

'This interview is being conducted under the terms of the Police and Criminal Evidence Act.' Montgomerie spoke clearly and deliberately. 'The time is 23.15, the date is the 22nd January. I am Detective Constable Montgomerie. I will ask the other persons present to identify themselves.'

'I am Detective Sergeant Sussock.'

A pause. Montgomerie said: 'State your name, Wayne.'

'Wayne Petty,' said hesitatingly, nervous.

'At this time we are within the rooms at P Division Police Station, Charing Cross, Glasgow.' Montgomerie paused. 'What is your name, your age and occupation?'

'I just told you...'

'Just say your name, keeps us right.' Montgomerie patted the recording machine.

'Wayne Petty... I'm twenty just turned. I've nae job. I'm on the broo.'

'In receipt of Income Support?'

'That, aye.'

'Your address?'

'You know that you . . . lifted me from there.'

'Your address.'

'Boghall Street, 132 Boghall Street, two up right, Ruchazie, Glasgow, Strathclyde, Scot—'

'All right!' Montgomerie glared at Petty. 'It's not funny.'

'It's daft that you ask my address when you lifted me from there just now.'

'Let's keep it right, Wayne. You'll get one of the tapes to give to your brief. I want to make sure that he hears we followed the rules regarding the interview.'

Petty shrugged his shoulders.

'You are going to be asked questions about the murder of Pam McArthur on or about June 6th last year. You are not bound to answer but what you do say will be taped and may be given in evidence. Do you understand?'

'Aye.'

'Right, Wayne. You have a decision to make about yourself, about your future, and we always say the same thing to people in your position and that is that you can make it easy for yourself, or you can make it hard. Your fingerprints were found at the locus of the murder of Pam McArthur, which as you know fine well was in the inside of a house that you had no legitimate reason to be in. When we called at your home, and explained our reason for calling, you stated before myself and before Sergeant Piper and PC Wandless, quote, "it wasn't me", unquote. Now understand this, Wayne, that and that alone means that you are going to be charged with the murder of Pam McArthur.'

Petty made to speak. Montgomerie held up his hand and silenced him.

'It may be, depending on the outcome of our enquiries, that the charge may be reduced, or dropped altogether, but tonight you will be charged with her murder, and detained in custody. So the time to start helping yourself is now. If it really, truthfully wasn't you, then who was it?'

Petty remained silent.

'Wayne, you're looking at life. You're twenty years of age and you're looking at life. All your twenties and a good lump of your thirties are going to be spent doing bird. Eating porridge, sewing mail bags. Nobody can survive more than eight years without getting institutionalized and when you've stopped thinking for yourself, you'll get transferred to an open prison where you can dig the gardens and fill the evenings playing children's games like "hunt the haggis" in the grounds. But that won't be until you get to a state where you stop dead in front of a closed door waiting for somebody to tell you to open it.'

'Fancy that?' Sussock spoke for the first time.

Wayne Petty glared at Sussock and then at Montgomerie. He was, it seemed to both cops, a scheme kid in the truest mould: pale, skinny, small face and sharp features. He looked up at the thick opaque glass in the small window, at the police mutual calendar on the wall, at the matt silver tape recorder, with the twin cassettes recording, the silence broken once by a wheezing cough from deep inside Ray Sussock's chest.

'That's a bad cough you've got there.'

'We're not here to talk about me,' Sussock snarled.

Petty looked again at the cassettes turning slowly, mesmerically. 'So what do you want to know?'

Sussock and Montgomerie relaxed. There was a noticeable lessening of tension in the small room. Montgomerie took a packet of cigarettes from his jacket pocket and offered them to Petty who snatched a nail and drew on it from the flame of Montgomerie's disposable lighter. Montgomerie slipped the lighter back into his pocket but left the nails on the table with the top open, tantalizingly. He was a non-smoker but he knew that cigarettes and a ready lighter are as indispensable to an interview as is a pen and note pad, as is an eagle eye ready to spot a flash across the eyes, as is an ear sensitive to the slightest change of pitch in a voice. Sussock, for his part, could have done without the smoke in the room. But he knew he had to endure it, and that was that.

'So you were there?' Montgomerie began to probe. Petty nodded and drew deeply on the nail which he held in trembling fingers. 'This will help me, aye?'

'Won't harm you, Wayne. Full confession, help us in our enquiries, if you plead guilty to a lesser charge, and the court accepts the plea, throw yourself at the court's mercy...' Montgomerie shrugged. 'Little previous track and none for violence, who knows, five years, and out in three if you keep your nose clean. Still be a young man, won't be institutionalized, still able to open doors. All depends on what happened, what you did, and what you tell us. You can start by telling us if you wore a beard at the time?'

Petty smiled and stroked his chin. 'No, I don't even shave. I just have never grown facial hair. Everything else is all right, I just don't grow whiskers. Suits me, saves me time, money, trouble.'

'So it was your mate that had the beard?'

'Aye. How did you know? Did someone see us?'

'Folk don't get much past us, Wayne. One of our scientists found it, and identified it as a hair from a beard. They're triangular in a cross-section, that's how he knew it was from a beard.'

Petty's eyes widened.

'And that,' said Sussock, fighting down a cough, and having read the developments in the case, 'was a hair, just over an inch long taken from a corpse which had decomposed for eight months.'

'As I said, Wayne, things do get past us, but not much, not often. So your mate. Who's he?'

'The Electric Gypsy.'

'The Electric Gypsy.' Sussock sat forward. 'That's a name I know. Known as "animal", I think.'

'Aye.' Petty nodded. 'That's your man. Animal, the Electric Gypsy. It doesn't surprise me that you know him. See Electric, he's been in and out of the poky since he was fifteen.'

'Now he's...?'

'Twenty-two. Two years older than me. He has a beard. So you found a hair from it, surprised you didn't find more. She tore some of the beard from his face, came out in clumps in her hands.'

Montgomerie picked up his pen. 'Plenty of time for details, Wayne. Let's start at the very beginning.'

'All right. Only I didn't kill her. I'm telling the truth. It wasn't me.'

'It was Electric.'

'No, no, him neither. It was yon Englishman. He filled her in. Not me, or Electric.'

'The Englishman?' Montgomerie looked at Petty.

'Aye. Well he said he was Scottish, but he spoke like an Englishman.'

'Name?'

'Never knew it, but Electric knows it.'

'Electric didn't tell you?'

'That's like Electric.'

'I see. So tell us, from the beginning, in your own words.'

Wayne Petty glanced at the cassettes turning slowly and began to speak. 'Electric told me there was a guy. And he said this guy was pure minted, Rolls Royce, the lot, and this guy wanted this lassie brought to a house— well, no a lassie, a grown woman—and there'd be money in it for us. See me, money...' Petty shook his head. 'There's not much I wouldn't do for money. So anyway, I went with Electric to see this woman at the Social Work Department, where she worked. I just sat there, while they spoke. Electric told her this guy had some information about the high-rises; he meant the two blocks of flats in Easterhouse, just across the road from where this woman worked. This woman was dead keen. So Electric fixed up a meeting for the following day.

'In the afternoon we went back to the woman's place of work. She was standing outside waiting for us, eating a fish supper from the wrapping. She'd just about finished it when we arrived. She screwed it up and tossed it behind her—talk about setting an example to folk. We jumped a taxi, she paid, took us to some house on the other side of the water—some house, like a castle. Anyway, she went happily, didn't know what was going to happen to her and she had one of they things—' Petty pointed to the tape recorder '—only not that big, a wee one, battery operated, and she had plenty of spare cassettes.

'So we get there, she paid off the taxi. The house was empty. I don't mean no one at home, I mean empty, deserted, nae furniture, nothing but floorboards and that. I thought we'd got the wrong address but Electric went round the back and we just followed. He seemed to know what he was doing and the woman was so keen she didn't seem to notice the house was deserted. Electric had a key for the back door. He went in. Then the woman, then me. We went up the stairs, and it's not like stairs in a scheme, it was wide, polished wood. Electric went into this room, we followed. In the room was this guy. He just stood there and smiled, then the woman realized what was happening and she screamed and turned to run but the guy said "hold her". Electric grabbed her and pulled her back and she started to struggle and kick and that's when she grabbed a lump of his beard out of his jaw. Electric yelled and smacked her one and she went reeling across the floor. See me, I just stood there not taking it all in. I was rooted to the spot...' Petty paused and looked at the floor. 'You'll need to believe me. I hadn't a clue that was going to happen.'

'Just carry on, Wayne,' said Sussock. 'You're doing fine.'

'Fine for you? Or fine for me?'

'Fine for all of us.'

Petty shook his head. 'It's the look on the lassie's face. I can't forget the look in her eyes. You know, the moment when she realized she'd been had, the way she looked at me and Electric... we'd betrayed her.'

'You had?'

'Aye.' Petty nodded. 'We had.'

'Just carry on.'

'Electric, he's a big guy, he can be a bit wild at times, and he does a few daft things. I'm not saying he's bad, but he's daft and wild. He's got a good side to him ...'

'So what did he do?'

A pause. Petty looked at the floor.

'Wayne, we know she was raped. Possibly by two men. Semen traces remain, even on eight-month-old corpses. Just as hairs from a beard remain. And not only that, they can tell whether or not they came from the same person. We'll soon know if the guy with the beard was the guy who raped her.'

'You can tell that, just from a hair and a bit of . . . ?'

'We can't. Our scientists can. It's called DNA profiling. Previously all they could do was identify blood groupings from such traces but now they can use DNA profiling. DNA is the stuff that makes you you and not the next guy, and we all have our own unique DNA signature. It looks a bit like a bar code that you see on foodstuffs in supermarkets. We were going to use the bar code on the whisky bottle to trace the outlet, by the way, but your dabs saved us that bit of bother.'

'You don't say.'

'And DNA doesn't deteriorate with age. They've recorded the stuff from fossilized dinosaurs, so an eight-month-old corpse doesn't present a problem, not for the eggheads in white smocks.'

'I can save them some trouble. Electric raped the woman.'

'Thanks, Wayne.'

The tapes wound relentlessly.

'See, Electric, he needs to be handled right, so he does, and that woman clawing at his beard, it set him off so it did.'

'What does that mean, Wayne?'

'Electric . . . well, he has this temper . . .'

'And he's a friend of yours?'

'Aye.' Petty dogged the nail. 'He helped me once. I got jumped by these neds. I was getting a kicking. He came along, got tore in, bounced a couple of skulls off the wall, the rest ran. I didn't have much to do with Electric before that, but since then...well, he's a mate. I owe him.'

'All right, so then what?'

'Well, Electric, he just flew at this lassie, slapped her face, sent her reeling so he did and he followed her across the room and began to tear at her clothes. She wasn't wearing a lot, it was summer... He kept tearing till they were round her ankles and hanging off her shoulders, and he was punching her all the while, putting her blood on the wall. She'd no time to make a sound, she was nearly out but he did it. Up against the wall of the room—couldn't manage with the bare floorboards, hurt his knees.'

'He tried?'

'Aye. Couldn't do it, so he hauled her up and pushed her against the wall, kept his hands under her armpits. She was all but out.'

'We think, we know, that two men ... two men were involved. Who was the other? You or the posh guy?'

A pause. Petty's eyes seemed drawn to the tape. 'Me,' he said, softly but with a clear note of relief.

'You?'

Petty nodded. 'But only after Electric told me to do it. I didn't want to, but Electric was in a mood to kill. I know Electric, if I had refused, he would have battered me senseless. So, aye, I did. But the woman didn't feel anything. She was held up against the wall with her head on one side, making this weird moaning sound. Electric had done all the damage. I thought there's nothing left of her to hurt, so I did it.'

'I imagine you actually believe that.'

Petty shrugged.

'So what about the guy that Pam McArthur was frightened of, the posh guy who spoke like an Englishman but reckoned he was a Scot?' Montgomerie offered Petty a cigarette.

'He stood there, just stood there in the corner of the room, just watching as Electric was tearing into the woman and knocking her head till it was flapping this way and that, and when I caught sight of him, the guy, he was just smiling all the time, smiling at what Electric was doing to this woman.' Petty took a cigarette and lit it from the flame of the lighter held by Montgomerie. He glanced around the interview room. 'See these walls, I bet they've heard some stories, eh?'

'Never you mind what they've heard,' Sussock said, with an edge to his voice, and irritated by the thought of more smoke. 'You just tell us your story.'

'Worse than this?'

'What happened next?' Montgomerie pocketed the lighter.

'Well...' Petty exhaled and paused. 'After...'

'After you'd finished. Is that what you're trying to say?'

'Aye. After I'd finished, she just slid to the floor in a heap. Electric grabbed one of her ankles and dragged her to the centre of the room. Well, then the guy, the posh guy, he calmly walks over, sort of squats on her, so he does, and he puts his hands round her throat. He had big hands, huge hands, but soft, not like a working man's hands. He feels her throat with his hands, sort of adjusting the position of his hands, calm as you please, as if he had all the time in the world. Then he starts to squeeze, light at first, but harder all the time until his forearms were solid bulging. The woman seemed to struggle at first but she's already half dead from the tanking Electric gave her. Then after a wee while her body shudders and I think that's it but this guy wants to make sure and he doesn't let up the pressure. I could see there was nae life left in her but this guy he doesn't stop squeezing. I glanced at Electric, and, see, Electric he was drained of colour, open mouthed, staring, gobsmacked, even he'd never seen anything like it.'

'We've all got our ceilings, son.' Sussock coughed. 'Even your pal the Electric Gypsy.'

'Then he cut off her head.'

The two cops glanced at each other.

'He did what?'

Petty drew on the nail and smoke billowed as he spoke. 'He cut off her head.' He studied the carpet, sombre brown, hard-wearing nylon. 'Not right away; afterwards he cut off her head. He said we had to wait. He reckoned there'd be less blood if we waited. So we waited. Electric was too frightened to argue with this guy. I just followed Electric. This guy was weird. Never raised his voice, but we found ourselves going along with it. Somehow he just controlled our minds. Unreal.'

'As you say,' said Sussock, 'unreal.'

'So we waited. This guy, he filled her in at about, I don't know, two o'clock in the afternoon, something like that, and we just sat there, four of us in the room, me, Electric, the guy, and the dead woman. The guy produced a bottle and we passed it round. He told us to drink because we'd need a good drink in us. He didn't tell us why we'd need a drink. I needed a drink anyway, after what had happened so I drank. Electric drank, but the posh guy, he didn't take a drop.' Petty drew on the nail before he continued. 'So we waited and waited and when it was dark, about midnight, the guy produced this hacksaw. You could see it clearly, summer's night, no curtains, streetlights shining, we could see all we wanted. He handed the hacksaw to Electric and said, "Cut her head off," or, "Saw her head off," something like that. Electric, he hesitated, he didn't want to do it, but the guy looked at him and said, "Do it." So the Electric Gypsy he takes the hacksaw and he rolls the woman over so she's face down and saws at her neck.' Petty shook his head. 'No blood, no blood at all. I thought it would come flooding out, but no. Not a lot anyway.'

'It's because she was dead,' Montgomerie said. 'Dead for ten hours at least by the sound of it. The heart had stopped and the blood was beginning to congeal. Go on.'

'So the guy knew what he was doing then?'

'Just continue, in your own words.'

'After that he told Electric to cut off her hands. So he did. Sawed them off, one after the other, just above the wrist. I suppose if you've cut a head off, a couple of hands are easy. The guy took the head by the hair, long red hair, and picked up the hands and put them in a black bin liner. He told me and Electric to pick up the rest and follow him. We pulled her clothes back on and I picked up her feet and Electric put his hands under her arms and we lifted her and took her downstairs. The guy was there waiting for us, holding the bin liner in one hand and looking at the back garden. He said that the back garden was more exposed than he thought. He said he didn't want to leave her in the front garden, but the fact was the front of the house was more sheltered from view. So he went first to make sure the coast was clear. Me and Electric followed and we took the body to some bushes and left it up against the fence. Electric said the body will start to decompose and give off a smell, and the guy said that that didn't matter because nobody walks these streets and the house won't be sold for a good while because the price is too high. So we kicked some leaves and branches over her and left her. The guy bunged Electric a wedge of brown and walked on to the street where he'd parked his flash motor. He put the bin liner in the boot, calm as you please, and drove off. Electric gave me twenty quid and we walked until we got to a main drag; we jumped a cab and went back to Ruchazie.'

'Twenty quid.' Sussock looked keenly at Wayne Petty. 'Is that all the Electric Gypsy thought you were worth?'

'He paid the taxi.'

'Big of him.'

Petty screwed the nail into the ashtray. 'We went back a few days later. The guy had contacted Electric, told him to return to get a watch from the body. He told Electric the watch could help identify her. So we went back. Electric was frightened of the guy. I went along because I owe Electric. We went back at night. I stood on the street keeping the edge while Electric went and lifted the watch. Just took a few seconds. Then we went back to Ruchazie.'

'Where's the watch now?'

'Electric launched it at a cormorant.'

'He did what?'

'He launched it at a cormorant. See the next day we went round a few shops in Barrowland. Electric thought the watch might be worth something because it was foreign, Russian, had a hammer and sickle on it. But we couldn't sell it for anything decent, so we walked back and crossed the water and were walking on the footpath in front of the Sheriff Court building by the river. The tide was low and a few wooden staves were sticking up out of the water and a cormorant was sitting on one and Electric he took the watch—it hadn't got a strap, just the watch itself was all he lifted—and he skimmed it at the bird. Good shot. He was a good few feet away and it skimmed past the bird's head. The bird took off and flew to another post that was sticking up—'

'In other words he threw it into the Clyde?'

'Aye.'

'Launched it at a cormorant.' Sussock shook his head slowly. 'OK, Wayne, time for details, names, addresses . . .'

'I don't know nothing else. Electric knows it all.'

'That's as maybe, but right now we're asking you. How did you get Pam McArthur to the house?'

'Told you. Electric said he knew a man that wanted to give her some information. Electric told her the guy was scared and would only meet her in a safe place. He knew a house that was empty and he wanted to meet her there. I went with Electric to see this woman to give her the message and she says: "I know why he's scared. Anybody that is prepared to blow the whistle on that lot would be scared too. I'm scared," or words like that, but she was keen to go and meet this guy. She seemed to trust Electric.'

'No comment.' Montgomerie doodled with his pen on his note pad. 'Did the Electric Gypsy ever give this guy a name?'

Petty shook his head. 'Never did to me, and I don't think he mentioned a name to the woman. But Electric knew him all right, seemed to feel he owed the guy

something for some reason that I don't know about—
sort of the same as I owe Electric for saving me from a
kicking that night.'

'All right. So this guy, posh as you say, could be an
Englishman, but he reckons he's a Scot. What did he
look like?'

'Tall, well built, slim, but strong. A good-looking
guy, thick head of hair, but neatly cut. Clean shaven.
He was casually dressed. He was tired, fighting off sleep
while we were waiting for the blood in the woman's
body to... what was that word you used?'

'Congeal,' said Montgomerie.

'Aye. During that time he kept squeezing his eyes and
shaking his head, kept getting up and walking about. I
think that if he had slept, me and Electric would have
cleared the pitch and he knew that, so he had to stay
awake.'

'You'd recognize him again?'

'Aye.'

'The interview is halted here. The time is 23.42.'
Montgomerie switched off the machine and left the
room.

Petty and Sussock looked at each other.

'This will help me, aye?' said Petty after a pause.

Sussock nodded. "It won't harm you, Wayne."

'I'd no idea.' Petty shook his head. 'You know that?
No idea at all. You know something else?'

'What's that?'

'I'm glad I've been lifted for it. Sounds daft but it's
true. I'm way out of my field here. I've done some daft
stupid things, but the murder of that woman. I couldn't
sleep at night...'

'Just tell us what you know, and all you know,' said
Sussock. 'It's the best sleeping pill I know.'

'Get it off my chest?'

'Aye, that's what I mean.'

Another pause, which became a period of silence, broken by the noise of traffic at Charing Cross and, a little closer, Sussock's occasional stifled cough.

The door opened, Montgomerie renewed his seat and switched on the tape recorder. 'The interview recommences at 23.46.' He took the computer graphic photofit, drawn up with the aid of Mrs Sloan, from a brown envelope and showed it to Petty. 'Production item McA/037, the photofit produced with the aid of Mrs Sloan, is shown to Wayne Petty. Wayne, is that the man you saw murder Pam McArthur?'

Petty nodded.

'You'll need to speak, Wayne.'

'Yes,' said Petty, holding the photofit at arm's length. 'That's him, sort of like him . . . I'd put the hair and the face a bit thinner, but if I glimpsed that face in the street I'd think I'd seen the guy who strangled the woman.'

'Photofits are like that, Wayne; they're never anything other than an approximation.' Montgomerie slipped the photo graphic back into the envelope. 'More an impression than a likeness. But this—' he patted the envelope '—is a reasonable likeness?'

'Could be his twin brother.'

'How old was he?'

'Older than me or Animal. I'm not good at ages. Younger than my dad, older than me.'

'A guy in his thirties?'

Petty shrugged. 'Could be.'

'What was he wearing?'

'Casual stuff. Jeans, trainers, shirt, summer jacket, American-style baseball cap . . .'

'Anything about him that you noticed, something special, unique?'

'Rolex watch, I noticed that. The guy had money all right. Rolls Royce and a Rolex.'

'Rolex watch helps.' Montgomerie scribbled a note. 'Anything else?'

'He was tired. I've told you that?'

'Yes.'

'But I mean really tired. Not just sleepy. But as if, should he keel over, he'd be out for days. And he seemed to know that. He seemed frightened of sleep but longing for it.'

'OK.' Montgomerie scribbled. 'I've got the picture.'

'He was left handed.'

'That's more like it. Left handed. You're certain?'

Petty nodded, then remembered himself and said, 'Yes. He carried his bag, the holdall with the hacksaw in, in his left hand. He handed the hacksaw to Animal with his left hand.' Petty paused. 'Aye, when he locked the door of the house behind us as we left he turned the key with his left hand . . . and, aye, when he walked to his flash motor, he carried the holdall and the bin liner, and the bin liner was the heavier bag of the two—it had the woman's head and hands in it; the holdall had only the hacksaw—and I'm pretty sure that he carried the bin liner in his left.' Petty shut his eyes as if reliving the scene. 'Aye, aye, he did for certain.'

'Well done, Wayne.' Montgomerie smiled. 'That's the sort of information we can use. You're doing well for yourself.'

Petty nodded.

'What happened to her handbag?'

Petty paused. 'The guy took it, yes, I'm sure. Yes, he was anxious to get at it. When Animal was knocking her about he was looking through it, not bothered about what Animal was doing. He took a kind of notebook, and a set of keys on a long chain and put those in his pocket...it's all coming back now... Yes, the first thing that went in the bin liner was the woman's handbag, big leather thing.'

'So the bin liner at the end of it all contained her handbag and the contents of the handbag, except her house keys and a notebook, her head, and her hands?'

Petty nodded. 'Aye. He kept the notebook and the keys separate. He seemed to want them.'

'How long did it all go on?' Sussock asked suddenly.

'All what go on?'

'From the time she entered the room and saw the Englishman, who reckons he's a Scot, to the time that guy got up off her, having strangled her. How long?'

Petty shrugged. 'An hour. About that.'

'An hour,' Montgomerie echoed as he and Sussock looked at Petty, both cops pondering the terror of Pam McArthur's last sixty minutes of life, softened as it may have been by her being semi-conscious, but terror nonetheless.

'Anything to ask, Sergeant?' Montgomerie broke the brief silence.

'No.' Sussock shook his head. 'No, not at present. We'll be talking to you again, Wayne.'

Petty nodded.

'Right, Wayne, listen to me. I am detaining you under section Two of the Criminal Justice (Scotland) Act—' Montgomerie looked intently at Petty, fixing eye contact '—because I suspect you of committing offences punishable by imprisonment namely rape and murder. My reasons for my suspicions are that in a recorded statement before myself and Sergeant Sussock you have freely admitted to being party to the unlawful sexual intercourse with and the unlawful killing of Pam McArthur.

'You will be detained to enable further investigations to be carried out regarding the offences and/or as to whether or not you should be reported to the Procurator Fiscal. You will now be taken to the charge bar where you will be informed of your rights in respect of detention. You are not obliged to answer any further questions but anything you do say will be recorded and may be given in evidence.' Montgomerie paused. 'Do you understand that, Wayne?'

Petty nodded.

'Can you speak? The machine can't hear that sort of answer.'

'Aye,' Petty muttered. 'I understand.'

'The interview is concluded. The time is 00.17 on Thursday, 23rd January.' Montgomerie switched off the tape recorder. The tension in the room lessened further.

'So now what?' asked Petty.

'You'll be kept here. We have until about 10.30 to decide whether to charge you. Depends on what we find out in the night.'

'You're working through the night?'

'Aye. We're going to chap the door of your friend Animal the Electric Gypsy. Bring him in for a wee chat. You'll get one of these cassettes of the interview to give to your solicitor. We keep the other.'

'What's going to happen to me? Off the record.'

'Off the record, we'll most probably be charging you with the rape and murder of Pam McArthur.'

'The rape, aye, but I was forced ... The murder, no, no way.'

'Wayne—' Montgomerie stood '—the interview is over. What you want to plead guilty or not guilty to, or offer pleas in mitigation to, is now something for you to talk over with your solicitor.'

'Aye, suppose.' Petty stood. 'Does this mean I'm a hard man now?'

'WE'LL ONLY BE ABLE to make the rape charge stick.' Montgomerie put his feet up on his desk and cradled the mug of coffee in his hands. 'I can't see the Fiscal proceeding with the other one; he'll put a red line through it. Petty, see him, just a wee ned out of his depth. He had no idea she was being lured to her death, he just went along with his mate Animal the whatever… Where do they get handles like that?'

'Beats me.' Sussock looked at his reflection in the glass window of the CID room and traced a line he hadn't noticed before across the width of his forehead. Beyond were the yellow lights of Finnieston.

'Well, we'll just prepare the report and send it up. The Fiscal will no pro the murder. Petty had no prior knowledge that it was going to take place and no part in it.'

Sussock ran his hands over his face. 'Wouldn't bet on it. He made no attempt to disassociate himself from the act, and guilt by association is a tough number to crack. Personally I'll lay good money that the Fiscal will proceed with it. I've seen it before, Malcolm. There's plenty of lags breaking rocks who went to the High Court with a defence along the lines of "it wasn't me, I just stood there and watched".'

'Maybe, but he won't be the hard case he wants to be. The lags don't go a bunch on rapists. He'll have to do his bird on Rule 43 and clock his porridge for ground glass each morning.'

'We'll let him find that out in his own time.' Sussock drained his mug of coffee and stood. 'Dalton Bayliss, a.k.a. Animal the Electric Gypsy, on the other hand, will be a tougher nut to crack. There's only two years between them but they were made in different factories. I know him, he won't come willingly. Doesn't know the meaning of the word "cooperate".'

'Well, I'll write this up and leave you at it, Sarge.' Montgomerie glanced at his watch. 'Three hours' overtime. Not bad. Could be worse.'

'Could be a lot worse.' Sussock left the CID room and walked softly down the corridor to his own office. The night stretched ahead of him.

HE REMEMBERED the day his life changed and he remembered it with clarity. He recalled the heat melting his suntan lotion; he remembered the blue sky and the equally blue Adriatic. He recalled the beach, the lines of deck chairs, the fighter aircraft that skimmed in pairs over the hotel rooftops and out towards the sun-hazed horizon. But most of all he remembered the olive-skinned girl with black hair and endless legs seen daily in her lime green costume. He never spoke to her but he sought her out each day and gazed at her from a distance. He remembered the warmth of the night, the street-side cafés selling huge steins of German beer, the relaxed atmosphere of the hotel bar; he recalled lying in bed listening to a rock band play in the adjacent hotel.

And he recalled that fateful day on the beach when, late afternoon, he and his friends decided to return to the hotel, wash and change for dinner. He reached for his sandals and fumbled with the buckle. His fingers had no sensation at the tips and he couldn't control them with the precise dexterity which had enabled him to unbuckle his sandals a few hours earlier. He had told his friends to go on ahead, that he'd catch them up. And he did, and said nothing about the reason that he'd been delayed, and found to his relief that he could handle the knife and fork and did so for the remainder of the holiday. But within three years he was bitten deep and completely disabled with multiple sclerosis.

At twenty-six years of age he lived alone in a ground floor, two apartment flat in Ruchazie and rested as much as he could; and when he moved he did so awkwardly on two stainless steel sticks which had cups to support his upper arms, and grips protruding at ninety degrees. He had also found that he couldn't sleep at night: Getting up at 2.00 or 3.00 a.m., he'd pull on some clothing and go for a walk, supporting his weight on his sticks and pulling his legs behind him. What arose from a need to do something because he couldn't sleep, proved to have an unexpected bonus. He found that he could walk for a mile in a circular route and not see another person, especially in winter. Heaven. Just him and the sound of his sticks, click, click . . . click, click.

He grew to depend on his night walk because outside, during the daytime, people would look at him with undisguised pity, or the children who didn't know what was ahead of them would laugh, sometimes out of nervousness, sometimes out of malice, but all would serve to make him self-conscious. At night he didn't have that problem; at night he could walk for an hour and return, exercised and with a lung full of fresh, west Scotland night rarefied air. And the people in the scheme knew him; lying in bed, also unable to sleep in the dead hours but disinclined to go for a night stroll, they would hear the distinct echoing click, click... click, click... click, click, as Roddy McGee made slow and painful progress up Bellrock Street towards the square bulk of the water tower at the junction with Stepps Road, and they then would turn over and murmur, 'Aye, there's that wee guy,' and continue the search for sleep. The beat cops in the cars knew him. At first they stopped him and questioned him as to his purpose and his welfare, then for a chat, getting to know him, or to ask if he'd seen anything on the occasions that something had gone down in the scheme between 02.00 and 04.00. Occasionally they would simply nod and flash their lights as they drove past him. As he walked, he would think of many things, but always he would ponder the holiday in Italy and the instant with the sandal buckle when his life had changed direction, and he would recall the olive-skinned girl in the lime green costume for his mind's eye had nursed her image into everlasting life.

At 03.05 on Thursday, 23rd January, Roddy McGee reached for his aluminium sticks and left his flat.

'DON'T KNOW. Why don't you tell me what's going on.' The woman clutched the thin robe around her neck and shivered, barefoot on the threshold of her flat. She had thin dark hair, a fading bruise on her left cheek which she made no attempt to conceal, and, thought Sussock, probably hadn't from the day it first appeared. It was often, he had noticed, the way of it in the housing schemes, as if the philosophy was: 'If you don't get a doing from your man you're just not married'. 'Anyway it's cold. It's the back of three. Are you coming or are you going? But see me, I'm closing this door.'

The cops went in: Sussock and two constables. It was dull inside the flat, a single sixty-watt light bulb on a sideboard illuminated the room. The carpet stuck to the soles of Sussock's shoes. Sussock glanced sideways into the kitchen as he passed and saw a sink full of unwashed dishes and empty tins on the working surface. It was, he thought, the sort of kitchen where plates are washed in ones and twos, only when they're needed; where tins were tossed aside when empty, not cleaned away and placed in the refuse.

Homes, it was Sussock's contention, emanate from the kitchen, read the kitchen and you'll read the house: a warm, cluttered kitchen will be part of a warm, cluttered house; a fastidiously tidy 'dead as the showroom' kitchen will be part of a fastidiously tidy 'dead as the showroom' house; and a kitchen which amounted to a health hazard, as Mrs Bayliss's kitchen appeared to him to be, would be part of a house which in turn amounted to a health hazard. He wasn't disappointed. The furniture was covered in popular striped upholstery with matching curtains. Empty special brew lager cans littered the floor, as did empty bottles of Buckfast Abbey and Thunderbird fortified wines; the ashtray on the sticky formica surface of the coffee table overflowed with ash and cigarette butts. Copies of the *Daily Record* lay strewn about the room. An aged gas fire hissed with angry flames.

The woman twisted and sank into the chair nearest the fire and extended a sparrow-thin hand towards a packet of nails which stood on the mantelpiece above the fire. She extracted a nail and stuck it between the silver bars of the gas fire, holding the tip in the flame. She pulled it away and drew deeply until the tip glowed, glanced at it as she exhaled and replaced it between her lips. She didn't look up at Sussock. 'I mean if you don't believe me, take a look. There's nobody here.'

'I'll take you up on that offer if you don't mind, hen.' Sussock turned and nodded to one of the constables who then detached himself and left the room.

'I don't know what's going down. Animal don't tell me nothing. Just gives me some money and expects me to pay all the bills and provide all the food—food to feed him like a lord. He's my man, I married him. It doesn't mean to say I'm happy. I'm still young, I might get out.'

The constable returned and shook his head. 'Empty, Sarge.'

The woman tossed her nose in the air. 'I hope it stays that way. Gonny tell me something, Inspector? Gonny tell me why women stay with men that treat them like dogs?'

'Beats me, hen,' said Sussock, 'but I see it all the time.'

'Bet you do—with your job, I mean. Got a thankless job so you have. Bet you see some awful things, eh?'

'All in a day's work, Mrs Bayliss. So where is your husband?'

'Is he in trouble, aye?'

'Aye, hen. He's in trouble.'

'Going to put him away?'

'We're going to lift him. It's the court that decides if he's to be put away.'

'I'd like to help you.' Sadie Bayliss smiled a sincere smile. 'I really would, believe me. Anything to be shot of that rat. What sort of trouble is he in?'

'Can't tell you, hen. Would like to talk to him though—we have a couple of questions for him.'

'But it's something serious?'

'Couldn't be more serious.'

'Murder?'

Sussock shrugged.

'Aye.' Sadie Bayliss nodded. 'It had to come sooner or later. See with him it's the blade, sees it as a craft, always carving people so he is. No wonder he's called Animal, and he likes the handle—"Animal the Electric Gypsy"—makes him feel hard. Even his dad's feared of him so he is, calls him "Animal", not "son" or "Dalton", but "Animal" with that wee note of respect in his voice. But he's been acting wary these last weeks, months really. Something on his mind. He's agitated, so he is.'

'Been like that for months, you say?'

'Since the white nights. Used to get phone calls at strange times during the white nights and have more money than usual. Other times we'd have to do without, mostly we'd do without because with him it's the bottle. If he had it it would go on the drink and I didn't mind that because I'm a wine muppet like other women in this scheme. We're all right if there's some drink in the bottle but if the bottle's empty our blood's on the wall. That's the way it is. So what's to be done?'

'Like I said, hen . . .'

'Aye, well, like I said, I don't know where he is. He took a phone call, at about midnight, took it from the father of that wee boy, Petty, Wayne Petty—he's one of Animal's Street Turks—anyway he's after telling Animal that Wayne's been lifted by the law and does he know what it's about? Said Wayne was lifted for murder. Is that the same murder that you want to speak to Animal about, aye?'

'Possibly. Can't really tell you.'

'I can add up. I can put two with two and make four.'
Sadie Bayliss drew on the nail. 'We had had a wee
drink. Well, he'd been having a wee drink but I've never
seen anyone sober up so fast as Animal did when he
took that call. Paled as well—I've heard of colour
draining from folk's faces but never seen it, but I saw it
tonight.'

'So what happened?'

'He made a call, well started to make a call then hung
up. Pulled on a coat, a plastic bag over his hair and said
he was away out to make a call from a public box. A
public box that works around here! He should be so
lucky. Anyway he went, and he went like death itself
was on his tail. Always fancied himself as a hard man
did Animal, but it was as if he'd met his match.'

'So he's on the scheme as far as you know?'

'As far as I know, aye, but see, what time is it now,
back of three, aye?'

Sussock looked at his watch. 'Three-twenty.'

'Well he took the call from Wayne Petty's father close
on midnight, a little before, I think. So I don't know
where he'll be. You can go a long way in three hours or
more.'

'Very well. You'll tell him we called? You'll tell him
we want to talk to him?'

'Aye, I'll tell him, but he'll not be looking to speak to
you. If you want him you'll need to find him.'

RODDY MCGEE walked on his sticks up Bellrock Street,
up the steep incline of a canyon formed by angular low-
rise tenements, glistening in the rain, with the satellite
TV dishes sprouting like mushrooms from the damp
walls. Click, click...click, click...click, click. He
walked towards the water tower, square, tall and im-

posing in the gloom, where he turned right down Skerryvore Road. Beyond he could see the lights of Edinburgh Road. It had ceased to rain as he turned into Skerryvore Road, and Roddy McGee swept back the hood of his anorak. Somewhere a dog barked, joined by another, then another, then silence save for the low rumble of traffic on the M8 behind him, and the sound of the occasional vehicle on the Edinburgh Road.

He walked on and saw an urban fox winding itself around a sapling, leaving its musk. The beast saw Roddy McGee and for an instant man and animal, both survivors in their own way, stared at each other across a space of perhaps twenty feet. Then the fox darted into the gloom, lean and fast. A car turned out at Langness Street, still some distance away. It hesitated at the junction with Skerryvore Road as if the driver was unsure of the locale, unsure of the direction to take. The car began to turn left, stopped when the manoeuvre was half complete, reversed, then turned right, driving slowly towards Roddy McGee, leaving two silver trails on the damp tarmac as it made its way up Skerryvore Road. Roddy McGee watched the vehicle as the headlights approached. The car swept up slowly, not in a hurry, and it slowed as it approached him.

McGee felt a sudden jolt of apprehension. A sudden chasm of vulnerability. It was the price paid for night walking; it's all very well to enjoy the streets when they're quiet and empty, but you do so without the protection of the natural policing influence of the crowd. He was alone with his obvious physical challenge: easy prey.

The car came on.

The headlights blinded him.

The car drew level and stopped. Roddy McGee's eyes readjusted to the gloom and he looked into the car, looked across the empty passenger seat at the driver. He saw that the car was a Rolls Royce; he saw the driver to be a handsome, well-built young man. For a brief period, one, perhaps two seconds, the two men looked at each other: one who had everything, it seemed by all appearances, and one who had little. One who was physically fortunate, the other less so. And the one who had everything and who was physically fortunate smirked at the one who was condemned to walk the streets of Ruchazie at night and in most weathers. Then they parted.

It was a smirk like the smirks that had driven Roddy McGee to night walking. He felt wounded, but as he walked he knew that sense of wounding would ease—it always did—and he'd carry on because it was all there was for him to do. He turned and watched the car. It disappeared from sight as it rounded the corner but he could see its headlights on the white buildings of the derelict industrial estate on the far side of Stepps Road. He watched the light spill leftwards as the car turned towards the M8.

He turned and walked down Skerryvore Road. A still night. No sound save his sticks and the distant hum of traffic.

He saw a mound in the road at the entrance to Langness Street.

He stopped and strained his eyes. Too large to be a bin liner. Maybe two lying together—bin liners often got taken out and left in the streets in Ruchazie. Then it moved. It became a man, lying in the road. He rose to a kneeling position, crawled a little way forwards then fell again and was still.

Roddy McGee felt alone in the world. He tried to shout but his voice had no strength. Strength was what he lacked. He had the strength to reach the man in the road, but what then? What could he do? He had no first aid skills; he would have no strength to go on and seek help. Behind him was a public telephone stand, a yellow box on a stalk. So he ran as best he could for it. Roddy McGee, who had been dealt a cruel blow in his early twenties, who had been forced to risk night walking because of endless taunts and smirks, and stares, and sniggering, turned and ran, on two aluminium sticks, uphill, to help his fellow man.

He moved digging the sticks into the pavements, so hard it jarred his hands and shoulders, dragging his feet behind him. The pain was greater than normal; his head hung on one side, his breath rasped in the chill night air. Yet still he moved forward. He saw the telephone, the yellow box on a stalk, but it seemed to get no nearer. He looked at the ground, he gritted his teeth, he carried on. Finally, after what seemed an eternity, he slumped against the phone, let one stick clatter to the ground as he lifted the handset and jabbed three nines.

RAY SUSSOCK SAT with his feet up on his desk. He allowed his eyes to close and entered a strange slumber-like state, as often before in the dead hours of a quiet night shift, not so much trying to sleep, but no longer trying to stay awake. It was a state of half sleep: his body was resting, his heartbeat slow and settled, his breathing soft and rhythmic. He was aware of his surroundings, heard noises both near and distant, but all noises seemed to have a detached quality. He was at all times conscious and could snap into activity in an instant. But his body was resting and enjoying sleep-like nourishment. Sussock felt no guilt about doing this, knowing fine well that the wild bitch of a city never sleeps, but it slumbers with one eye open and can rise up snarling. So whisper who dares, and don't poke her with a stick, let the City of Glasgow sleep because she is easily angered and her claws are deadly.

He shuffled in the chair. He heard a door open and close again further down the CID corridor. He heard a heavy goods vehicle on the street. He heard twin klaxons, likely, he thought, to be the fire brigade exercising. In the schemes, where the City of Glasgow abuts the countryside, it was Sussock's experience that people, some very young, who had little with which to fill their lives, would become burdened by the monotony and aimlessness of life, would retire to their beds in the afternoons and would slumber and induce a dream, but who could and would retain just sufficient consciousness to dictate the progress of their daydream and would push it in the direction they wished to go. It was a method of escaping the poverty, of escaping a future without hope.

His phone rang. The bitch city never ever sleeps for long. Now it was stirring. He opened his eyes, swung his feet off the desk and reached for the handset. 'DS Sussock.'

'Control, sir.' The voice on the other end of the line was crisp and alert. 'Tango Delta Foxtrot has attended a three nines call from the member of the public and is reporting a Code 41.'

'Where?'

'Ruchazie. They've requested an ambulance: victim is an adult male, apparently deceased. He'll be taken to the GRI.'

'Ask Tango Delta Foxtrot to remain at the locus. I'm on my way.'

At the locus, and if only at the locus, Sussock found that the slumbering beast had stirred. A few people stood in the street, but mostly they leaned on the balconies of the flats which stood at the junction of Langness and Skerryvore; in the gods of the street theatre.

'Gentleman in the car called in, Sergeant,' said Hamilton, a solid methodical cop in Sussock's view: twenty-four years old, married to a nurse, or so he believed; Hamilton who wrote how, why, what, when, where, who, in front of his notebooks and mentally ticked them off as he took notes and information; Hamilton who plodded round whatever incident he had attended until he'd covered every inch of the issue. 'We know the reporter, a disabled gentleman who lives in the scheme.'

'Disabled?'

'Multiple sclerosis. He walks the scheme in the dead hours, we often see him between three and four. He won't walk about like that during the day, folk being folk.'

'Aye.' Sussock sighed knowingly.

'He's still exhausted. He saw the victim from a wee distance, sized the situation up and took himself on his sticks to the phone box on near Bellrock Street, there.'

'Did the gentleman tell you anything?'

'Not a great deal, Sarge, still shaken and all in. He didn't see the incident itself.' Hamilton spoke matter of factly. 'But he did mention a flash car, a roller, leaving the locus in such a way as to suggest the driver didn't know the best way out of the scheme. Mind you, it's not every Rolls Royce owner in the city that knows his way about Ruchazie.'

'A roller, you say?'

Hamilton nodded. 'At least that's what the reporter said. A Rolls Royce or a Bentley—they're identical side on and from the rear which is how he saw it, side and then rear as it drove off. The victim was a white male, early twenties. It was a knife job but not like any knife wound I've seen—he was laid open in a dozen places. No pulse but we called an ambulance anyway.'

'A cleaver job perhaps?'

'Aye.' Hamilton visualized meat falling away under a butcher's cleaver. 'Aye, that's the sort of wound. The attack seemed to be in the doorway.' Hamilton flashed his torch, over the front of the tenement, 'Largely empty, as you see, Sarge. Two ground floor flats boarded up with those metal plates they use. Most of the blood in the entry to the close, as you see.' Hamilton drew his torch beam along the path between the close and the street. 'Reckon there's a good eight pints of red stuff there. He was seen in the street about there at the end of the trail of blood.'

Hamilton's cynicism and dispassion surprised Sussock—'young' Hamilton was clearly finding his feet.

Sussock pondered the tenement block from which the victim had staggered, or crawled, oozing life as he did so. A half empty tenement, in the early hours, ideal for a fatal rendezvous. It was clearly well chosen by the man who had wielded the cleaver. 'Wash the blood away,' said Sussock. 'You and your mate. These people will lend you the materials.'

'Very good, Sarge.' A note of resignation in his voice. 'There's no ID as yet, Sarge.'

'Won't be a problem, laddie, won't be a problem. I spoke to his wife less than two hours ago, she won't be sorry at this news. His name was Dalton Bayliss, a.k.a. Animal the Electric Gypsy.'

In the southeast a silver sliver rent the night sky.

SIX

'HE WAS DOA, sir.' Sussock reclined in the chair in front of Donoghue's desk. He felt tired, dishevelled, grimy, especially so when he compared himself to Donoghue: fresh, neat, clean shaven, a whiff of after-shave. Donoghue sat back in his chair and pulled contentedly on his pipe with its gently curved stem, listening attentively to Sussock feedback. Just, in fact, as he had listened attentively to Sussock twenty-four hours earlier, when the elderly detective sergeant had related the incident of the motorist who had swerved instead of braking in a straight line. 'He bled to death, apparently, massive blood loss. Early reports indicate that he was hacked to death, possibly with a machete or a similar implement.'

Sussock winced as the smoke from Donoghue's first pipe of the day reached his lungs.

'And you say the witness didn't see a great deal?'

'Well, hardly anything, but what we did see dovetails neatly with what other witnesses have offered. They're hazy, but within that haze there is distinct corroboration. We haven't been able to locate any other witnesses. We asked the crowd that gathered when the police vehicle and ambulance arrived and did a door-to-door; everybody was up and leaning on the balconies, clocking the spectacle. The rain didn't put them off any.'

'But nobody saw the incident itself?'

Sussock shook his head. 'Nobody.'

'So tell me what bits corroborate?'

'Largely Wayne Petty's statement that the felon is a Rolls Royce owner, a young male, also seems a calm character—a cool customer, according to the witness. He emerged from Langness Street quite slowly, turned in the wrong direction, so he thought, reversed, and then drove slowly up Skerryvore Road, calm as you please, calm enough to slow down and stop as he drew level with the witness, clocked the witness and let the witness clock him.'

'I see.' Donoghue took his pipe from his mouth. 'A reliable witness, Ray?'

'Yes, I think so, sir. He suffers from MS and ran a good length of Skerryvore Road on his aluminium sticks to phone three nines. When the cops found him he was in a state of near collapse.'

'What was he doing out at that hour?'

'The beat cops know him well, sir. He gets hassle if he goes out during the day. You know what it can be like in the schemes.'

'Sounds a noble sort of a man. I'll ask Elka Willems to nip out today and take a full statement and show him a copy of the photofit that was offered to us by Mrs Sloan.'

'And as corroborated by Wayne Petty,' Sussock said, and then added, trying to hide the pleasure in his voice, 'It's actually WPC Willems's day off today.'

'No matter. Abernethy then; he can take a ride out to Ruchazie. What's the state of play at the moment, Ray?'

'In terms of what is happening where? Dr Reynolds is doing a PM at the GRI, otherwise work on the McArthur murder is awaiting allocation. There's the usual gamut of burglaries, car thefts, assaults, no other

major inquiry in progress, just the McArthur murder.'
Sussock's eyelids felt like lead.

'Ray, I appreciate you staying on like this; it does help
the handover. It's difficult for me to get an overview
otherwise. Let's kick it about a bit.'

'Delighted,' said Sussock wearily.

'Good man.' Donoghue rekindled the tobacco in his
pipe with a blast of flame from his gold-plated lighter.
'So,' he said, 'we have a body discovered, sans head and
hands, discovered some eight months after the murder.
The body transpires to be that of one Pam McArthur,
a deeply unpleasant woman by all accounts, the sort to
have enemies and who was, and I quote, "working on
something"; she had, she believed, stumbled on
"something big" that happened in Glasgow thirty years
ago, or thereabouts. Something that she wanted to expose but she brought nothing to us?'

A pause. Sussock realized he had been asked a question. 'Sorry.' He shook sleep from his brain. The sound
of the rain on the window became louder. 'No, she
didn't bring anything to us.'

'Try and stay with it, Ray. So she was going it alone,
not even enlisting the help of a colleague or a friend.
Though of course she had few friends.'

'It didn't appear so.' There was an edge to Sussock's
voice. He was stung by Donoghue's rebuke, feeling it
unfair and truculent.

'She was just asking questions and beavering away in
her flat, putting all the information on discs on her
computer. But the fact remains that she was getting
somewhere; she had succeeded in frightening someone, or some persons, who lured her to her death with
the promise of information. I've listened to the tape of
the interview with Petty—he sounds genuine to me.'

'I think this. Frankly, I don't even think Bayliss a.k.a. "Animal" knew what was going to happen. Bayliss seems to have been carried along with the current until he got deposited at the bank as it were, by which time it was all over and his hands were bloodied.'

'Like your analogy, Ray. The fact remains that our man in the flash motor had every intention of murdering the McArthur woman and even when Bayliss and Petty threw in the rape he just sat back and let them get on with it. Maybe out of a sense of vindictiveness. But whatever, you know what really comes over? The sense of the man's calmness, the settling back to let something unplanned run its course as if he had all the time in the world.'

'Or as if his self-assertion was weakened,' said Sussock suddenly, throwing something into the discussion.

'What do you mean?' Donoghue raised an eyebrow.

'I recall Petty saying that the man was tired, exhausted. You may be right, sir. You may be quite correct in interpreting the reason why the man sat back and allowed Bayliss and Petty to rape McArthur, but you know, I think there's another way of looking at it. If he was so tired he had all on to keep awake, then he wouldn't have had the energy to oppose Bayliss and Petty.'

'That may be a valid point.' Donoghue teased the tobacco in his pipe bowl with his ballpoint pen. 'We'll keep an open mind about that. Anyway the body was discovered, we traced Petty because of a latent on the whisky bottle that they had left behind—careless of them—and Petty led us to Bayliss.'

'Who is now deceased.'

'As you say,' said Donoghue, 'as you say. Now what interests me is that Petty's father phoned Bayliss, told him that Wayne Petty had been arrested and why he'd been arrested. This, according to yourself, via Sadie Bayliss, succeeded in rattling Bayliss's cage to the extent that he sobered fast, started to make a call, then went out to make the call. This at shortly after midnight.'

'Before, I think.'

Donoghue waved his palm imperiously. 'Around midnight. The exact time is not of importance. So the next thing we hear is some three hours later, when a member of the public sees a Rolls Royce manoeuvring casually in Ruchazie, at about the locus where and when Dalton Bayliss's body is shortly to be seen. Fair enough?'

Sussock nodded wearily.

'Now.' Donoghue lit his pipe. 'Now, Ray. I'm going to play a dangerous game. I'm going to make some assumptions.'

Sussock began to despair of getting home and, seeing the blue cloud begin to screen his immediate superior, he began also to despair for his lungs.

'The first assumption that I'm going to make is that Petty and Bayliss were not involved with whatever happened in the town thirty years ago—pretty safe assumption that one, neither of them being alive thirty years ago.' Donoghue grinned at his own joke. 'More seriously, I believe it safe to assume that Pam McArthur had stumbled onto something; in fact, I thought at home last evening that those missing tapes would explain everything. They hold the key which is of course why they were purloined from her flat.

'Now the man in the Rolls Royce intrigues me. He too, like the McArthur woman, is by all accounts far too young to have had anything to do with whatever happened thirty odd years ago, but he seems caught up in it, so much so that he is clearly prepared to kill for it. It's safe to assume that he killed the McArthur woman because she was going to spill the beans. I think that the person whom Bayliss left his house to phone was the man in the Rolls Royce who agreed to meet him, that night, in the scheme where Bayliss lived, but he intended to meet him only so as to chop the life out of him. He did that because Bayliss was clearly frightened and frightened people have loose tongues. Reasonable so far?'

'Very.'

Donoghue pursed his lips. 'This character in the Rolls Royce...'

'Intriguing, isn't he?'

'Very. He's calm, he's calculating, he doesn't mind being seen. He's pukka—remember Petty believed him to be an Englishman, though he claimed to be Scots. He wasn't at all anxious to get on with the murder of Pam McArthur, fatigued or not; he let Bayliss have his retribution, and he let Bayliss and Petty have their fun and then he calmly strangled her, after which he handed a hacksaw to a shaking Bayliss and told him to chop her up. But did that only after the body had lain for ten hours or so, long enough for the blood to begin to congeal. Then he carried the bin liner containing her head and hands to his car and drove away, untouched by it all. We know that he kept in touch with Bayliss because he phoned him a week later and told him to return to the corpse and recover a distinct watch that she had worn. Bayliss did what was asked of him—not a pleasant task, but it does indicate the sort of hold that this gentleman has over Bayliss a.k.a. "Animal the Electric Gypsy".'

'We'll likely never know the nature of that.' Sussock yawned. He was past caring about protocol.

'But a considerable hold—the man in the Rolls Royce wouldn't go to McArthur's corpse to check up on whether or not he had removed the watch.'

'He wouldn't have to. If we had found the watch we'd publicize it and that would likely have been sufficient to cook Bayliss's goose. But you're right. Bayliss was more than just a ned hired for a one-off job. There was some unsavoury relationship between Bayliss and the Rolls owner.'

'To further assume, Ray, I think this chap in the Rolls Royce is running scared, despite his coolness. A single call from Bayliss was sufficient to summon him to Ruchazie at some godforsaken hour and he did so to chop Bayliss because he'd outlived his usefulness. He evidently lives within two hours' drive of the east end of Glasgow, probably somewhere in the country.'

Sussock threw a questioning glance at Donoghue.

'Think of the blood, Ray. Think of the blood that flowed when he chopped Bayliss up. No clean strangulation here, no waiting for the heart to stop and the blood to congeal. No, on this occasion he waded right in with a serious blade and he would have been covered in the stuff. If he lives alone he wouldn't necessarily have to have somewhere to change his clothes, but if he's married, he would have had to change before returning home. Bayliss phoned him, we'll say, after midnight; he was probably chopped at about 3.00 a.m.'

'Nearly three hours to get from his home to Ruchazie, by fast car...could put him most anywhere in
Scotland and the northern counties of England.'

'Only if he was ready to move on receipt of the call,
and only if he knew the quickest way to Langness Street.
In the first instance he wouldn't have been expecting the
call. He may have been disturbed from his sleep or in
the middle of a drinking session, one or the other; he'd
have taken some time to wake up, and dress, or throw
black coffee down his neck until he was sober enough
to drive. And he may have had to disengage from some
person or persons and find an excuse for doing so.
Could take an hour, and I'm betting that while he may
well know Dalton Bayliss and have some dread hold
over him, he won't necessarily know all the nooks and
crannies of Ruchazie. He probably told Bayliss to wait
for him at some discreet place and Bayliss, thinking in
terms of his immediate vicinity, would probably have
said "corner of Langness and Skerryvore, half empty
close" and put the phone down, leaving the Rolls Royce
owner to thumb through the Glasgow *A-Z*, which he did
because he wanted to get to him before we did, and you
know what those schemes are like—trying to find your
way round a scheme at night, if you don't know it...'

'Might as well be on another planet.'

'Right, so he'll take some time finding Bayliss.'
Donoghue placed his pipe in the ashtray. 'I'll bet he
lives about an hour's drive from Ruchazie. And that's
at normal driving speed; he wouldn't draw attention to
himself by speeding.'

'Makes sense.'

'You know, Ray, I want to lift this guy. He has a cold
and a callous disregard for human life. Not a pleasant
individual, not pleasant at all. The trouble is, that even

if we did know his identity, we still haven't got a safe conviction. So far it's only Petty's word and a photofit, and the photofit is an observation of him ex-locus, as it were.'

'Footprint in the blood, sir,' Sussock offered, 'as I recall.'

Donoghue smiled. 'Good, if it's his that would clinch it. Can't explain that without difficulty. But only if it's his. It could have been made by Petty or Bayliss and thinking of it, it is likely to be Bayliss as he kneeled to chop the McArthur woman, or the corpse of same. This man is cautious. He would not get too near the blood.'

'Do we go public with the photofit?'

Donoghue shook his head. 'Could work against us. Don't want to tip him off. But I'll have it distributed to the beat cops. Can't be that many good-looking young men driving Rolls Royces in Glasgow. But you know I'm right, the key to this whole affair is the project that the McArthur woman was engaged upon. I'm going to revisit that flat of hers. The cool customer may well have walked up to her flat and let himself in and walked away with her discs, but the flat hadn't been turned over. I bet you he left something. I bet you that there's something in that flat for us, Ray.'

Wearily, finally, and with a sense of a weight sliding off his shoulders, Detective Sergeant Ray Sussock walked out of P Division Police Station. It was, by then, mid-morning, dull, overcast, rain falling lightly yet incessantly; water ran down the walls of the tenements, plunged through down pipes, ran deeply and swiftly in the gutters and caused a thin film of grease to form on the road surface. He walked across the car park at the rear of the police station, collar up, hat screwed down, to where he'd parked his car.

In the car, the seats had no spring remaining, and rain seeped in between the doors and the car body, and the engine, because of the damp, and because, thought Sussock, it was his car, refused to start. He leaned forward and gripped the steering wheel. He was within an ace of retirement and he lived like *this*. He abstracted himself from his body and wished himself many miles away. Something somewhere had gone wrong, more, much more, than his separation could account for. He leaned back in the seat and closed his eyes, and brought himself back to the present, back to Thursday morning, 9.15 a.m., in the yard in the rear of the police station at Charing Cross. In the rain. But, he thought, there was light at the end of the tunnel: a divorce would come through any day now, then he'd be able to instruct his solicitor to raise an action for division and sale, just as he clung to tired expressions like the last mile is always longest and the darkest hour is just before dawn. He held on to the promises inherent in those words, action for division and sale: sell the bungalow in Rutherglen, the shrew and the pathetic Samuel could fend for themselves, and he would have enough left to buy a room and kitchen in a sandstone tenement in Langside, for him, him alone and no other. He pondered on the headlong, lemming-rush of young people into marriage: it rarely lived up to its expectations. He, at least, subscribed to that view.

He got out of his car and slammed the door behind him having run down the battery trying to start a damp engine. Batteries, he knew, are strange animals, leave them alone for a few hours and they'll recharge themselves. Not fully, but sometimes just enough to turn the engine over, and if he returned with a spray can of damp-start, it should then fire. He strode away from the car. Leave it for a few hours, he thought. That would sort it.

He held his coat collar together and his battered trilby on against the gusts of wind. Normally he'd take a bus, or a suburban, orange liveried train, whirring smoothly between stations with magical names like Mount Florida, Crosshill, Queen's Park, Crossmyloof and Shawlands, but tiredness did strange things to him and one of the things it did was to reduce his willpower and this made it easy for him to spend money. There was a dull pain across his eyes as he walked towards Anderston Station for a train south of the water and he felt in a strange zombie-like state. Normally a taxi would be an inexcusable indulgence, an unjustified extravagance, but his resistance was low, it was in fact non-existent, and he raised his hand at the first fast black he saw and asked the driver for Baker Street, Langside.

The driver undertook the journey with his head at forty-five degrees to the road, one eye on the road and one eye on Sussock, sensing Sussock to be a ready victim for his opinions on all things, to which Sussock, in his state, could only reply at appropriate intervals, 'Aye, s'right, Jim.' He glanced at the Clyde as the taxi crossed Kingston Bridge, the water a dull grey and extensively rippled with the vertically falling rain. On Pollokshields Road, the steamed-up buses with colours of many companies moved slowly, nose to tail, and the bars were beginning to prepare for the day's drinking trade. At Baker Street he climbed a common stair, and stopped on the second floor, at a heavy wooden door painted in gleaming gloss black, with 'Willems' on the name plate. He pressed the bell.

Elka Willems opened the door and welcomed him with a radiant sunbeam of a smile. She hooked a slender finger under the collar of his coat and tugged him gently over the threshold of her flat. Her blonde hair, always up in a tight bun when in uniform, now hung down over her shoulders; her blue eyes and high cheekbones hinted at her Dutch ancestry. 'You look all in, old Sussock.' She shut the heavy door behind him with a homely, reassuring clunk.

'I am.' Sussock took off his hat and ran his hand over his damp scalp. 'The slave driver wanted to, and I quote, "kick things about a bit".'

'Well, you're home now.' She peeled off his coat and hung it, with his hat, on a peg behind the door, allowing it to drip onto the linoleum.

'Hope you haven't been waiting for me.'

''Course I have. What on earth else would I do?' She kissed him and ran the tip of her finger along his jaw line. 'Don't worry, I know what Fabian can be like. The bed's made up with clean linen; you wash, and then collapse into it. It's my day off and I don't have plans. I'll be around when you wake up.'

'I MUST SAY, I feel relieved not to have had to attend at the locus.' Reynolds smiled. He was tall, silver haired, lean of figure and feature. 'To be able to come straight to the hospital was a treat. No soil samples or fly larvae to collect. The gentleman died from a massive loss of blood. His heart stopped in the ambulance, according to the ambulance crew; no pulse on arrival, couldn't start the heart. He just had run out of the red stuff. Hearts don't work unless they have something to pump. We can't transfuse into an empty system.'

'I didn't know that.' Donoghue sat opposite Reynolds and listened attentively as the pathologist summarized from his notes.

'Happens to be a fact of life, or death, depending on your point of view. You can survive, just, with only two pints of blood. If we can stem the bleeding that can keep the heart pumping and give us time to identify the blood group, then we can hook you up to an alternative supply and if we can pump in more than is coming out you'll eventually recover. We'll stitch and suture the wounds, and coagulation will eventually occur at the wounds and the bleeding will stop. That's basic medicine. The body has a natural tendency to recover and so we help it along all we can. There's no magic wand in respect of surgical intervention, it's logical and mechanistic. But, and it's a big but, you need a life force to begin with. If that life force is spent both in terms of the heart no longer beating and all the blood being spilled   ' Reynolds waved a hand in the air. 'In this case the body was in the hospital, the blood was in the ambulance, but mostly it was five miles away in a street in Ruchazie. He was logged DOA or ''condition purple'' in ambulance crew speak. It obviated the need for the police surgeon to attend; a senior registrar can start the ball rolling.'

'Even so, I do apologize for having to ask you to attend so early in the morning.' Donoghue supped a hot liquid from a plastic cup. He had obtained the drink from a vending machine outside Reynolds's office in the Glasgow Royal Infirmary. It purported to pass for coffee, white without sugar.

'It's part of the job, unsocial hours come with the territory. My wife and I play a game. She's a light sleeper, she actually suffers from insomnia, and anything can wake her. She had a bad beginning to her, she'd told me. Because she couldn't sleep she saw herself as being ill, some sort of freak, and she tried to

knock herself out with drugs and alcohol just in order
to sleep for eight hours like the rest of us. But overnight, apparently, her attitude changed, sensible woman
that she is, and the solution, simple as it is brilliant, was
that she accepted that if her body didn't need eight
hours' sleep, then it just didn't need it. So she had six
hours a day extra to herself that most other people
didn't get. She looked upon it as effectively lengthen-
ing her life. It gave her time to study. She took an ex-
cellent degree, with the increased study time she had,
and now uses her extra hours to study foreign lan-
guages.'

'As you say.' Donoghue placed the plastic cup on
Reynolds's desk; with the best will in the world there are
things up with which he would not put. 'It's all a question of attitude. I have a very good friend who, when in
the RAF some years ago, was stationed in the desert and
was confined to barracks for some misdemeanour. Part
of being c.b. apparently involved reporting to the guard
house hourly, dressed in different kit, and he had to report at 5.00 a.m. in the first instance. Going out at that
hour he saw the desert at night, and he experienced its
coolness and tranquillity, the things which leave as the
sun rises, yet they are the things which I understand
make men return to the desert. So after his seven days'
c.b., he took to getting out of his pit at 5.00 a.m. and
just sat or strolled about, enjoying the desert until rev-
eille. He looks back on that with great fondness. Mind
you, it's rare to suffer an identifiable complaint that can
be turned so strongly to one's advantage.'

'Indeed, my wife is lucky in that respect, Mr
Donoghue, but, as I say, we play a game. I know fine
well that your calls in the night have not woken her. I
put the phone down quickly and quietly and leave the

bedroom to dress. She pretends she is sleeping soundly so as not to upset me. Only when I have been gone five or ten minutes or so does she rise and let Gustav into the garden.'

'Gustav?'

'Our St Bernard. Then she percolates some coffee and curls up with a novel or her language texts for four or five hours to herself before the children have to be up. I know because there is evidence of her being up many hours when I return. Gustav doesn't want to go into the garden, there are vast amounts of percolated coffee waste in the bin in the kitchen, and large amounts of unwashed mugs in the sink. My wife will never rinse a cup or a mug for a second cup of coffee but always reaches for a clean one, and when there's no clean ones left she "blitzes" the washing up. So if I leave the house in the middle of the night and return at 6.00 a.m. and notice eight or nine unwashed mugs in the kitchen sink which weren't there when I left, then that gives me some indication of how long she's been up. It's a secret that isn't a secret, if you see what I mean. I dare say every marriage has one.'

'Even the most successful marriages.' Donoghue became aware that the clock was ticking and that time was marching ever onwards. 'But we have to disturb you because in murder investigations the importance of time diminishes as we move further, in time, from the incident. The first few hours are of crucial importance, especially if the corpse is fresh. We have to start work immediately or the inquiry loses its momentum.'

'I'm afraid I don't have a good deal to report.' Reynolds allowed himself to be brought back on the rails. 'You'll get my report in due course, but glancing at my notes, I can tell you that he sustained a frenzied attack with a large, heavy, sharp-edged instrument.'

'Such as a cleaver?'

'Such as a cleaver. I gather that you know his identity?'

'Dalton Bayliss,' said Donoghue and Reynolds scribbled the name on his note pad. 'Yes, his wife made a positive ID this morning. She was not too upset by all accounts.'

'Well, anyway, young Dalton Bayliss died from loss of blood caused by five incised wounds, as opposed to stab wounds; incised wounds are longer than they are deep, stab wounds are deeper than they are wide. He sustained five wounds, as I said, and I think it's possible to put them in some sort of order. The first wound to be sustained was the one to his genitals.'

'His genitals!' Donoghue winced.

'Yes, I felt for him too,' said Reynolds. 'Hardly bears thinking about. It was a wound which split his testicles and split the base of his penis. It seems to have had an upward motion, as if the perpetrator approached the deceased while concealing the weapon in some way and the deceased, standing facing the perpetrator, was not aware of any danger, nor wearing the sort of garment that offered protection, such as a long coat, which he wasn't. The perpetrator then came within striking distance and suddenly brought the cleaver up into the victim's genitals.'

'Horrible.'

'But effective. It's a ploy which has two advantages, for the perpetrator, that is. In the first instance it is, as you can imagine, utterly disabling, like a kick in the same area, and like a kick it would induce a groan and so stifle a scream.'

'Being the second advantage.'

Reynolds nodded. 'Then the chopping began. Two blows to either shoulder, again useful—they would have prevented the deceased making full use of his arms to defend himself—and they severed an artery in the left shoulder and missed the artery in the right, but that one severance of the artery was probably the fatal blow. He then appeared to have gone for the neck, trying for the carotid artery; he missed, otherwise the deceased would have died within ten seconds of that blow being struck. Finally he laid the stomach open, not fatal, but again utterly disabling. The deceased then crawled a few feet, about twenty feet, into the road, I understand, where he was seen and the alarm raised.' Reynolds turned a page in his notebook. 'The attack would have been over in a matter of seconds, only one instrument was used, indicating one perpetrator, and would have occurred only minutes before he was seen. He actually died in the ambulance. The ambulance crew reported a pulse, but he was DOA. The deceased was a drug abuser.'

'We didn't know that.' Donoghue sat forward. 'It might prove an additional line of enquiry. Equally it might be irrelevant. He's not known for drug-related crimes.'

'Well, he's definitely a drug abuser. He punctures himself with dirty and broken syringes going by the craters in his arm. He's probably HIV positive.'

'Yet he bled in the ambulance.'

Reynolds nodded. 'I'll advise the ambulance crew but they treat every "bleeder" as being HIV positive. The crew wear surgical gloves, the blankets and sheets will probably already have been incinerated and the vehicle taken out of service to be sanitized.'

'So he was a druggie,' Donoghue said, standing.

'Do you think that's connected with the murder?'

'I don't.' Donoghue shook his head. 'I don't actually. I think he was used and then murdered when he became an inconvenience.'

'Dare say he ought to have chosen his friends with a little more care.'

'Well, if you fly with the crows you'll be shot with the crows. That's the way of it.'

MALCOLM MONTGOMERIE once had occasion to listen to a radio magazine programme whilst driving his car. It was, he recalled, while driving north along the A74 from Dumfries to Glasgow having spent a day at Dumfries Sheriff Court, summoned as a Crown witness. He had spent the day on a hard bench in a small room with a window which looked out onto a rooftop and a high wall beyond, and then been told by the usher that his evidence was not, after all, required. So he drove home in the rain, leaving Dumfries at 5.00 p.m. and had switched on his car radio. A component of the radio programme was that a listener could phone in and, after a few minutes' chat with the programme host, would attempt to identify a 'mystery voice'. The same voice repeating the same short sentence was played each evening until it was identified, at which point a cash prize was awarded, and the longer the voice remained unidentified, the greater the value of the prize until it reached a certain cut-off point and another mystery voice would be played. On the day that Montgomerie drove back from Dumfries, a new mystery voice was introduced and played for the first time and the listener on the line had said, 'Er, um, yeah, er, it's that guy... What's his name? Yes, Che Guevara...'

Silence.

Just the swishing of the windscreen wipers.

Finally the programme presenter said, 'Well...I don't know what to say...I'm flabbergasted... You're right...I'll see if we can approve more than the first night's prize which would be ten pounds. Yes, the producer is signalling through the window...fifty pounds... Well, I'm truly lost for words...'

Montgomerie felt a little like he imagined the radio programme presenter must have felt at the moment when he went to speak to Tuesday Noon at the Gay Gordon, at the Round Toll, bottom of Garscube Road, Glasgow G21.

He had slept late, tired after the interview with Wayne Petty which had obliged him to put in three hours' overtime. He woke leisurely, allowing himself a period of 'slumber' before rising, and then he had soaked in a hot bath. It was, he had found, one of the compensations of shift work, that on occasions he could rise slowly and leisurely. He shaved after he had bathed and as he did so he savoured his image in the mirror, drawing the razor lovingly over his face. He had been found handsome since he was seventeen, when he had gone to university in Edinburgh to read law. In the event he found the smugness of the legal profession alien, gave up his studies and had returned to his native Glasgow, joined the police force and had, as he was fond of saying, 'dropped on his feet'. Now at twenty-seven and a detective constable, he felt himself where he should be on his career path, with a flat in the West End of Glasgow, just off Highborough Road, a series of women friends but far from settling down. He was all in all not an unhappy man. But occasionally his employment demanded inroads to be made into his free time and responding to Fabian Donoghue's request to have a word with his snout was just one such occasion.

He took the tube from Hillhead to St George's and walked up St George's Road to the Gay Gordon which stood on the corner of Garscube Road and Possil Road. It stood alone, surrounded by rubble and marram grass. Once it had been a corner pub in a tenement block. The tenements had been cleared and, as so often happened in cleared areas, the pubs were left standing, isolated outposts in a sea of rubble. Beyond the Gay Gordon, striding across the skyline, was the grim edifice of the Galloway Road housing scheme: not the most sought after housing in the city. It was ten past midday; rain fell slowly from a low grey sky. Montgomerie pushed open the heavily stained and polished door of the Gay Gordon. He wore a multi-coloured hiking jacket, comfortably out of place.

The barman eyed him with distaste. Some barmen like cops to pay a call, helps to keep the peace; others, those with time behind them, those with mates in the gaol, those with a sideline with one of the city's 'firms', definitely don't care for cops in the sawdust and the barman of the Gay Gordon was one such man. Montgomerie felt reassured. He had got to know the barman over the years of calling on Tuesday Noon and felt that if the man ever took a liking to him, then he would have cause to be deeply worried about himself.

Tuesday Noon sat in the corner. He sat underneath a wall-mounted television which had both the sound and the colour turned up too loudly, at the moment broadcasting a current affairs programme. Beside the television was a stained-glass window which softened the image of the day outside and doubtless encouraged the punters to remain inside and part with their money.

Montgomerie walked up to the gantry and ordered a whisky and an orange juice. No other words were spoken. He was served in a dour, sour manner. He dropped a five-pound note on the wood and scooped up a pile of lead; he carried the drinks over to where Tuesday Noon was sitting with his back to the wall, close to where a tuft of horsehair had been pulled out of a slash in the upholstery. Over in the opposite corner sat a man with a deeply lined face and matted silver hair, staring into a world of his own.

'Tuesday.' Montgomerie sat opposite him on a chair which was chained to the floor. If the chairs and tables were not chained down they'd be used as weapons in the inevitable Saturday night rammy or carried home as newly acquired items of furniture. That's how it was in parts of the city and Montgomerie accepted it. He placed the glasses on the formica table top, sticky from the previous night's spillage.

Tuesday Noon grabbed the whisky and sank it in one and gasped a breath of hot air towards Montgomerie. Montgomerie winced and looked into Tuesday Noon's mouth, a gaping red hole with a few yellow pegs going up and down, surrounded by silver whiskers and flabby folds of flesh. 'Mr Montgomerie.' He pushed the empty glass towards Montgomerie.

'Maybe.' Montgomerie looked Tuesday Noon square in the eye. 'You know the rules, Tuesday—all depends on what you can put my way.'

'I don't know anything about it, Mr Montgomerie. Haven't heard anything.'

'Anything about what?'

'Yon stabbing in Ruchazie. It's the only thing that happened in the night.'

'How did you hear about it?'

Tuesday Noon grinned and tapped the side of his jaw.

Montgomerie just had to hand it to him. 'OK. It's that that I'm here about, Tuesday. Young boy got chopped up.'

'I'll keep my ears open.'

Montgomerie nodded. 'Counting on you, Tuesday. Tell me, do you know of a guy with a Rolls Royce?'

Tuesday Noon grinned at the joke.

'I'm serious, Tuesday. Good-looking young man, could be mistaken for being English by his accent, but he's a posh Scot. Runs a roller.'

Tuesday Noon nodded, raised a finger in Montgomerie's direction and said, 'Aye. That guy. Oh, him. Aye, aye. Marjerison, that's his name, Marjerison.'

Silence.

Montgomerie suddenly knew what the presenter of the radio programme had felt like all those years ago when the mystery voice was identified at its first airing. He let his jaw drop a little.

'What do you know about him, Tuesday?'

Tuesday Noon shook his head. 'Not a lot. He was pointed out to me one time. Me and this guy were standing in a doorway near the *Herald* building, passing a bottle of buckshot between us, and the boy, he says, "That's a guy called Marjerison." There are lots of Rolls Royces in Glasgow, Mr Montgomerie, but not that many driven by boys. This car is jet black with a grey roof. You tend to see him around the Merchant City.'

Montgomerie took his wallet from his jacket and dropped a fiver on the table. 'Tuesday,' he said, 'Tuesday, you're beautiful. I really mean that.'

Montgomerie left the Gay Gordon and phoned P Division from a public call box. He asked to be put through to DI Donoghue.

'Just about to take my lunch, Montgomerie.'

'I think you'll enjoy it more when you hear this, sir.' Montgomerie paused to allow an orange Strathclyde Regional Council bus to whine past, kicking up spray as it did so. 'I really think I have something here.'

Donoghue reached for his pen. 'Go on.'

'I have a name for the guy with the Rolls Royce. It may be a guy called Marjerison.'

'Marjerison. Same name as supplied by the estate agent.' Donoghue spoke as he wrote. 'Anything else?'

'Just that he's the only known youthful owner of a Rolls Royce in Glasgow, according to Tuesday Noon, and that he's often to be seen around the Merchant City.'

'Well, your snout's been right before. Right, Montgomerie, come straight in. You can start the back shift a wee bit early, do your soul good. You can dig up all you can about young Mr Marjerison.'

'You know, I thought you might say that, sir.'

'Just get your tail in here, Montgomerie.'

'IT COULD BE the gentleman.' Sara Sinclair's scarlet claws that had the day before spidered across the spines of files in the top drawer of her filing cabinet while assisting Richard King now held at arm's length a photofit compiled with the assistance of Mrs Sloan. 'But after so many months . . . but yes, I think it is he.'

Abernethy took the photofit and slipped it back inside the stiffened brown envelope. 'Thank you.'

'Well, you see it's not so much the appearance I recall,' said Sara Sinclair, 'rather it's his youth.'

'Oh.' Abernethy, gauche, and young for a CID offi-cer, had the distinct impression that the painted, coif-fured, scented woman was forcing conversation to keep him in her office, desperate to know what had hap-pened at the large old house on Sherbrooke Avenue that two police officers should call on her within the space of twenty-four hours.

'Well, yes. Houses like that, if they are in the posses-sion of single family occupants, tend to be bought by people in their middle years, at least.'

'At least.'

'But this gentleman appeared to be in his early thir-ties. He seemed genuine, he could handle class and he had the delicious pungency of "old money" about him. You see, each and every job has its drawbacks that have to be lived with. In this line of work, we have to put up with wide boys who string us along as much as they can. They enjoy being pampered and wooed, especially if they are looking upmarket in a buyer's market. We drive them about, sometimes take them to lunch and then they pull out at the last minute. But that chap—' she nodded at the envelope that Abernethy held '—he seemed to be the real thing, young but genuine. He was class, top-drawer stuff, as I told your colleague yester-day.'

'That's important to you is it, Mrs Sinclair?'

'Yes, it is.' She raised an eyebrow, but the attempt to look imperious didn't come off and Abernethy found the gesture somewhat pathetic. 'You see I didn't go to school and the name on my birth certificate is Sadie Crosby. The name on my marriage certificate was Sa-die Smith, can you beat that? I come from Castlemilk and I married a jobbing carpenter from Nitshill. I changed my name when we got divorced and moved into this business. I learned the trade from another company and started up alone. I'm sending my son to school, the fees are expensive but he'll move up a couple of notches and his son will move up a couple of more notches. That's how I see it.'

'Fair enough.'

'Is that wrong?'

'No, no. It's neither right nor wrong: personal values are a private matter.'

'But this man, he's just how I'd like my son to turn out.'

'I think you'd better hope that you're wrong there.' Abernethy stood. 'Thanks for your time.'

'What do you mean about being wrong?'

'Can't really explain.' Abernethy walked to the door. 'But, well...' He tapped the envelope. 'Charm and good manners are all very well, but this is probably one man you don't want your son to turn out to be like. We may be wrong, of course...'

'But you don't think you are?'

'I've already said too much.' Abernethy smiled.

He returned to P Division and wrote up his visit to Sara Sinclair, a two-line entry into the growing Pam McArthur file, now cross-referenced to the Dalton Bayliss file. Two lines, dated and timed, confirming Mrs Sinclair's identification of the photofit as being of similar likeness to the man she knew as Marjerison, c/o Littlejohn, Houston Ltd, and who had requested keys to the property at Sherbrooke Avenue about the time of Pam McArthur's disappearance, and at which locus Pam McArthur's headless and handless body was subsequently found some eight months later.

It was 12.15. He signed off and returned home by bus to a modest three apartment in the south side. He opened the storm door, then the main door, he peeled off his dripping waxed jacket and hung it in the hall of dark stained wood and threadbare carpet; it had changed little since his earliest memories. He padded down the corridor and entered the living room. A bald head at the top of the back of an old armchair greeted him. Beyond the chair and the baldness was a flickering coal fire.

'Hello, Dad.'

'Son,' said the voice belonging to the bald head. 'What time is it?'

'Just the back of one, Dad.'

'In now for the day?'

'Aye.'

'Good. What time is it?'

'One o'clock, just gone.'

'Still raining?'

'Aye. Easing off though.'

'In for the day?'

'Aye.'

'Not going out again?'

'Not until the morning.'

'Still raining?'

'Not as much, but yes, it's still coming down.'

'What time is it?'

'One o'clock.'

Then the head nodded and was silent. Abernethy shut the door.

RICHARD KING FELT deeply embarrassed. The man's joy at serious and unexpected company, at having a role to play and being possessed of a voice deemed important enough to be heard, was all too evident, humblingly so. Yet his joy was marred because his private world, where he could escape, was now, to him, being scrutinized, and there was also, he believed, the inescapable fact that his important voice stemmed from his situation. King felt deeply for the man, sensing both his delight and his awkwardness. He saw a sharp mind in a body, still young, but wasting cruelly and as relentlessly as an unstoppable decay. The man sat in a wheelchair, beside him was a table with a place set for one and beside the plate with deepened sides, but not yet a bowl, was a knife and fork with hugely thick handles to facilitate grip. Outside the window Edinburgh Road rumbled with traffic; it lay beyond a service road, and beyond a grass bank, yet the rumble and hiss of tyres on wet tarmac were clearly heard in the man's room. There was no other sound.

'I have good days and bad days,' said Roddy McGee, tapping the padded black arm of his wheelchair. 'Sometimes I think I have just bad days and bad days, but rest is the key. My muscle energy is all but spent; I mustn't use it up needlessly. If I rest during the day and sleep in the afternoon I can drag myself out at night on my sticks.'

King nodded, continuing to be humbled by the man's courage.

'But I do enjoy my walk at night. I like the clean fresh air and I like the scheme when it's still.'

'You certainly walked last night, early this morning. The cops said you were in a state of near collapse when they found you.'

'I think I was driven by panic. Seeing a dying man seemed to be worse than what I imagine seeing a dead man must be like.'

'Oh yes.' King knew what he meant and leaned forward slightly and smiled behind his close-clipped beard as he warmed to Roddy McGee. If a man or a woman is dead there is little to do, but if a person is dying all the responsibility in the world is dropped in your lap. King had been there a few times: RTA victims mangled under wheels, neds with knives in their ribs, the fashionable scarlet blouse which revealed itself to be white on closer inspection…and the time he'd held his palm over a severed throat until the ambulance crew had arrived. Yes, he knew fine well what Roddy McGee meant. 'Anyway, it's the guy in the flash motor, Roddy, he's the guy we're keen to trace.'

'Aye, a Rolls Royce. Not many of them in the scheme.'

'That's for sure. I've got a photofit here. I wonder could you take a look…?' King probed a reinforced brown envelope and handed his copy of the photofit to McGee.

'It's not like you see in the films. I thought you made them up section by section, you know a mouth, then a nose…'

'Dark Ages, Roddy. Dark Ages. It's all done by computer graphics these days; produces a single, whole image rather than the old-fashioned composite. Anyway, recognize him?'

'Well, it could be him. I didn't get a good look, and it was dark. I can say it's not unlike him, if that's a help.'

'It's a great help.' King slid the photofit back inside the envelope. 'These things are never supposed to be more than an approximation, an impression if you like. Photofit is a poor term, gives the wrong suggestion, you know, "photo" and "fit", but it'll be a good few years before I get up to the sort of level that will allow me to introduce far-reaching changes of that sort, that is changing long-standing terminology.'

'Well, in that case, it's a close impression of the man I saw. And he didn't mind me seeing him. He stared at me and sneered, me all twisted on my sticks in the rain, him looking like a fashion model in his Rolls Royce.'

'I'm sorry.' King couldn't think of anything else to say.

'I've learned to live with it. I dare say I'm better off than the guy I saw dying in the street. I mean I'm alive and he's not, and I've lived for longer than him. I read in the *Record* that he was only twenty-two. But I wish people could stop comparing themselves to each other, me included. Most days I make the best of what I've got, but occasionally I read about some tragedy and I say "well at least that's not me".'

'It's a normal attitude.'

'It's not healthy. It's selfish and immature.'

'Like the guy in the Rolls Royce and his sneer. That's an extreme example.'

'Aye, even so, but he was full of himself, that one. You know how a glimpse, a flash of insight, can reveal so much. He liked life well enough did yon in the Rolls. Life had dealt him a good hand of cards all right.'

'Nice for some.'

'Aye, but I didn't envy him. Strange to say.'

'Not?'

Roddy McGee shook his head. 'No. There's me leaning on my sticks in the rain, old clothes, him and his setup, but he just hadn't lived: he'd smoothed his way through life without having to meet an obstacle or a setback. That's how I saw him in a split second. But me, I've lived. I know what it's about. He didn't, like he thought he couldn't be touched. I suppose he knifed the guy I saw?'

'Aye.'

'Well, after doing that, he can still turn this way and that, reverse back the way finding his road out of the scheme; then he draws up alongside me and stares at me and sneers, after doing *that* to a guy, calm as you please. He must believe he can't be touched. I'd hate to have that attitude.'

Richard King left Roddy McGee's ground floor flat, glancing into the kitchen as he walked down the corridor and noting the lowered sink and cooker, adapted for the needs of the physically challenged. He noted too the single mug, next to the small teapot.

'If you think I can be of any further help—' Roddy McGee wheeled himself to the door '—then do call back.'

'Thanks.' King turned and smiled as McGee closed the door behind him.

On the pavement, a young boy about ten years old sat astride a chopper bike, with his arms folded, blue anorak. He looked at King with self-satisfied eyes. 'Have you just given him a wee visit?' he asked.

IN THE DRAWING ROOM of a large house in the vicinity of Helensburgh two women sat in an awkward, tense silence as a young child, an infant male, crawled about the floor. Both were called Mrs Marjerison, both sat upright in their chairs, held long empty cups which had once contained tea and looked out of the drawing room windows to where two men walked with the accompaniment of a bounding Dalmatian. In the room the clock ticked and the women would each occasionally clear her throat. One was much older than the other.

In the expanse of the rain-sodden garden the two men on whom the women in the drawing room cast their gaze were similarly both called Marjerison and similarly were of differing ages. Dissimilar to the women in the drawing room, the men walked in close company and chatted amicably, yet the elder of the two was troubled: he liked his son, the younger man, but felt deeply uneasy about the reason his son should like him.

'Haven't heard from that dreadful McArthur woman for some time.' Marjerison the elder broke a brief silence in the conversation.

'Been about six months since you heard last from her.' The younger man picked up a stick and skimmed it into a shrubbery causing a cascade of water to fall. The dog bounded after it.

'Longer I think. I did tell her that she might well have got on to something but it was something she could never prove. I think she must have come to that realization herself and thrown her energies in a different direction, and heaven knows they needed throwing in a direction. The woman was burning up with bitterness and resentment about some personal injustice or other and if she didn't have something to drive at she would drive at herself, send herself deranged.'

'Oh, I think she was there already.' The younger man took the stick from the Dalmatian's jaws and threw it back into the shrubbery. 'Maybe that's why you haven't heard from her. Maybe she's in a locked ward some place.'

'Maybe. I do hope they can help her. It doesn't do to allow yourself to burn up like that. You get nothing out of life because you put nothing in.'

'Rain's coming on again,' said Marjerison the younger. 'Shall we join the ladies?'

SEVEN

'SOMEWHERE,' said Donoghue, 'somewhere in this flat is a key piece of information.'

'Certainly hope so, sir.' King closed the door of Pam McArthur's flat behind him.

I have no idea what it looks like, or what it will tell us. We've lost the discs; the tall man whom I believe to be Marjerison will have destroyed them by now. But there will be other information here.'

'I'm sure he has,' said King. 'I would if I were him.'

Donoghue nodded. 'He pops up in all the wrong places, Richard, and there are too many people identifying him, as though he feels himself invincible. I can't fathom why a man in Marjerison's position, Rolls Royce owner, civil engineer with...what was that company?'

'Littlejohn, Houston.'

'That's the name. Why should he be so afraid of a shrew like the McArthur woman is reported to have been that he murders her? And what was it that went down in this city thirty or more years ago, when both Marjerison and McArthur were pre-school, that made them want to destroy each other? I don't want to rush this one, Richard, I've a feeling that we could lose it if we did that. I dare say we could lift Marjerison now with what we have, but I don't want to tip him off before we have at least an inkling of his motivation.'

'So let's look for it.'

'Right. If you could start in the bedroom, Richard, I'll take the study.'

King walked into the bedroom of the late Pam McArthur and again saw the mattress on the floor and the posters of Stalin and Karl Marx. He looked about him and then began to open the drawers in a chest of drawers, starting with the bottom one first and working upwards, sifting through clothing. In the top drawer he found joss sticks and a generous tablet of cannabis. Also in the top drawer was a brown envelope on which 'Pamela McArthur' had been written in a full round hand. Underneath the name the same full round hand had written 'this is what you want'. Inside the envelope was a typewritten report entitled 'Reema Blocks', compiled by one Liz Hext who enjoyed the designation Research Coordinator. King stood and read the report, scanning it quickly in the first instance, noting that one or two lines had been highlighted with a yellow felt-tip pen and that notes had been scribbled in the margin.

The report transpired to be about a block of high-rise flats and King took especial note of the words and phrases that had been highlighted: 'dampness', 'damage could not always be attributed to vandalism', 'lift shafts flooding, short circuiting and activating the lifts', 'a mixture of fresh water and dilute sewage', 'cracks and fissures in service pipes' against which a note had been scribbled: 'poor structural integrity'. King turned the page and read on: 'structural investigation refused so as not to cause panic', 'structure at risk in high winds or fire', 'fire doors unable to hold flames', 'fire and fumes could spread from flat to flat due to the cracking between wall and floor panels', 'tenants needed additional heating and are resorting to calor gas', 'serious doubts on structural safety', 'all steps to be taken to re-assure tenants that the blocks are safe to live in'. King folded the report and showed it to Donoghue.

'Could very well be it, Richard,' Donoghue said, having glanced over the report. 'We'll talk to the author, Liz Hext. No contact number or address. Still it won't be too difficult to find her. We'll hand that to Montgomerie, perhaps you could . . . ?'

'Certainly.' Richard King folded the report and slipped it into his jacket pocket.

Outside on the landing Mrs Sloan stood on the threshold of her door, cigarette in her mouth, brazenly curious. Both cops walked past her and down the stairs without a glance, or a single word being spoken.

RAY SUSSOCK AWOKE. A pleasant gentle sea of pastel blue met his opening eyes, as did a wide bed of clean linen and a mattress which accommodated his awkward posture, half on his side, his arms and legs, it seemed, everywhere. He closed his eyes and opened them again. He was lying in the double bed in the recess of Elka Willems's room. He recalled the beginning of the day, the end of the graveyard shift, being kept back by the aftershaved, neatly-iron-shirted, fresh-as-a-field-of-dawn poppies, pipe-smoking Donoghue to 'kick it about a bit'. Leaving P Division dull and tired, too tired to face public transport, and taking a taxi after his aged car had refused to start because of the damp weather. Elka Willems hooking her finger under his collar, pulling him over her threshold. He felt refreshed after a good, nourishing, alcohol-free sleep and glanced at his watch, 15:17 by the digital display: six hours thereabouts, that would do.

He rolled over and lay on his back, looking up at the high ceiling. That would do, he thought, that would do very nicely. Sussock had learned that, after almost a full working life of shifts, it is not the length of sleep that is important but the quality: four hours of solid, undisturbed rest was, in his experience, far more refreshing than eight hours of fitful, alcohol-contaminated tossing and turning.

He looked around the room, the clean young person's comfortable furnishings, the bowl of fruit on the sideboard, the reeds of pampas grass in the earthenware vase, the Van Gogh print on the wall. This, he felt, was an ideal use of a room and kitchen, for a single young person living alone, with the occasional overnight guest. Sussock had grown up in a room and kitchen, not in calm, self-controlled Langside, but in the old Gorbals, the Gorbals of global infamy, now cleared save for one or two pubs which stand like decaying boxes between Eglinton Street and the waste ground behind. He had been one of six children. He well recalled the shared toilet outside on the turn of the stair, and the screams in the night and the pools of dried blood in the morning.

A woman walked on the pavement outside, under the window. A car moved slowly in the opposite direction. All seemed calm outside, under a pale grey sky.

He yawned loudly as Elka Willems entered the room dressed in a short yellow towelling robe belted tightly at the waist and giving at the hem to silken smooth endless legs. 'Move over,' she commanded with a smile, tugging the knot of her towelling belt.

MONTGOMERIE PUSHED open the door of the Long Bar on Great Western Road. A bronze orange bar, it seemed to him: orange carpet right up to the gantry; polished wood, most likely, he thought, to be veneer and chipboard as was most often the case in the new bars in the city. Brass beer engine handles, upright, static, just for show. The girls in pink dresses pressed a button under the pump to obtain the beer, the lager, the Irish Stout; choice of Murphy's or Guinness. The mirrors, edged in brass, and soft lights completed the image of walking into a long yellow-brown cavern, and behind, the deeply tinted glass of the door served to shut out the day. No clock in sight, no TV on the wall here, as in the Gay Gordon. Everything in the Long Bar was designed to separate the customer from reality: soft colours, music, gentle lights, girls in pink frocks. It all served to encourage punters to remain, and remain parting with their shekels.

The bar wasn't busy when Montgomerie entered, a few retired punters sitting in front of half-pint glasses and a glass of whisky, pulling on empty pipes. It being a Thursday there were a number of Giro dependants who lived in the hostel on Hamilton Park Avenue; these, it seemed to Montgomerie, lived for their Giro on Thursday and blew it on the drink, and then somehow lived through to the following Thursday when they got smashed again. Montgomerie had also noticed that in the Long Bar, as in other long, deep bars in Glasgow with only one entrance and exit, the Giro dependants prefer tables near the door, while the middle classes of the locality, and the students, favour the tables in the furthest recesses of the pub. Odd, he thought. No reason for it that he could detect, but it was the same in all such bars in the west end.

Diana saw him as he opened the door and allowed a split second of eye contact before she turned away with a swirl of flowing pink and stacked 'sleeves' on the rack of clean glasses underneath the spirit rack. Montgomerie walked across the carpet with long, effortless strides, and ignored the glares and sneers of one or two of the Giro-dependent young men who had evidently been lifted by the law and who recognized the unmistakable stamp of the CID when they saw it. He stood at the gantry. She plunged a sleeve in the glass wash and pumped it up and down and didn't look up when Montgomerie said, 'Hi.'

Pump, pump, pump, angry pump, pump. Eventually she said, 'So what happened to you?' Curtly accusatorial.

'Had to work, hen.'

'You said you didn't start till mid-afternoon. That's what you said. Plenty of time for an early lunch, that's what you said.'

Montgomerie levered himself onto a bar stool, twin shades of orange upholstery on a fixed aluminium tube. 'Just had to work,' he said. 'That's the way of it sometimes.'

'I was waiting from 11.30 till 12.30.'

'I'm really sorry. Can I have a soda and lime? Heavy on the lime.' He was served. He laid the lead next to a bar towel. It was swept up angrily and the change placed down on the veneer, next to his open palm.

'Not even a phone call.'

'I finished late this morning, had to see an old guy, my snout...'

'Your what?'

'Informant. Had to go up to Round Toll to a pub—'

'I don't believe I'm hearing this. You know I'm waiting for you in a bar in town, but you go up to St

George's, of all places, to meet a guy that clypes on his mates?'

'No road round it, he laid a pile of gold dust on me. I phoned it in and got told to come in early. I should be there now but I took a detour to call in here to explain...'

'That's big of you. I missed lunch because of you. I am not the sort of woman that gets stood up. Men don't stand me up, Malcolm.'

'I didn't...' He took a drink. It was light on the lime, no taste to speak of.

'I was waiting for you with two other girls, otherwise I wouldn't have waited the full hour...friends of mine...you didn't show. I felt so embarrassed. They're always gossiping about me now, be all round the year group at the university.'

'Look, it wasn't so easy to phone. I didn't think you'd wait that long anyway and, besides, I'm sticking my neck out to come here as it is.'

'Then go.'

Montgomerie drained his glass. 'That's it then.'

'That's it.' She marched off and served a customer.

Montgomerie eased himself off the stool and walked towards the swing door of tinted glass and onto Great Western Road. 'Easy come,' he thought, 'easy go,' but Diana must be something of a record: he'd known her for only twenty-four hours and had achieved the elbow already. Never touched her, never known her surname. He felt a strongly misplaced sense of achievement.

He stood at the kerb in the drizzle, pondered a bus but jumped a fast black and asked the driver to take him to Charing Cross.

He walked across the car park to the rear door of P Division, and saw Ray Sussock's car standing isolated, as though no other officer wanted to park next to it; he noted it was rust streaked, rain streaked and one tyre was clearly badly deflated. Montgomerie signed in and checked his pigeonhole. Nothing there, and that pleased him. He felt himself satisfied with his rank at his age, but he wasn't a careerist. Something in his pigeonhole invariably meant work or a 'see me' note from Donoghue, which invariably meant he had to think on his feet in order to explain something and so, for Montgomerie, happiness was an empty pigeonhole.

He took the stairs two at a time up to the CID corridor and entered the office he shared with King and Abernethy.

'You're a bit late.' King's smile made his comment a little less barbed than it might otherwise have been.

Montgomerie glanced at his watch: 15.30. 'I've been working since 11.30.' Montgomerie peeled off his hiking jacket.

'Want a coffee?' Montgomerie advanced on the kettle and selected the least dirty mug.

'No thanks, I'm away home. Want to grab a nap on the sofa before Rosemary brings Iain in from the child minder's.' King leaned back causing his chair to creak. 'Fabian wants to see you as soon as you come in.'

'I know, I've got to do some digging about a guy called Marjerison.'

'How do you know about him?'

'Tuesday Noon.' Montgomerie stirred the brown liquid; slightly sour milk floated to the surface in white globules. It was, he told himself, the sort of drink that didn't taste bad if you pretended you were dying of thirst in the Sahara.

'It'll be about that, he's connected with both murders.'

'Murders?' Montgomerie sank into his chair.

King nodded. 'This has moved while you slumbered. You recall the ned you lifted last night?'

'Wayne Petty.'

'He mentioned a pal of his.'

'Dalton Bayliss, or Animal the Electric Gypsy. They were both present when the McArthur woman was slain.'

'Well, Dalton Bayliss or Animal the Electric Gypsy is no longer with us.'

'You're kidding.'

King shook his head. 'I'm as serious as a heart attack. Read the file if you don't believe me.'

'I believe you. What happened?'

'Shortly after you lifted Petty, Petty's father phoned Bayliss and told him what had happened—fair rattled Bayliss's cage according to the not very distressed Mrs Bayliss, who will doubtless be out at the dancing tonight celebrating and looking to pull a replacement man. Anyway, Dalton started to make a phone call from his house, thought the better of it and went out to use a public phone. He never came home.'

'My God.'

'Member of the public was walking in Ruchazie in the wee small hours, saw a guy stagger and fall and dialled three nines. Turned out the staggering guy was the dying remnants of Dalton Bayliss. The PM was done this morning. Dr Reynolds reckons he went up against a cleaver and took the second prize. The cops took Mrs Bayliss to make the formal ID at about 8.30. She apparently said, 'Aye, that's him the bad swine,' and walked out of GRI and was seen going into a bar with a breakfast licence—to have one or two super lagers to celebrate her freedom, I would imagine.'

'This I dare not believe.'

'Not only that . . .'

'There's more?'

'In the immediate vicinity of the locus, contemporary with the incident, was seen a Rolls Royce manoeuvring slowly, as if lost. It eventually left the scheme via Bellrock Street and the M8 westbound. A Rolls Royce, a calm, carefree manner . . . Ring any bells?'

'Deafeningly. Driven by a young good-looking man . . .'

'I showed the computer composite to the witness. He said it could be the guy in the roller.'

'That means Petty is only safe where he is. He's in protective custody, in a sense. So why isn't Fabian moving on Marjerison? We know where he works, Littlejohn, Houston Ltd, we have Petty's ID of him, Mrs Sloan's ID of him at McArthur's house just having removed McArthur's computer discs, we think. It would be good enough for me.'

'That's your answer,' said King. 'What is good enough for you isn't good enough for Fabian. Fabian is nothing if not cautious. I think he knows that Marjerison isn't going anywhere, and with Petty inside no one else appears to be at risk. I think he wants to be able to identify the motive for murdering Pam McArthur before moving on Marjerison. He wants to know all the answers to his questions before he asks his questions of Marjerison. He hasn't said as much to me but I believe that's how he wants to play it, knowing Fabian.'

DONOGHUE LEANED BACK in his chair, dressed in white shirt and dark blue waistcoat, his jacket having joined his homburg and Burberry on the hat stand. He pulled lovingly on his briar and said, 'This is how I want to play it.'

Montgomerie listened attentively.

'Point one, it hadn't occurred to me that our number one suspect would chop Dalton Bayliss, but in fairness to us things have moved at some speed. It's difficult to believe it was only yesterday morning that a motorist ran into a shrubbery and started this whole thing off, but I can't identify anyone else who might be at risk from this gentleman, Mr Marjerison, save young Petty and he's safely banged up. He'll go before the Sheriff in the morning; the charge is murder and rape so he'll be remanded as a matter of course. It may well be that the Procurator reduces the charges to a single charge of rape, given the circumstances, but the point is he's safely out of harm's way: can't harm others; no harm will come to him from Marjerison although the other lags will give him a hard time—they don't like rapists in the slammer.

'Point two is that what strikes me as the biggest obstacle for us is the apparent coolness of this creature, Mr Marjerison. Consider the premeditation that has gone into this crime, consider how he was prepared to let the planned proceedings be interrupted while Bayliss first gives the unpleasant but nonetheless unfortunate McArthur woman a good tanking and then while Bayliss and Petty perpetrate rape. Only then does he strangle her which is what he intended to do all along. Then consider the coolness with which he waits, and upon his insistence, Petty and Bayliss also, for hours, from early afternoon to midnight, in the presence of the body of the McArthur woman, until he's certain that her blood has congealed sufficiently to allow him to chop her up with a minimum of blood flow. Then he calmly places the bag containing her head and hands into the boot of his Rolls Royce and supervises the concealing of the body at the front of the house. He disposes of the head and hands—they'll never be found—and then realizes that McArthur possessed a distinctive watch so he orders Bayliss to retrieve it. So he does, goes back and rolls over a week-old corpse, and rescues the watch.'

'So he's cool. And he has power over people. A real chancer.'

'The watch could have identified her, and when everything else was so well planned... No, Montgomerie, he's not a chancer.' Donoghue laid his pipe beside his ashtray. 'No, he's too meticulous to be a chancer. I deduce him to have built an alibi. I deduce him to be waiting for us, and waiting with a cast-iron alibi.'

'I see.'

'That's what I anticipate. I fully expect Mr Marjerison to have an alibi which places him in someone's presence or at least a long way from Pollokshields on the 6th June last year. But the nice thing about alibis, if they are false, is that they can work as much against you as they can for you. A huge and powerful alibi can be destroyed by a hairline fracture. So we'll have some checking to do at some point in respect of Marjerison's movements on or about that date.'

'Very good.'

'Point three is that we'll have to determine what we can about Marjerison's motives for murdering the McArthur woman. Consider that he despised her so much that he was prepared to let her last experience of life be violent assault and multiple rape. And all because of something that happened in this town thirty years ago, before either suspect or victim had started school.'

'Find that and we're on our way.'

Donoghue smiled. 'Richard King has...I think he has anyway.' He handed Montgomerie the report King had found in the drawer in Pam McArthur's bedroom. 'Read it over. It's all about a jerry-built block of flats in Easterhouse, which were built about thirty years ago. Marjerison gave his business address to Sara Sinclair as care of a firm of civil engineers. I can see a faint glimmering candle flame in the gloom, a pinprick of light in the darkness. Forget about digging up what you can about Marjerison. I want you to find the author of this report, find her and get us nearer that source of light.'

Richard King drove home. He was tired. Dog tired. But that, he often told himself, was the nature of police work. Relentless round-the-clock, on a shift pattern which is immovable, which crushes everything before it, regardless of days of the week, so that a cop knows which shift he'll be on in ten years' time. There just isn't a shift that slides smoothly into the normal frame of human existence, of 09.00 to 17.00, Monday to Friday. But there were compensations, like journeys home and to work taken outside the rush hour, as today when King drove home on clear roads, on a traffic-free Springburn Road, up towards Bishopbriggs. At Bishopbriggs he turned off the main drag and into a neat enclave of semi-detached houses, gardens to the front and to the rear, clipped lawns and roses growing in lattices, either side of the front door. His own house needed work to finish it off, and he was often embarrassed at being the owner of the least tidy house in the street, it having a 'make do and mend' quality. The lawn was 'kept down' rather than mown tidily in alternating strips of light and dark and weeds grew in his flower beds. But Richard King's household was the only household in the street with a young infant, and with more planned. He had to place the issues in his life in order of priority. When Iain and subsequent children were grown and away, like the children of his neighbours, when he was enjoying a comfortable retirement, like his neighbours, then he would address himself to the state of his lawn, and the weeds amongst his daffodils; like his neighbours.

King left his car at the kerbside and with his hands plunged deep into the pockets of his waxed jacket he ran through the rain and up to the front door of his house. It was empty, and silent save for the radio Rosemary insisted on leaving playing when the house was deserted as a burglar deterrent. She had been burgled once, before she was married, when a young professional living in a rented flat. She lost little, and suffered minimal damage, but the sense of violation was profound and long lasting. She did not wish to repeat the experience. He went into the kitchen and switched the radio off.

He hustled a mug of tea on the low table in the middle of the floor, settled backwards and allowed himself to begin to doze. He no longer fought off sleep. Soon he could have all the sleep he wanted but he wanted also to be awake when Rosemary and Iain returned, with him in his light blue romper suit and sensible shoes, and her in a flowing skirt. He wanted to speak to them both when they returned and then he would wash, and undress and slide into bed with the curtains closed against the gloom of the afternoon. As he sat his eyes remained closed and sounds seemed further and further away.

THE MAN STOOD. He had found himself daydreaming. Again.

It didn't look good. He had a pile of reports to read, he had a list of reports to write. He had a project to cost. And he had a personal and a family reputation to uphold. But yet again he found himself leaning back in his chair, looking at the arms of his angle poise or out at the rain-running windows of the other buildings in the Merchant City, which, like his, were burning lights in the middle of the afternoon. A secretary would walk past and stare at him curiously; a senior partner would frown. The man stood, he wanted to make a deliberate movement so he stood. He went to the men's washroom. He leaned against the marble top of the sink unit and looked into the mirror above the gold tops with fern plants at either side. He adored his image, yet his brow was furrowed of late.

He wondered if he had thought of everything? Yes, no, yes, yes. At least everything he could do. So they had found the woman, not gone public yet, nothing on the radio or TV. It had taken them longer than he had thought it would have, long enough to cover his tracks. They had identified her more quickly than he had thought possible but it didn't matter, he had done all he could do. Those few days: how he'd kept himself going still amazed him; the temptation to resort to amphetamines had been almost beyond his control, but he'd resisted them. Snatched catnaps, here and there.

He wondered if they could link him to the murder? Two neds had watched him. He'd bought their silence for a few hundred pounds and the threat of life imprisonment for conspiracy to murder, and had sealed the contract by handing the hacksaw to one of them to do the chopping. Now one had been lifted—how they had traced him didn't matter, the fact is they *had* traced him. The other heard about it, began to panic. He had to be chopped. No road round that one. That left one to identify him. One's word against another's. He could cope with that. That might be good enough for some countries but not Scotland with its need for corroborative evidence in its criminal proceedings, two independent streams of evidence, or whatever the phrase was. The word of a ned against the word of him, a professional man from an Old Glasgow family. He smiled: yes that he could well live with, that he could cope with. He had after all the strongest of alibis and there was nothing, nothing at all, to link him with that... that... thing McArthur. Nothing at all.

The man, the ned—what did he call himself? Animal, Gypsy, something utterly Street Turk stupid—he'd done the right thing by phoning him from a public call box, not from his home, because in these days of itemized calls such calls would be logged. No one had seen him chop Animal or whatever his name was. He had crumpled with a groan. Then there had been only the poor creature on sticks hobbling about the scheme in the dead of night. All that guy had seen was a guy in a car, he'd got a brief glimpse, but not enough to nail him. Or was it?

No, not another murder. It had to stop somewhere and it would stop here. Two was sufficient. Two was one too many, in fact.

He turned on the hot tap and let it run. He enjoyed the steam on his face and enjoyed the delicate beauty of it condensing on the fern leaves.

He wondered if his alibi would stand up? No 'ifs' about it, it just had to. He had kept the counterfoils of the air tickets he had to keep, he'd destroyed the tickets he didn't need. His wife had been away from the house. She wouldn't have noticed he'd borrowed the car—that had been a risk, but he hadn't been seen, and he just had to get behind the wheel. Like sliding on a silk sheet, he thought, that's what driving a Rolls Royce is like. He had to drive it, like a druggie needs a fix, especially after those hire cars and Greyhound buses. He'd dropped the bag containing the woman's head and hands into a skip at the roadside; it would have been covered with other rubbish then incinerated or dumped in the Clyde.

Pity about his passport being stamped in Toronto—that he could have done without—but he'd got round it neatly by destroying his passport and reporting it as missing. The passport being stamped twice would have blown his alibi. No, his alibi couldn't be broken, couldn't, and the burden of proof rested with the police. No, he was safe, he was safe, he was safe. The problem was that it was now that the sweating began and the next few days would be crucial. If the police didn't interview him in the next...next week, then they never would. Hey, this was Glasgow, more murders here than strife-torn Belfast. Once the trail went cold, another murder would divert the attention of the police... and they'd still never link him with the woman, now he had her tapes. Left that a bit late in the day, bit of an afterthought, but he'd taken them and they had gone the same way as the head and hands, dropped in a skip and removed by the City Cleansing Authority. Thank you kindly.

All he had to do now was keep calm and stay cool. All he had to do now was play for time, let the trail start to chill, keep remembering that he didn't have to prove a thing and the cops had to prove everything. They might not even link the murder of McArthur to the murder of Animal the ned. Wouldn't that be convenient? Wouldn't it just?

The door of the men's room swept open as he grabbed a paper towel to wipe his hands and face.

'Toby,' said the man entering the room.

'Nigel,' said the first, screwing up the towel and tossing it into the waste bucket. He left the washroom and returned to his desk. His phone was warbling. He snatched it up. 'Marjerison,' he said.

MONTGOMERIE GLANCED at the clock on the wall above the door in the Detective Constables' room: nearly four. He knew from experience that it was at about this time that the welfare types start to drift home, about the time of day when they write 'visits—not back' on the blackboard, or in the movements book, and go home. Some 'visits'.

He reached forward and picked up his phone. Consulting the growing file on the murder of Pam McArthur he looked up the office number of McArthur's line manager. He dialled the number. His call was answered by a woman who surprised him by the unusual amount of aggression in her voice, especially for an employee of the Social Works Department. The sort of woman, he thought, who believes that she is unheard unless she shouts. Even on the telephone.

'He's in a conference,' she yelled.

'I'd like to speak to him,' said Montgomerie calmly, finding that he had to resist sliding into the violent manner of the receptionist.

'He's in a conference,' she said again as though that explained everything.

'This is a police matter.' Montgomerie allowed a firm edge to creep into his voice. 'It's in connection with a murder inquiry and I insist on speaking to Mr Deakins, and I insist on speaking to him now, conference or no conference.'

'Oh . . .' The line clicked and fell silent. A full minute passed and a man's voice, softer and gentler than that of the receptionist, said, 'Hello. Deakins speaking.'

'Mr Deakins, police here, sorry to disturb you in a conference . . .'

'No matter.' Montgomerie had a sense of a man settling into a chair. 'I'm grateful to you, in fact. It couldn't have been received at a better time because I was taking some flak about a decision I had made—this has given me time to think. When I go in for round two I'll be prepared for them. How can I help you?'

'Liz Hext.'

'Who?'

'Oh . . . it's not a name you know?'

'Sorry.'

'I was hoping you could help me trace her.'

'Liz Hext . . . I wouldn't know where to start.'

'She compiled a report about the quality or lack of quality of workmanship that went into two high-rise blocks of flats in Easterhouse.'

'McIntyre Heights. I know them. I can see them from my office window. They're falling apart.'

'So it appears by reading Ms Hext's report. She gave her designation as that of Research Coordinator.'

'Ah. I don't know her but I do know where she's most likely to be based.' Montgomerie heard a notebook being turned page by page. 'Yes, if you'll try this number...'

Montgomerie tried the number given by Deakins. It rang out. He let it ring and was about to hang up when it was answered. 'Hello,' said an uninterested voice.

'Police,' said Montgomerie, rapidly growing unimpressed by the telephone manner of Regional Council employees.

Silence.

'I'm trying to contact a Liz Hext. I was advised she may work at this number.'

'She does.'

'Then,' he said with restraint, 'may I please speak to her?'

'Speaking.'

Montgomerie felt like banging the handset on the desk top. Hard. 'I'd like to come and speak to you. Nothing to be worried about. You're employed in the city centre, going by your phone number?'

'In Charing Cross,' said the voice.

'Well, how convenient. I'll be there in ten minutes. What's the address?'

'I've got to go out.'

'I'll be there in ten minutes. Where exactly is your place of work?'

'But...'

'This is a murder inquiry.'

'IT'S A SCAM that's as old as the hills,' said Liz Hext in a flat voice. 'In fact the Tay Bridge disaster in 1869 was down to the same script.' She was, Montgomerie found, a small woman, difficult to age, but perhaps in her late twenties. Short hair, centre parted, spectacles, poor dress sense: ill-matching colours, bright skirt, dark top.

Her office was spartan, with not a single attempt to soften it that Montgomerie could detect; this was quite unusual in his experience, especially for a woman.

It was Montgomerie's immediate impression that the title 'Research Coordinator' did not imply the same dynamic get-up-and-go live-wire quality that it might in a university. He thought that perhaps he ought to have known better, this was after all local authority territory, the last refuge of endangered species of cobweb and deadwood. His immediate impression, and his final and lasting impression, was that Liz Hext, Research Coordinator, was a very dull woman indeed.

'So what's the story about McIntyre Heights?'

'Well, the residents were always complaining about water seeping in, lifts going up and down by themselves as if operated by ghosts—the water caused short circuits and that's why the lifts did that. Folk couldn't get warm, ran up huge fuel bills and still sat about in overcoats, couldn't get hot water for a bath. So we catalogued all the complaints and tried to put pressure on the Housing Department to get things put right.'

'Fair enough.'

'Well, I have a friend who has a friend, and at a party once she met this guy who'd actually been a civil engineer on the project. He was eighteen or nineteen then, a trainee civil engineer, doing it the hard way, on-the-job training and night school courses rather than a prestigious university course.'

Montgomerie nodded. Behind Liz Hext was the graceful red sandstone sweep of Charing Cross Mansions.

'To let you understand, in the old days, all the local authority building was supervised by the Direct Works Department and for them it was a huge job to replace rotten window frames in a single four-storey tenement block. So to ask them to supervise the building of massive schemes and high-rise tower blocks after the slum clearance programme was just not on, they were way out of their depth.'

'Oh...' Montgomerie could see what was coming, but he let Liz Hext continue in her own flat monotone.

'So the City engaged the services of a number of consultant civil engineers to supervise the building of the new Glasgow. When the consultant civil engineers, who were responsible for the supervision of a particular scheme reported that, for example, Phase D had been satisfactorily completed, then x million pounds would be released to the building contractors to allow them to build Phase E. See, Tim—'

'Tim?'

'This guy at the party, the trainee civil engineer?'

'Yes?'

'Except he's now a librarian.'

'Yes, yes.'

'He told my girlfriend that he remembered Mac-Intyre Heights being built and it was his job to check that the steel reinforcing mesh went in place as they were laying the concrete floors, so many sheets for each floor right up to the twenty-fourth floor. The specifications were exact, and also exact about the size of the metal sheets, grade of metal, everything. And Tim says he was just too naive to realize what was being said to him when the steel-fixing foreman came up to him and said, 'Away into town, young sir, and let the boys show you a good time, I'll make sure the steel goes down.'

'But Tim said "no" because he wanted to do a thorough job and he wanted to write the project up for his work study thesis. Anyway he was pulled off the job

when the block he was on was only three floors high and
sent to supervise the laying of pathways in a cemetery.'

'A comedown in more ways than one.'

Liz Hext's thin mouth cracked into a brief flicker of
a smile. Montgomerie had the impression that it was not
a practised gesture. 'I hadn't thought of it like that.'
Then she continued, 'So that's what happened. The
designs were good, the specifications clear. The city
paid for top quality buildings and got jerry-built rubbish. The contractors and the consultant civil engineers
were in cahoots with each other. They shaved millions
of pounds and shared it between them. The navvies
knew what was going on but they were silenced with
cash.'

'Sounds like a police matter. Why didn't you report
it?'

'We had no hard facts, and it didn't involve every
contractor and every firm of consultant civil engineers.'

'That's still really up to the police to find hard facts.
If you even suspected that something of that sort had
gone on you should have reported it rather than carry
out your own investigation. I mean, this is beginning to
sound as though it's going to make every financial
scandal in recent years look like two little boys who stole
a packet of sweets from Woolworth's.'

'It's even bigger.'

Montgomerie raised his eyebrows.

'After Glasgow had been thrown skywards, the cir-
cus left town. The same outfits followed each other
around the country. Went on to rebuild Aberdeen,
Edinburgh, the English cities like Newcastle, stopped
off in places like Dundee, and Falkirk to give them the
odd high-rise so they wouldn't feel left out. But like I

said, it didn't involve everybody, so it appears, because there are some schemes and some tower blocks that just don't throw up problems. They're clearly the ones that were built to specification. Then we were told that it wasn't our remit to investigate the cause of the problems, it was our remit to investigate the extent so that the tenants' association could put pressure on the Housing Department to repair the flats.'

'I see.'

'It was a bit unfair because the Housing Department can only work with what it's given in terms of housing stock. To ask the Housing Department to put things right is like trying to repair a fractured limb with a sticking plaster.'

'So how did Pam McArthur get involved?'

'Oh, her.'

'Her.'

'She heard about it, wanted to expose it all. Came round here to this room breathing fire and demanding all we had, so I gave her an early report I'd written and she went away happy. I heard she'd been found. I have a friend who works in Easterhouse. The rumour has spread. They say murder.'

'The rumour's right, about her being found, that is. At least her body has been found. I won't be drawn on whether it's murder or not.'

'I see. Well I heard she began to chew away, like a dog with a bone, and actually interviewed people who were involved. Now *she* was doing your job if anyone was. One old guy she pestered until he gave her an interview, and she came away stunned by what he had told her. A full account of the scam. But he really only told her what she already knew. She went back after him. She'd tasted blood, I think.'

'I think I'd like to speak to this elderly gentleman.'

'He's a man called Marjerison,' said Liz Hext. 'Lives at Helensburgh. I don't know the address itself.'

'Now that's a name I've heard before.' Montgomerie rose from his seat.

EIGHT

Thursday, 17.40-Friday, 09.34 hours

DONOGHUE DROVE westwards out of Glasgow along the
road which follows the northern bank of the Clyde, out
towards well-set Helensburg. Montgomerie sat in the
front seat. They didn't speak during the journey—there
existed a professional and a personal tension between
the two men. It was not born out of an unresolved conflict, or even of mutual dislike: it was simply that the
two men felt uneasy and uncomfortable in each other's
presence. It was an unease and a discomfort which
would disappear if a third person joined the company,
but if Montgomerie and Donoghue were alone with
each other, then a certain tension was present.

Montgomerie tried to relax but he found that he
couldn't. He involuntarily moved into a stiff and rigid
posture, and found that all he could do was to keep his
eyes fixed on the road which he felt was far too narrow
to accommodate the amount of traffic it was obliged to
accommodate. The rain fell vertically. The windscreen
wipers swept backwards and forwards; the lights of the
oncoming vehicles dazzled and hurt the eyes.

Donoghue drove his Rover with smooth effortless
movements. In himself he was more relaxed than
Montgomerie. He had seniority, he was at the wheel, it
was his case. He was in control, but he would have preferred the company of another officer other than
Montgomerie: Richard King, for instance.

'What's the address again?' Donoghue broke the silence as they entered Helensburgh.

Montgomerie shuffled in his seat as he reached into the storm pockets of his multi-coloured waterproof jacket. 'Lomond Road,' he said. 'Tabara, Lomond Road.' Here houses are named, not numbered.

Donoghue slowed the car and inched past imposing gateways where the house names were picked out in paint on the stone gateposts, or worked into the wrought-iron gates. Eventually Montgomerie said, 'Tabara.'

Donoghue turned the car between two gateposts and drove up a gravel drive which, according to the spill of his headlights, was bordered by lawns which gave way to neatly trimmed hedges and bushes. A Dalmatian barked a welcome in front of a stone-built house, taller than it was broad, deeper than it was tall. Stone stairs, pillars either side of the front door, square sash windows. A double garage stood off to the left, part of a parcel of outbuildings. Donoghue turned the car round so that it pointed towards the gateposts; it was a habit he had picked up when still on the streets, one of the hints passed on from cop to cop: always leave your car parked in such a way that you can make a quick getaway in the event of an emergency. Never leave anything in the back of your car that can be used as a weapon against you, is another such rule that doesn't appear in the training manuals.

Donoghue and Montgomerie left the car and walked up towards the front door of the house, accompanied by the barking, tail-wagging Dalmatian. The door opened before they reached it. A woman stood on the threshold, illuminated by the light from within. She was tall, grey haired, poised, a diamond brooch spoke of wealth but did so tastefully and softly. 'Can I help you, gentlemen?' She had a homely, warm Scots accent: Scots from the Glen, rather than Scots from Ferguslie Park. She added by means of explanation, 'I heard Ben, and the car on the gravel.'

'Police.' Donoghue showed his ID. Montgomerie offered his. The woman held up her hand to Montgomerie. 'No, I'm sure if one of you is genuine, then the other is. Detective Inspector, I'm impressed. How may I help you?'

'We'd like to speak to Mr Marjerison, please. If he's at home.'

'Oh, he's at home. He rarely goes anywhere these days. Is he expecting you? I presume not.'

'No,' said Donoghue. 'No, he isn't.'

'I do hope there's no trouble.'

'We think that he could help us with an inquiry. He may be able to throw some light on a matter.'

'I see,' she said slowly, thoughtfully, pausing and displaying great skill at controlling the interaction. 'Then you'd better come in.' She stepped backwards and sideways but retained a gentle hold on the door handle.

The cops stood in a large hallway: Corinthian columns, an old but valuable carpet on a parquet floor, oil paintings on the walls, a large vase on a heavy oak table. A grandfather clock.

'If I could ask you to wait here, please, gentlemen. I'll advise my husband that you are here and wish to speak to him.' The woman walked down the hallway and entered a room via a door that was built into the panelling and which was not immediately obvious.

Montgomerie and Donoghue stood in silence, avoiding eye contact. The clock's tick echoed.

Presently the woman returned with a calm, measured foot-fall. Her expression was stern, serious. 'My husband will see you,' she said.

A cynical response flooded into Montgomerie's mind; he remained silent as it seeped out again.

'He's in the drawing room. I must advise you, gentlemen, that my husband has a serious heart complaint. Any undue distress or excitement could be fatal, or so we have been advised by our doctor.'

'We'll bear that in mind, Mrs Marjerison,' said Donoghue.

The woman nodded and said, 'I'm sorry, I've forgotten your names.'

'Donoghue. Detective Inspector. This is DC Montgomerie.'

'Donoghue and Montgomerie.' The woman repeated the names. 'If you'd like to follow me, please,' and she echoed on hard heels back along the hallway. She opened the door of the drawing room with a flourish which to Donoghue's eye seemed a little over-theatrical and said, 'Messrs Donoghue and Montgomerie of the police to see you, dear.'

'Thank you.' The well-built man stood by a log fire. He was dressed in a comfortable-looking cardigan and equally comfortable-looking corduroy trousers. He had thin, wispy white hair and a heavily mottled complexion. The room was darkly furnished: a thick red-brown carpet, panelled walls, solid furniture, soft lighting. The log fire threw out dancing shadows and thick curtains partially hid floor-to-ceiling windows.

'Can I offer you a drink, gentlemen?'

'Thank you, sir, but we can't drink on duty.'

'Ah, wish I had that excuse. You don't mind...?' The man held up a crystal decanter of golden liquid.

'Not at all, sir.'

'The doctor says I should knock this habit on the head but I've snorted this stuff all my life. I'm eighty this year and I'm not going to stop now. I'd like to go on a bit longer, especially when I can still control my bodily functions and remember what day it is and all the rest of it, but at eighty I won't be drinking myself into an early grave, and if I drink myself to death before I become a vegetable, then at my age it's still a won game. Eskimos have the right idea.'

'Eskimos?'

'Fellows in igloos. As soon as they feel they're a burden on their family, they run off into the snow, go for miles, and I mean miles, before they drop, taking themselves as far as possible as a matter of pride. I was up in the Arctic once, far north of Canada at an Eskimo settlement. There it was all Portakabins, rather than igloos, small supermarkets full of white sliced bread and four-wheel-drive pick-ups, but...' Marjerison paused as he jetted soda into his whisky. '...but while I was there an elderly couple decided that it was their time, decided that they had become a burden and so they ran off hand in hand into the night. Never seen again. Lived as partners since they were little more than children and died together in their declining years. That's the way of it among the Eskimos. It's why the Eskimo doesn't have burial grounds. The Eskimo will hang around while he or she believes he's making a contribution but as soon as they believe they're a burden they do the noble thing. And we in the developed world fill ourselves full of medication in order to cling on to a few more months of space-wasting existence. So how can I help you?'

'We're investigating a murder, Mr Marjerison.'

'Oh!' The man seemed genuinely surprised.

'It's the murder of a woman you may have spoken to sometime last summer. A woman by the name of McArthur.'

Marjerison looked stunned. His eyes narrowed, his right hand went up to the left side of his chest. He slid sideways into a chair. His whisky spilled. He looked at flames licking a log in the grate; he seemed mesmerized, as if absorbing some dreadful realization.

'Are you all right, Mr Marjerison?' Donoghue stepped forward.

Marjerison held up a hand to stay Donoghue. He nodded his head. 'Take a seat, gentlemen, please. I think we have some talking to do.'

The cops sat slowly, silently. Marjerison relaxed back in his chair and put his hand to his head.

'What can I tell you, gentlemen?' Marjerison sank a deep draught of whisky.

'You did speak to Miss McArthur?'

Marjerison nodded. 'Several times. You know I don't think I have ever met a more unpleasant woman. How can I forget her, though I would very much like to. I recall a tall gangly female, with a small trunk, or torso, and long thin arms and legs, wearing black leggings and a black T-shirt, red hair done up in a tight bun. Her appearance and her toxic personality always left me feeling as though I had played host to a tarantula. I always felt poisoned too, still do, as though she had managed to inject some venom into me somehow. I still have that feeling, after more than half a year. She came here about four or five times.'

'I'm surprised you gave her house room, sir.'

'To be perfectly honest, gentlemen, I did it for selfish reasons, at least in the beginning. Eventually I was relieved that she stopped calling. I'm not a Catholic, but I know now the value of confession. I felt a lot better for telling her what I know. She lapped it up, scribbling notes with a gleam in her eyes. After a while I was just repeating what I had already told her but she seemed to refuse to believe there wasn't more information. That's why I was pleased she had stopped coming. We were good for each other in the first instance: she like a shark in feeding frenzy, me feeling a weight sliding from my shoulders.'

A pause which became a silence prompted Donoghue to move the interview along. 'What did she want to talk to you about, Mr Marjerison?'

'The massive defrauding of the City of Glasgow thirty years ago or thereabouts. I don't know how long ago, maybe a little more than thirty years, thirty-five maybe.' It was a statement made with disarming honesty.

'Mr Marjerison.' Donoghue spoke firmly. 'I feel that I have to caution you . . .'

Again Marjerison held up his hand. 'No need for a caution. Far be it from me to tell you your job, but you'll probably take a statement from me, if not to-night then at some point in the near future; you may even charge me, but I doubt if the Fiscal will proceed with it even though we're talking millions of pounds in today's money. I really do doubt that you'll be able to proceed and that's what I advised Miss McArthur. I told her she could have all the information I could give her, verbally, but she wouldn't be able to do a blessed thing with it and when I said that the gleam in her eye turned to a flash of rage. A statement from me is only half the battle; she just wasn't in a position to do anything with it. When I pointed that out to her she stormed off in a temper and I confess I've never heard language like that from a woman. But she wouldn't take "no" for an answer, came back a few days later, wanting more details, more information. I gave what I could but it was largely repetitive.'

'So what did happen?'

Marjerison poured another shot of whisky. 'Well, she'd done her homework; she'd followed a trail with dogged determination which led her to my front door and made Ben growl. He took an instant dislike to her.'

'But it was concerning McIntyre Heights?'

'So you know?'

Donoghue nodded. 'They were jerry-built.'

'Yes, they and other similar projects. Though McIntyre Heights were the only ones in Glasgow that were not built to specification that I know of. There were six of us involved: myself, my partner in our consultancy, and four senior executives from the civil engineering company. The plot was hatched in this very room, in front of this very fire, while we drank whisky from this very decanter. The plan itself is as old as the hills, and has been practised since man has been building buildings. Simply, you don't build to specification and nobody is the wiser until the building collapses as it did in Dundee in 1879.'

'The Tay Bridge disaster?'

'That's it. A similar plan. Except I don't think we have caused a loss of life—yet. You see, the City of Glasgow paid for architectural drawings which called for specific materials in specific quotas and of specific quality, but the City hadn't the expertise amongst its public service officers to supervise the buildings on the scale that was called for after slum clearance. So the

City engaged the services of a number of firms of consultant civil engineers.'

'Being yourself.'

'One of many. Just as the civil engineering contractors were one of many.' Marjerison drained his glass. 'So, as I said, six of us met in this room, having spent that day looking at the drawings. The contractors said that they could build under specification and still create a building which would look well, and it would last for forty or fifty years before problems began to be noted. Our part of the scam, the consultant civil engineers' part, was to monitor the building and dutifully report that it was being built and finally completed to specification. The City then paid for a building which was in fact worth about seventy-five per cent of the purchase price, perhaps more than seventy-five per cent. Basically if the tower blocks cost ten pounds each if built to specification, the contractors shaved costs here and there—not putting reinforced steel mesh in the concrete which formed the floors of the tower block was a common practice; so was diluted cement mix or aggregate in the cement instead of pure cement; cheap thin wiring, that sort of thing—and built the tower blocks for eight pounds each. So a saving of two pounds was creamed off. The contractors took eighty pence, we, the consultant civil engineers, took eighty pence, and the forty pence left was distributed among the workforce as hard cash over and above their wage packets. The workforce knew what was going on and their silence had a price. But if for two pounds, you read two million pounds in today's money, then you get an idea of the scale of the fraud.'

'You realize what you're saying, sir?'

A log cracked. Flames flared and then died.

'Aye.' Marjerison nodded and replenished his glass. 'And before a witness too.' He held up the decanter. 'You're sure . . . ?'

'Sure.'

Marjerison sank back in his chair. 'Aye, I'm sure and once again I find myself enjoying a confession—more so since I'm talking to officers of the law, whereas Ms McArthur wanted the information for her own use. She wanted to profit from my criminality. But it was, and still is, only half a confession, or a safe confession because I won't be prosecuted.'

'You can't be too certain. A fraud of that magnitude, even thirty years ago . . .'

'More than that. Remember our actions have cost the City of Glasgow dearly, as it pays for repairs that wouldn't have been necessary if we hadn't defrauded it into paying through the nose for jerry-built tower blocks. That's money that comes out of your pocket. It's why your local taxes are so high.'

'The practice wasn't confined to Glasgow, I understand?'

'No, we hit the road, Jack. We did much the same thing in other Scottish cities and not a few north of England contracts came our way, and we skimmed some real money. I mean some real money. You see we were men in our fifties then; we thought if we could build buildings that would last forty years instead of the design life of one hundred or so, we'd all be well out of it before cracks began to show. It seemed perfect, foolproof. There were six Rolls Royces in my driveway on the evening that the plot was hatched. Our problem was that we were too greedy. The further under specification we built, the more money we creamed off. We should have built closer to specification and settled for less.'

'Or you shouldn't have done it at all.' Montgomerie spoke suddenly, angrily. Donoghue shot a glance at him for speaking out of turn, but he had to concede that Montgomerie had hit the nail on the head.

'You don't know how right you are, young man.' Marjerison nodded at him. 'But we decided to build so far under specification that the problems started to show within fifteen years. Not too bad at first but now they can't be ignored, and are getting worse all the time. And there is another reason why we should not have built under specification and that is the concept of global warming.'

'What has—?' Donoghue suddenly recalled a conversation he had had with his son about the possibility of flying kites in hurricanes.

'What it has to do with it—' Marjerison cut Donoghue's question short '—is as follows.' He sipped his whisky and continued. 'Even thirty-five years ago there were financial constraints and the specifications that the architects drew up were the least expensive; the specifications that we should have built to were already the absolute minimum needed for safety. One of the things that the tower blocks were supposed to do was withstand the strongest anticipated wind speeds and so the climatic records were consulted. At the time they went back two hundred years and the buildings were duly designed to withstand the strongest winds ever recorded in the west of Scotland. One of the consequences of global warming is that the average wind speed is increasing. In the not-too-distant future it is highly likely that Scotland will experience winds far stronger than it has experienced before. That means that even if McIntyre Heights had been built to specification it would not now be strong enough to withstand the winds it may have to withstand.'

'Oh . . .' Montgomerie's jaw sagged. He put his hand to his forehead.

'That's right, young man,' said Marjerison. 'As it is McIntyre Heights are badly substandard, unsafe now even in a subgale. It's only a matter of time before a disaster occurs.'

A silence as Donoghue and Montgomerie absorbed the implication of what Marjerison had said. Then Donoghue asked: 'How widespread was this practice?'

'That I don't know. But it seemed to bring with it its own form of natural justice. There is a strong sense that no one got away with it, no one got away with anything. The firms of contractors who built to specification and the firms of consultant civil engineers who didn't compromise their professional integrity are still going strong, valuing their reputation. The contractors who built McIntyre Heights went to the wall some years ago and our consultancy failed, the work just stopped coming in. I was going to hand my share to my son but . . . anyway, I was forced out of the business, I took early retirement; my partner carried on alone but he too went under. All the money I made from the fraud I lost in a series of dreadful business ventures and stupid, ill-advised investments. This house is bought and paid for by more honest endeavours and money from my wife's family, left to her. We have little in the bank and we keep going by trickling a few antiques or oil paintings onto the market and raising loans using the house as security. The creditors will have the house when we die and my son will inherit some loose change and my taste in cars. We both love Rolls Royces. In fact his Rolls

Royce is worth more than his house. You know, of all the men who met in my house that night thirty odd years ago—'

'The night when all the Rolls Royces were in the drive?'

'That's the night. I am the only one left alive. All the others, the other five, not only died comparatively young in their fifties or sixties, but all seemed to die as a result of the money they had misappropriated. One bought a light aircraft and crashed while landing in fog, another took a dream holiday to the Seychelles where he drowned in the surf. My erstwhile partner died of a heart attack shortly after he went under. Never knew what he did with his money—didn't leave his wife much, that's for sure. One chap got divorced and his wife fleeced him, and he didn't resist because she knew what had happened and threatened to blow the whistle on him. The other chap gambled and lost and drank himself to his grave. That left me, not a rich man despite these trappings and not able to look back on a working life with any sense of pride or satisfaction.'

Marjerison paused, considered his whisky and swallowed a generous measure.

'My father was a churchman. A minister in the Church of Scotland. A good man, gave a lot to me, and because of his influence I knew that not only should I not go along with the fraud but that I'd regret it. I should have listened to myself. I feel that by doing what I did I betrayed my father's trust and faith in me. That's eating me away from the inside. And when I think of those families living in cold, damp high-rises which they can't heat, having to climb the stairs because the lifts keep failing, existing in buildings which may well collapse in the first serious blow…all brought about by six men in comfortable middle years, each already wealthy enough to own and run the finest car in the world, and each of whom wanted even more. So I sit here with my whisky and look back with regret, and live with a sense of having wasted it all. You know many people in the building industry go out of their way, literally, to visit a building they had a hand in building, whether as a bricklayer or as a senior site engineer, or architect. But I avoid the east end of Glasgow in case I catch sight of McIntyre Heights and if I do see them I get a pang of guilt followed by a sense of surprise that they're still standing.'

Another pause.

'And my son, Toby, you know we never seemed to get on. He never seemed to like me. Even from the earliest days there was conflict. He's a civil engineer too, works for Littlejohn, Houston, a reputable firm. He's done well to get there, but about a year ago, perhaps eighteen months, I told him what had happened, the story that I have just related to you gentlemen about the scam behind the building of the twin towers of McIntyre Heights. I told it to him to get it off my chest. I felt he ought to know what his father is, or was, really like, and you know you would be forgiven for thinking I was telling him of a personal triumph or an act of heroism. His reaction was almost worshipful. It took a confession of being party to a serious fraud and to compromising the living conditions and safety of my fellow citizens before I was able to win the respect of my son. And me the son of a minister who grew up in a manse. Toby was a late baby for me and my wife. I was forty-three when he was born. He was always special despite the conflict... but to respect me for the first time in his life because of what I told him about the fraud... I mean, what manner of man have I sired?' Marjerison lapsed into a long silence, and seemed to enter a world of his own as if reliving some past incident. The fire cracked. Outside rain lashed the windows, wind moaned through the trees. 'And now it seems that my son is caught up in it all somehow. When was the McArthur woman murdered?'

'Last summer.' Donoghue spoke softly. 'Though we found the body only yesterday morning.'

'You're certain she was murdered?'

'Certain.'

'And Toby is implicated?'

'We can't say for certain but we . . . well, we'd like to talk to him, in due course.'

'If he is, I have brought that on him and on myself. Nobody profited from the fraud, misfortune befell us all. I have sat here for many years thinking that because I had been coerced into being party to it, rather than a prime mover as it were, and because I lost all that dirty money, then less misfortune had befallen me. It's the way an old man's mind works, trying to find reasons for everything. Now I find that I have not yet begun to pay my penalty if Toby has acted inappropriately trying to protect me from that McArthur woman.'

'Do you think he may have done that?'

Marjerison shook his head. 'I really don't know. I feel stunned. He and his wife and child visited us only this afternoon. We walked together in the garden during a break in the rain. He said that I wouldn't be hearing from McArthur again. It was said in response to something I'd said, but at the time I felt there was something weighted about it, as though he knew something that I didn't know. I hope I haven't compromised him by telling you that?'

Donoghue shook his head. 'No. In itself it means nothing.'

Marjerison grunted as if relieved. 'I had told him months ago that we should leave her to find in her own time that she can't do anything with my statement and let her find another issue to fight. She couldn't have proved anything for the same reason that I don't fear prosecution and never did. You see my statement is useless without corroboration. Nothing of the fraud was documented and the money was laundered. The only way you can obtain corroboration is to dismantle the towers of McIntyre Heights. I don't mean demolish them, I mean dismantle them, bit by bit, and as you do, check the materials against specifications. Quite impossible. And you'd have to make upwards of four thousand people homeless in the process and that in a city where homeless families are being put up in hotels because there aren't enough houses in the first place. And even if you did get that sort of proof, would it be in the best interests of the citizens to know that their high-rises are probably unsafe? That would be the real cost of a much publicized trial. The people would evacuate their homes en masse. That's the sort of argument that was voiced in this room that evening all those years ago and it has to be said it was a solid argument. In terms of the law we got away with it. In terms of our private lives and personal circumstances we got away with nothing.'

On the journey back to Glasgow Donoghue and Montgomerie sat in silence. Then Montgomerie said, 'It was an afterthought. I've just realized it was an afterthought.'

'What was?'

'On Marjerison's part, going to McArthur's to remove the computer discs. The time lapse between the murder and him being seen by Mrs Sloan leaving McArthur's flat is a period measure in weeks. He must have had an afterthought that she may have recorded something which could tie his father into the scam.'

'Probably,' said Donoghue, 'though he did take her keys from her at the time of the murder. He did that for a purpose.'

'Aye, I hadn't thought of that.'

'Afterthought or part of the original plan, it's an action that has made our job a bit more difficult but not impossible, because now we have a motive. It'll depend if we can break his alibi.'

'You think he'll have an alibi?'

'I'm certain of it.'

They didn't speak again until they reached Glasgow.

Friday, 09.30 hours

KING SAT AT his desk. Abernethy at his. Montgomerie at his. Sussock sagged against the wall. Donoghue stood by the door. Each nursed a mug of coffee. Smoke hung in the room, jackets were slung on chairs, ties were loosened.

'So—' Donoghue broke the silence '—that's it. We all had a part to play, we've all fed back. There was a huge scam in the city some thirty or thirty-five years ago, McArthur found out about it, Marjerison the elder told her what had gone down but she kept coming back. Marjerison the younger thought she was giving too much grief to his father, so last summer he hired two neds and lured her to an empty house with the promise of more information and there he filled her in. Her body, or what remains of it, wasn't discovered until forty-eight hours ago. We pulled one of the neds, his father tipped the wink to the other who was about to squeal, so Marjerison chopped him with a cleaver. Which brings us here, and why I've called you together. Thanks for coming in in your free time, Montgomerie.'

Montgomerie nodded.

'I'm not sure how to proceed,' Donoghue continued. 'I'm open to suggestions. My guess is he'll have an alibi.'

'We must assume that he knows we're getting close,' said Abernethy. 'He'll be wary.'

'He'll also be nervous,' said Montgomerie, 'and we must assume that by now there will have been contact between father and son. By now he'll know that we know of the scam; that means he'll know we know of his motivation to murder McArthur.'

'To protect his father when in fact he didn't need protection.' Donoghue pulled on his pipe. 'Marjerison the elder was right. McArthur couldn't harm him with his confession alone, and neither, I doubt, can we. I don't like it any more than you do but he'll escape prosecution for the reasons he gave to Montgomerie and myself yesterday evening. So Marjerison the younger is going to be ready for us. We're going to speak to him and we're going to speak to him today. The question is do we do the soft-shoe shuffle or do we go in with all guns blazing?'

'I can see advantages and disadvantages in both.' King leaned forward. 'But as I see it, if we arrest him we can hold him without charging him for twelve hours. Now he's unlikely to cough so we won't get the evidence we need in the interview room, but arresting him would keep him isolated for twelve hours. He won't be able to fine-tune his alibi, for example; it will be as strong as he left it before we lifted him.'

'We could also have a look at his house,' said Montgomerie. 'I mean, even if we have to release him without charge on this occasion—'

The phone on King's desk rang. He snatched it up. 'Look, we're in a conference . . .' He paled and cupped his hand over the receiver. He glanced at Donoghue. 'Gentleman at the uniform bar, sir,' he said. 'Gentleman by the name of Marjerison demanding to know why we're harassing his father?'

NINE

'NO.' THE MAN SMILED and shook his head gently. 'No, I'm a Scot all right, but it's true I'm often mistaken for an Englishman. After Fettes I went to Heriot Watt, training in Glasgow, did a few overseas jobs and then took up my present post three years ago.'

'It is of no consequence.' Donoghue leaned back in his chair and considered the pleasing features of Toby Marjerison: smoothly shaven, well built and in good shape; expensively dressed; thick mane of black hair, trimmed neatly; the sort of man who'd go to a ladies' hairdresser or to a trendy west end or city centre unisex salon, or so Donoghue thought. And the man's manner was slippery, permanently smiling a salesman's smile, leaning confidently forwards with his forearms on the desk, forcing Donoghue and King to lean backwards until both officers realized, as if at the same instant, what effect the man's manner was having on them, and they leaned forwards, together, challenging him, a clear assertion of their authority. Marjerison held his posture and his face froze into a smile.

He reminded Donoghue of a time-share promotion he and his wife had been sufficiently unwise to attend, and especially of that instant when the salesman's charm and glinting, gleamy-eyed smile and his overflowing warmth had, upon the Donoghues saying they would 'think about it', rapidly inverted to snarling hostility. It had prompted Mrs Donoghue to observe: 'Well, you've changed your attitude;' bringing the response: 'I'm only nice to you if you buy something from me.' That had actually happened though Donoghue had stopped relating the tale when he realized few people were believing him. And Toby Marjerison reminded him strongly of that time-share salesman: pleasant when he was in control and getting his own way. He wondered what it would take to make Toby Marjerison snarl and spit. Not much he thought, not much at all. 'It's of no consequence what nationality you are.'

'Of course it's not, and neither are we here to discuss my accent. I really have to protest about your intimidation of my father yesterday evening. He's an old man, he has a bad heart. He wouldn't have told me but Mother phoned me. I've spoken with my solicitor. He advised me to take the matter up directly but to come back to him if I didn't get satisfaction.' He leaned back smiling, giving the impression that he was well satisfied with his delivery and also the impression that he had much in reserve. He glanced at the police mutual calendar on the wall of the interview room.

'I see.' Donoghue hid his amusement at Marjerison's sudden transformation into an angered consumer complaining to a shop manager about being sold deficient goods—'if I don't get satisfaction'—indeed. 'Did Mrs Marjerison tell you why we called on your father last night?'

Marjerison shook his head. 'No, my mother couldn't tell me, but she did say that he was agitated and upset when you had left and had clearly drunk too much whisky. He wouldn't tell her, and I've been unable to speak to him. He's been in his study all morning and refuses to come to the phone. He's clearly deeply troubled by something.'

Beside him, Donoghue felt King stiffen as the implication of what Marjerison had said registered. If he was telling the truth he did not know of the content of the discussion between his father and Donoghue and Montgomerie. He did not know of the extent of the knowledge held by the police. But only if he was telling the truth. Donoghue didn't know whether Marjerison was a fly blundering into a fly trap, or whether Marjerison was a shrewd and sharp-witted predator who would play a game but never take the bait. It was a time to look for giveaway signs, a flash in the eye, a quiver of a lip, because here, thought Donoghue, sit two adversaries, and one was badly underestimating the other.

He looked steadfastly at Marjerison.

Marjerison looked steadfastly at him.

Donoghue's eyes were serious.

Marjerison's eyes were dilated, smiling, warm, as if approving of Donoghue.

Donoghue had the impression of being sucked into a wholly unhealthy collusion. He felt the rug of professional detachment being eased from under him. He was glad of King's presence.

'Well,' he said, 'let me say first of all that the police did not harass your father—he agreed to see us. We had a calm conversation during which he offered myself and my colleague whisky, which we were obliged to decline, and during which he did far the greater part of the talking. Mrs Marjerison advised us of your father's heart condition and we were constantly sensitive to it.'

'I see.'

'Tell, me, Mr Marjerison.' Donoghue sat forward; he couldn't avoid the issue any longer. 'Since you are here, can I ask you if the name McArthur means anything to you?'

Toby Marjerison pursed his lips and shook his head slowly. And that gesture Donoghue knew now set the scene and pointed the way ahead. It was to be denial from the outset. Toby Marjerison's response also, he thought, and King, sitting silently, also thought, cast doubt on his claim that he had not spoken to his father following the police visit to Marjerison the elder. From this point both cops knew that they must assume Marjerison to be fully informed as to the extent of their knowledge. Of course this man knew someone called McArthur—his father had told him of her and Wayne Petty had lured someone called McArthur to her death at the hands of this man. But the fact that it was to be denial from the outset telegraphed to Donoghue and King that they had their man. Had he said, 'Oh yes, I know Pam McArthur, she's more known to my father...' or similar, then the cops would have an uphill struggle, but as it was they then knew they were looking at a multiple killer.

Donoghue sighed. He'd been here before and all he could ponder was the awesome gulf between guilt and proof of guilt.

'Can't say it does, especially,' continued Marjerison without a flicker of conscience—a man, Donoghue and King saw, who could hold eye contact while lying through his teeth. Donoghue had the sensation of being at the foot of a long, hard climb. 'No, I know a chap at a school of that name, chap I met in Australia...but not a name that holds significance for me.'

'I see. Bayliss?'

'Sorry?'

'Bayliss. Dalton Bayliss, sometimes known as Animal the Electric Gypsy. Is that a name that means anything to you?'

'No,' said calmly, displaying no emotion. But Marjerison was a worried man. He was regretting blustering into the police station, regretting his decision that attack should be his best form of defence. He was regretting it because he had to stick with it; he was regretting it because he couldn't now suddenly remember something and leave. But he was mainly regretting it because this police officer, the older of the two, the one who did the talking, smartly dressed like a banker or a civil servant, the one who called himself Donoghue, was not like any police officer he'd met before. He wasn't like the constable who said 'Yes sir, second on the right, then first left and you can't miss it. Good day, sir', or even the constable who didn't smile and said 'Can't park here, sir. Drive off now—please', not like that at all. This man Donoghue was calm, controlled, well spoken, well mannered, but he had the eyes...the eyes... My God, yes, he had the eyes of a wolf.

'Where were you the night before last, say about 3.00 a.m.?'

'In my bed,' said Marjerison.

'In your bed?'

'That's what I said. Can I ask what this is about?'

'It's about murder, Mr Marjerison. It's about two murders believed to be connected. About 3.00 a.m. yesterday morning, about twenty-one hours ago, perhaps more, one of the people I mentioned, Dalton Bayliss, was found in a crumpled heap, oozing crimson, and doing so in great quantities.'

'I see. I'm devastated to hear it, but I can't help you.' There was a slight hardening of the look in his eyes—not an overreaction; nicely done, in fact, Donoghue had to admit. A look which spoke of concern about where this might be leading, but not a look which indicated guilt or implication. Marjerison was impressing both police officers as being cold, ice cold, and very detached. But he said nothing, letting Donoghue do all the work.

'What sort of car do you drive?' Donoghue tried a sudden change of tack.

'Am I under some sort of suspicion? Am I, as I understand the expression to be, "in the frame" for something?'

'We have an open mind.'

'I'm so pleased to hear it.'

Outside traffic growled around Charing Cross Interchange. Occasionally a squeal of brakes and an angry horn pitched above the dull rumble. Behind, the deeper hum of the motorway traffic was clearly distinct.

'So your car?'

'A Rolls Royce,' said in a matter-of-fact way. 'I wouldn't drive anything less.'

'Colour?'

'Black and silver.'

'If I were to tell you that at about the time and place of the murder of Dalton Bayliss, a man was noticed driving away in a black and silver Rolls Royce, would you understand our interest in you? The witness to that also identified the driver of the car as being similar to a photofit description of the person wanted in connection with the murder of Pam McArthur. And I have to say that that photofit bears more than a passing resemblance to yourself.'

'Oh, really.'

'Yes. Really.' A hardness crept into Donoghue's voice.

'So I am "in the frame"?'

'If you like, Mr Marjerison. But it's a big frame, plenty of room for others. At this stage all we are doing is trying to eliminate rather than implicate.'

Marjerison smiled.

And that, in Donoghue's mind, damned him. The denial of knowing anyone called McArthur fixed in Donoghue's mind the certainty of Marjerison's guilt. But he had then offered Marjerison an escape route; he'd said something to ease the pressure and Marjerison had smiled the relieved smile of a guilty man who had been offered a reprieve. A man with nothing to hide, Donoghue reasoned with himself, would have nodded understandingly and would have continued with serious-minded cooperation.

'Your father—' Donoghue began to reapply the pressure '—had some degree of contact with a lady called Pam McArthur. Not contact of a positive or a warm nature, quite the opposite in fact. Ms McArthur became something of a thorn in your father's side, as indeed by all accounts she was a thorn in the side of all who knew her. Do you know what the story was there?'

'No.'

'Well, I'll tell you. At least I'll tell you what your father told us.' And Donoghue explained about the fraud surrounding the construction of McIntyre Heights in Easterhouse, where Pam McArthur was employed as a community worker; about the building company and the consultant civil engineers skimming off the money saved by deliberately building under specification.

'I find that difficult to believe of my father. He wouldn't have had anything to do with that.'

'I think you're right,' Donoghue said. 'It was and still is my impression that your father is a man of integrity.'

'Thank you,' said drily.

'But the fact remains that, his integrity notwithstanding, he was drawn into something about thirty years ago, perhaps more, which may have been the only occasion in his life when he compromised his ethical steadfastness, but it was a compromise of awesome enormity which now plagues and tortures him.'

'I still find it all difficult to believe.'

'Nevertheless it appears that Pam McArthur got onto a scent of what was happening and succeeded in interviewing your father, who quite fairly told her that his admission was in itself insufficient evidence to prove anything, but she wouldn't let go of it.'

'How interesting, but again I fail to see what it has to do with me.'

Donoghue took his pipe from his jacket pocket. 'Do you mind . . . ?'

'Not at all.'

Donoghue took his time lighting his pipe, playing the flame of his gold-plated lighter over the bowl, over his special mix of Dutch base with a twist of dark shag to give a deeper flavour and slower burning rate. He was beginning to feel more in control of the interview, finding sure footholds in all the shifting sand.

'I'm curious, Mr Marjerison.' Donoghue pocketed his lighter. 'I'm curious as to why you say you haven't heard of the fraud or of your father's involvement in it, when your father told myself and another police officer that he had told you fully of the fraud.'

'Well he didn't!' A snapped angry retort.

'And not only did he tell you of this, but it was only when he told you of this that for the first time in your life you exhibited some respect towards him. It appears to have been deeply wounding to your father that he, with his observation of the moral code, should have had to be in serious breach of that code, become a large-scale criminal, before he won his son's respect.'

Marjerison gripped the table, his knuckles whitening, his jaw set firm; he glared at Donoghue. 'I think this interview has gone far enough.'

'I think it has,' said Donoghue. 'Toby Marjerison, I arrest you for the murders of Pam McArthur on or about 6th June last year and Dalton Bayliss on Thursday 23rd January this year. You are not obliged to say anything but whatever you do say will be taken down and may be given in evidence. Mr King.'

Richard King stood and laid his hand on Toby Marjerison's shoulder.

'CONFESS THAT that took me by surprise, sir.' King walked by Donoghue's side down the cell corridor, back towards the charge bar; piles of clothes and footwear stood outside each cell door.

'Rather took me by surprise, Richard.' Donoghue grinned. 'It just seemed to be the right thing to say and the right time to say it. I think I felt we were pussyfooting around and that we needed to get some sort of structure and direction into this. So now we've got twelve hours to charge him or release him. I know that we can rearrest him later but to release him carries the danger that he'll cover his tracks and go to ground, maybe even clear the pitch completely. I wouldn't put it past him to have an escape route planned, false passport, different name, another identity to assume at the drop of the hat, and survival money salted away somewhere.'

'First step?'

'First step, Richard, is that you and I will visit Toby Marjerison's home. See what we'll find and take it from there. Do you know if Montgomerie has left the building? If he hasn't he can conduct the PACE interview with Marjerison. Abernethy can organize an ID parade.' Donoghue lifted the hinging counter at the side of the charge bar and passed into the area behind the uniform bar. Here four desks nosed together, on which stood typewriters; officers sat at the desks attending to members of the public who called with queries or complaints. When not speaking to the public they hunted and pecked at the typewriters, slowly completing incident reports. In an anteroom a computer console glowed dull green. Montgomerie stood at the uniform bar chatting to Phil Hamilton.

'Montgomerie,' Donoghue called.

Malcolm Montgomerie turned to Donoghue and his face paled.

'Don't wander too far, Montgomerie. In fact you could join us in the DCs' room upstairs—at your earliest convenience, of course. We've got until 22.00 to wrap this up. I dare say she'll wait.'

Montgomerie glanced at Phil Hamilton and raised his eyebrows in the universal gesture of exasperation, and Phil Hamilton shrugged his shoulders in the universal gesture which said 'love to help you . . .'

Montgomerie followed Donoghue and King, climbing the stairs to the CID corridor.

'WE SLEEP SEPARATELY.' The young woman spoke in a matter-of-fact manner. 'Things have not been right between us for some time. So I wouldn't know if my husband did or did not leave the house at 3.00 a.m. the night before last.'

To Donoghue's eyes she was a good-looking woman, finely featured, good posture, held her spine and legs rigid and straight. She wore a yellow shirt and blue jeans; her hair hung loosely down to her shoulders. A child gurgled in a playpen amid soft toys and stimulating 'Early Learning' items. At the far end of the room a gas fire hissed relentlessly. Beyond the rear window an immature and a small garden typical of 'new build' properties stood green and brown, dank and depressed, under a moody January sky. The interior of the home was not to Donoghue's taste, nor to King's: puffed black furniture, bleached pine bookshelves full of books with shiny covers clearly bought from a book club, a loud red carpet and a digital clock over the fireplace. Not a typical Bearsden household where, in his experience, all is solid and staid.

'My mother-in-law, she's suspected for a wee while now that things are not so good between me and Toby. She's become cold and distant. His father's a pleasant old man and I think he believes us to be happy, so I suppose Toby's parents don't talk to each other a great deal. He always seems to be preoccupied with something, does Toby one.'

'Toby one?'

'That's what they're called; all three are Toby Marjerison. My Toby, he's Toby two, his father is Toby one, and this—' she smiled at the child who at that moment sat in the corner of the playpen banging the head of a toy rabbit on the bars '—is Toby three.'

'I see, no confusion there.'

'Well, there would be if the family just talked about "Toby", but if we talk about Toby "one" or "two" or "three" we all know who we're talking about.'

'Fair enough.'

'It's about the only thing that is fair. See all this, it's doing my head in, so it is. It's pure torture, my marriage. My mother said I shouldn't have married so far out of my class, so she did, and she was right. I grew up in a scheme in Barrhead and it was hostility between me and Toby's mother from the start. He was their only one and they pure doted on him. Me, I'm one of four and the youngest at that. Always the last to get any attention, always the last to get my own way, but that's just the way it is for last-born children. But Toby, see the attention he got. He was spoiled rotten and he calls his mother "little Mummy", like I get half an hour's notice that "little Mummy's" coming to "dinner"—he means tea but he calls it "dinner". So she comes in all fur and ostrich feathers and sits and watches me, never lifts a finger to help. She sniffs at everything I do and when I put the meal down she pokes it with a fork and pushes it away from her. Toby one, he eats and pretends to enjoy it, but her . . . see this, I can't go on.'

'Not a pleasant situation. I'm very sorry.' Donoghue was genuinely sorry. He had pulled himself out of the Saracen G22 and he knew fine well the invisible barriers of class. Surmounting the barriers is only the beginning. Once over and accepted for yourself, there still lies ahead years and years of feeling awkward and gauche. Or so it had been for him when visiting his in-laws in their mansion in Morningside.

'Not a pleasant situation. That's putting it mildly. He's making it really difficult for me.'

'Oh?'

'Well aye, see his attitude, it's mental cruelty. He makes it impossible to stay and impossible to go. See if the mental cruelty was physical cruelty I'd be a bag of splintered bones but he's careful not to lay a hand on me. He wouldn't do that, that would work against him. He once told me to go if I wanted to go, but I had to leave Toby three. I can also have a divorce anytime I want so long as I agree to a "no maintenance" clause. I mean what sort of deal is that? I'm not leaving my wean and I need money to survive. I've paid a wee bit into this home, I've got a bit coming back. See me, when I was a wee girl playing in the street in the scheme in Barrhead . . . I mean who would have thought that I'd find myself in this mess?'

The gas fire hissed.

'See, he's as good as told me that if we get divorced and I get any half-decent settlement, he'll wait until the dust settles, then I'll get "snuffed out" maybe about two or three years later.'

'Snuffed out? Is that what he said?'

'Uh huh. Snuffed out. He said he'd leave it until it appears he's accepted the settlement and that he's paid regularly without complaint and then he'll make "it" look like an accident—you know, a front bumper job with a Land Rover one night. There was a fatal hit-and-run at Bearsden Cross a few months ago.'

'I remember,' said Donoghue, 'a young student walking home; he'd been at a party and missed the last bus.'

'Aye, well that put me in mind of what Toby two said he'd do to me.'

'You think he's capable of that?'

Rose Anne Marjerison nodded. 'We had a wee dog, a puppy. We couldn't house-train it, but Toby just didn't give it enough time; it had the makings of a smashing wee dog. One day it just wasn't in the house. Toby was unconcerned, said it had gone for a wander and that it would come back. I knew I wouldn't see it again and I've been proved right. It's been away over a year now. Toby got rid of it, I know he did. I just hope he took it to the Dog Rescue so they'd find it a good home but I think he would have killed it, battered it to death and left it out on the Campsies for the foxes. That's more Toby's style than is taking it to the Dog Rescue.'

'So you take his threat seriously?'

'I have to. I don't know what to do for the best. I'm just putting off a decision until things seem clearer. I sleep in the back room and he has the front. I pop a couple of pills to help me sleep once I've made sure

Toby three is fed and changed. Once I pop them I go out and I mean out. Toby two could bang about all he likes and I wouldn't hear him. So that's another reason why I wouldn't know if he left the house that night.'

'I see.' Donoghue mused and then asked, 'Could we have a look at his room, please?'

The woman shrugged. She had a beaten, wary look. But was finally able to ask, 'What's all this about anyway?'

'We hope your husband can help us with some enquiries.'

'Oh.' A flat response and both officers had the impression that Rose Anne Marjerison had been prescribed pills to help her through the day as well as the night. 'This way,' she said.

'DO I GET a copy?' Marjerison nodded to the tape recorder with the twin cassettes whose spools were rotating steadily and silently.

'Of course.' Montgomerie nodded. 'That's the whole idea. You get a copy of the tape of this interview to give to your lawyer should we decide to charge you. It's part of the Police and Criminal Evidence Act. It's a simple device to prevent ourselves from concocting statements.'

Marjerison smiled.

'And more importantly—' Montgomerie's tone was stern '—it prevents you from alleging that we concocted anything. Shall we get back to it?' he added as Marjerison's smile waned.

'Suits me.'

'Pam McArthur?'

'Who?'

'The young woman who annoyed your father.'

'Oh yes, the other officer mentioned her.'

'As did your father.'

'To you?'

'No, to you.'

'Did he?'

'So he told us. We can always go back and ask him to confirm that he told you about her.'

'Really rather you didn't. He's got a heart condition.'

'We can pin down the date of McArthur's murder to being the 6th June last year. Where were you on the 6th June last year?'

'In Canada.'

Silence. The spools turned. Phil Hamilton sitting behind Montgomerie stared hard at Marjerison.

All three men knew the answer had come too freely, too quickly, to be truthful; it had the unmistakable ring of a fabricated alibi. Marjerison looked stunned, knowing what he'd said, looking as though he wanted to be thirty seconds younger so he could play the scene again.

'Sure of your dates?' Montgomerie asked.

A pause, as if thinking. 'Yes,' said Marjerison, 'I'm sure.' But the damage was done.

'I mean I only suggest that because I think that if I had been overseas seven months ago and somebody asked me where I was on a particular day, when I was abroad, I'd have to think and check the dates.'

A flash of anxiety crossed Marjerison's eyes. 'I remember the date well,' he said, attempting to recover ground.

'Why?'

'Why what?'

'Why do you remember the date well?'

'I just do.'

'Why?'

'Is it important why?'

'It could help your credibility.'

'Is it at risk?'

'Frankly, yes.' Montgomerie held his pen over his pad. 'You'll forgive me but your statement that you were in Canada has the impression of being a prepared alibi. I have not been a police officer for very long but I have noticed that legitimate alibis tend to emerge, whereas fabricated alibis tend to be pushed under our noses. Just as you pushed yours just now.'

'I did?'

'Yes. You look like a man who's just realized that he's made a dreadful mistake. Do you wish a solicitor to be present?'

Marjerison glared at him. 'No, I don't want a solicitor.'

'Just so long as you know that you are entitled to one.'

'I don't need a solicitor.'

'It won't be taken as an indication of guilt,' Montgomerie said. 'In fact, it won't be taken as an indication of anything at all.'

'I don't want a solicitor. I was in Canada on the 6th June last year. I know because I spent the entire month of June in Canada. That's why I was certain where I was on the 6th. Simple as that. I knew I flew out on the 1st June and I came back on the 30th June. I know those dates because the receptionist at the travel agent commented on the dates; she said something about going out on the 1st June and coming back on the last day. She said it was "neat".' But Marjerison's indignation was a little too theatrical for either Montgomerie or Hamilton to give it great credibility.

'Doubtless your passport will have stamps of entry at whatever airport...'

'Toronto. It did.'

'Did?'

'I lost it. I lost it shortly after my return. I did report its loss, as I understand I am obliged to.'

'So, we'll have a record of that?'

'I would hope so. Pretty poor police force if you haven't. I still have the air tickets—the counterfoils, that is, of the flights. I keep them as keepsakes. I also sent postcards home to my family friends and colleagues. I think that's good enough to put me in Canada on the day you mention.'

Montgomerie nodded. He had to concede a point. Perhaps. 'You travelled alone?'

'Yes. I went alone and returned alone. Over there I was with people most of the time. It was a business trip combined with a little pleasure. If you see what I mean?'

'I don't.'

'Well, my wife and I are not too happy. I have to take my pleasures when and where I can.'

'I see.'

'Knew you would if you tried.'

A cold eye-to-eye contact. Brief and mutually hostile.

A pause.

'We'd like you to take part in an identity parade.'

Marjerison raised his eyebrows. 'Do I have to?'

'No, we can't force you. But if you refuse you then invite us to think what we must think, and maybe lay before the court the fact that you refused to take part and so invite the jury to think what it must think. But only if it gets that far.'

'You leave me no option.'

Montgomerie nodded. 'The interview terminates at 11.35.' He switched off the machine.

Hamilton escorted Marjerison to the cell corridor. He returned to the uniform bar where Elka Willems was taking details from a distraught elderly lady who had lost her wee terrier. Montgomerie half sat on a desk consulting his notes. He looked up as Hamilton approached.

'All banged up,' said Hamilton. 'Not saying anything.'

'Didn't think he would. You know, Phil, this one's a cool customer.'

'Seems like it.'

Montgomerie tapped his note pad with his pen. 'Tell me, Phil. If Marjerison did fill in Pam McArthur, yet flew to Canada six days prior to her death, sent postcards from Canada as well, then how did he do it?'

Hamilton mused. 'You're the one with the degree. I left school at sixteen.'

'I didn't complete my degree,' Montgomerie said with a grin. 'But I can't see how he did it. We'll be able to check the postcard bit, but if the postmarks tally and they're clearly in his handwriting...'

'He may have had an accomplice?' Hamilton suggested. 'Someone to bring postcards from Canada, or post them to him. He returns them with messages on the back and his friend posts them on an agreed date...'

'Maybe...but he'd still have to fly to Canada. It's not possible to have someone fly under your name because passports are checked against air tickets.'

'A puzzle.'

Montgomerie smiled. 'No, it's not. It would be exhausting but not impossible.'

'What would?'

'To fly there, then return, do the business, fly back to Canada and return as planned on the 30th June.'

'The visa requirements would prevent it.'

'That's the beauty of it. If you hold a full British passport you can fly to and from Canada as often as you wish. No visas are necessary. My aunt does so regularly to visit my other aunt. Once or twice a year she hops on a plane to visit her sister for a natter, like any other woman would hop on a bus to visit her sister for a natter.'

'As you say, exhausting but not impossible.'

'I recall Petty saying that the man who murdered McArthur was sleepy on the day. I also recall that Mrs Sloan—'

'Who?'

'A witness who saw our man, now in the cells, leave McArthur's house some weeks after she was reported missing. He murdered her, flew back to Canada and when he returned to Scotland on the 30th June he took a risk and went to McArthur's house and removed her computer discs. This is beginning to fall into place. Now, we're five or six hours ahead of Canada...sorry, Phil, I'm just thinking aloud here...if he flew into Prestwick on the morning of the 6th June he'd be in a position to murder McArthur and fly out again on the same day. Prestwick's only one hour from Glasgow by bus or train.'

'Could be done.'

'It would explain why he "lost" his passport. If the customs in Canada stamped it on his second arrival he couldn't use it as an alibi.'

'Fits.'

'So if he left Canada on a flight which left Toronto for example at shall we say 6.00 p.m., local time, on the 5th June, not only would he arrive in Scotland at 8.00

or 9.00 a.m. on the 6th June, but he could post post-cards at the airport, and if he missed the last collection of that day, then the cards would be postmarked the 6th June.'

'Thus giving him a strong alibi.'

'Very strong. Postcards in his writing, postmarked Canada, 6th June. Allegedly putting him in Canada when we believed he was in Glasgow wringing Pam McArthur's neck in front of a stunned audience comprising Dalton Bayliss and Wayne Petty.'

'Clever.'

'Brittle, I'd say. Because unless he went to extraordinary lengths to obtain a false identity, fly out on one passport and back with another...I don't think he'd do that. He'd trust to luck that we wouldn't twig or wouldn't have the resources to check the passenger manifests of all flights flying from Canada to the UK between the 2nd and the 6th June...so he'd fly back under his real name.'

'We could narrow it down a lot...'

'We could narrow it down to one flight, Phil. If we're lucky. Can I ask you to do that? I'll have to write up the interview in the file.'

'Certainly.'

'Phone Prestwick Airport flight information. If a flight arrived from Canada on the morning of the 6th June last year we'd like to know the carrier. If it's a British carrier, phone them direct; if it's a Canadian carrier, you'll have to go through Interpol. What we want to know is if a passenger by the name of Toby Marjerison appears on the passenger manifest for that flight. They'll keep records going back that far, and further, in fact.'

'Very good.'

'I'm not too bothered about his exit date. Right now we just need to place him in Scotland on the morning of the murder and his alibi is out of the window.'

EIGHT MEN STOOD in a line in the muster room of P Division Police Station. All eight were white European, all eight were in their early thirties, all eight were well built with dark hair, and all were neatly dressed. It had taken two hours for uniformed officers to trawl the streets of Glasgow town centre for seven men who met the appearance requirements and who were willing to give up an hour of their time. Toby Marjerison had been brought into the room as the eighth and final man in the line-up. He elected to stand at the end of the line. Two constables stood in attendance.

The door opened. Mrs Sloan entered, accompanied by Abernethy. She stood and surveyed the line of men and then confidently walked up to Marjerison and grabbed his upper arm. She turned and beamed at Abernethy as if pleased with herself.

Sara Sinclair, with scarlet fingernails, walked up and down the line. She once paused in front of Marjerison and then walked on. Finally she looked at Abernethy and shook her head. Abernethy glanced at Marjerison just in time to see him smirk.

Wayne Petty entered the room in the company of a warder from Polmont Borstal. He stood and glanced at the men and then he walked boldly up to Marjerison and touched his shoulder. Marjerison glared at him.

Roddy McGee entered the room, unsteady on two aluminium crutches. He glanced along the line and shook his head. 'I'm sorry,' he said. 'It was dark and raining. I couldn't be certain.'

'It's no worry,' said Abernethy, 'no worry at all.'

DISAPPOINTMENT. Both Donoghue and King felt deep disappointment as they entered Toby Marjerison's bedroom.

Save for a small rug, the floorboards were bare, not even varnished as is fashionable among householders of Toby 'two' Marjerison's generation, especially those who live near the university. The bed was a metal-framed affair painted yellow. A cabinet which appeared second-hand stood beside the bed. A walk-in wardrobe lined the wall opposite the door. Donoghue opened it. It contained row upon row, rack upon rack, of fashionable and expensive clothing. He shut the doors of the wardrobe with a series of clicks.

'See, that's my husband.' Rose Anne Marjerison appeared to read the officers' thoughts. 'All image and no substance. Even his beloved car is worth more than the house. His clothing is worth more than the rest of the contents of the house combined, including my clothing.'

Donoghue looked at Rose Anne Marjerison and smiled in an understanding manner. He turned away and walked to the window, peeled back the net curtains and looked out again on the small garden to the rear of the house. He saw a garden shed to the left-hand side which had not been visible from the downstairs room. The door of the garden shed flapped and banged in the breeze. It looked out of place in such a house.

Rose Anne Marjerison came up and stood beside him and followed his gaze. 'It's not like him to leave it ajar. I'll sort it later. Maybe the latch is away.'

'Mrs Marjerison—' Donoghue turned to her '—do you know where your husband was on the 6th June?'

'This year past, you mean?'

'Yes.'

'June . . . yes, aye, how could I forget? He was away in Canada. I can't remember the exact dates, but he was away for most of the month. I know because I spent the entire month with my mother in Barrhead. Just me and Toby three; it was pure heaven. See marriage . . .' She shook her head. 'He sent us a couple of cards from Toronto, then he came back and my so-called marriage started up again.'

'He left the car here?'

'Aye, and you know there's a thing, he's only the one set of keys for the thing and he won't let anybody drive it. He's so possessive of it that he even took the keys to Canada with him. But the car was moved when he was away.'

'It was moved?'

'Only a couple of feet, back up the drive, against the incline so it couldn't have been the brakes slipped a wee bit and it rolled forward.'

'You certain?'

'Certain. Positive certain. See I'd call back once every two or three days to check the house and pick up the post, and for the first week I had to walk on the front lawn because I couldn't get between the Rolls Royce and the gorse bush, not without tearing my tights to shreds. Then I called at the house and found I could walk between the gorse bush and the car—the car was just a couple of feet further up the drive, you see.'

'I see. Can you remember the date that you first noticed that the car had been moved?'

'Yes . . . it was the 8th June. The next day, the 9th, is my mother's birthday. I had to go into the town to buy her card and a wee present. I did that and then drove out to Bearsden and found I could get between the bush and the car quite the thing.'

'When were you last at the house before that?'

'I don't recall. Maybe four or five days. No, not as much as five days, maybe three or four.'

'So on the 4th or the 5th of June, when you called at the house you had to walk on the front lawn because you couldn't walk up the drive between the car and the gorse bush. But when you called on the 8th you could, in fact, walk easily between the car and the gorse bush.'

'That's what I said. Couldn't understand it because cars don't move uphill by themselves. Somebody had to have driven it, but the only keys were in Canada with Toby two. I could only assume that Toby had given a spare set of keys to someone without telling me.'

King asked: 'Did you mention the fact that you had noticed the car to have been moved to your husband at all?'

'No.'

'Sure?' asked Donoghue.

'Certain. We don't talk at all. I knew what he'd say if I had mentioned it. Something along the lines of the Rolls Royce is his business and his business alone.'

'The postcards he sent you,' King asked, 'did they come here or to your mother's address in Barrhead?'

'To my mother's. Toby knew we'd be staying there.'

'And that nobody would be living here during the month of June?'

'That's right. What is all this?'

But Donoghue didn't seem to hear her. 'The postcards he sent. Do you still have them?'

'They're in the wardrobe behind you. He sent them to us but kept them for himself for some reason, clipped to the air tickets.'

Donoghue turned and opened one of the wardrobe doors.

'Other end I think,' said Rose Anne Marjerison. 'Near the ties. I found them when I was putting the ironing away.'

Donoghue went to the other end of the wardrobe and found the cards among the ties. He glanced at the postmark on each and handed them to King. 'Is that your husband's handwriting?'

'Yes. They're from him all right.'

'Sixth June,' King said, a note of dismay in his voice. 'One was posted in Toronto on the 6th June.'

'So I saw,' Donoghue replied. 'Can we keep the cards and the airline tickets, please?'

IN THE CAR, driving back to Charing Cross, Donoghue broke the silence: 'The card clears him, Richard.'

'Would seem to, sir. Funny how the date is so convenient. There's a card posted on the 2nd.' King looked at the postcards. 'Ties in with his arrival. One on the 5th, one on the 6th. Then nothing until the 14th. Then they seem to be once every four or five days until the 27th.'

'So we don't know where he was from the 6th to the 14th?'

'Not by these cards. But the important thing is this one card, and I suppose others he sent to friends, relatives and colleagues, which places him in Toronto on the day of the murder in Glasgow. Seems so cast iron.'

'Too cast iron for me,' Donoghue growled.

ROSE ANNE MARJERISON sat in the chair in the living room. Toby three stood in the playpen. Normally she didn't occupy this chair, normally it was his chair, but after the police officers had left it seemed the appropriate thing to do.

The garden shed door banged in the wind.

Why? she thought. Why had the police called? Wanting to know dates. Wanting to know about her husband.

The garden shed door banged, insistently. Invitingly. Invitingly.

She rose slowly. She said, 'It'll be all right, Toby, promise,' and left the room. She had an aching feeling in her stomach. Her knees were weak. She slipped into a waterproof jacket and went outside to the garden shed.

Just inside the shed door was the spade. The one garden spade they possessed. It was not in its usual place, especially in the winter months—in the winter months it was not so close to hand. And the blade of the spade was smeared with clay soil, damp clay soil.

She stepped backwards and shut the shed door. She glanced to her left and surveyed the garden. She noticed freshly tilled soil in the bottom right-hand corner.

She hesitated.

Would she dig it up? Whatever 'it' was. Would she rebury 'it', if she did dig 'it' up? Would it then become like most everything else in her marriage, happened, or happening, but unspoken of?

How long could it go on like this, for her and Toby three? Rain pattered against her head and streamed down the waterproof jacket, making her jeans cling soaking to her legs.

Eventually she unlatched the door and reached for the spade.

'TWO POSITIVE identifications of Marjerison, sir,' said Abernethy as Donoghue peeled off his raincoat and hung it and his hat, dripping, on a peg. King unzipped his jacket and kept it on while he listened. 'Mrs Sloan...'

'She would,' said Donoghue icily.

'. . . and Wayne Petty. That's an actual eyewitness to the murder.'

'Or mistaken identity.' Donoghue sat heavily in a vacant chair. 'We're just come from the Marjerison home in Bearsden. We've got a postcard which puts Marjerison in Toronto on the day of the murder. You have it there, Richard?'

King handed the cards to Donoghue.

'Here we are. The CN Tower in Toronto, by night, if you please.' He turned it over. 'Postmarked Toronto, 6th June last year. In Marjerison's handwriting. The Fiscal won't proceed against this evidence.'

'Oh, I don't know,' said Montgomerie. 'When I interviewed Marjerison he seemed too certain of his alibi, so I pondered, I had a notion. Phil Hamilton's doing some telephone work . . .' and he explained to an attentive Detective Inspector Donoghue the nature of his notion.

'Blimey,' said King.

The phone rang. Montgomerie answered it and then said, 'Thanks, Phil, thanks a lot.' He replaced the receiver and smiled. 'Who said long shots don't pay off.'

Donoghue played the flame of his lighter over the bowl of what he then knew would be a very satisfying pipe. 'So tell us.'

'Had to go through Interpol in the end, but a Wardair flight from Toronto to Prestwick arrived on the 6th June at 9.00 a.m. The passenger manifest contains the name Marjerison, Toby.'

'Well, that's one alibi down the tubes. Well done, you.' Donoghue pulled on his pipe. 'We'll go and have another chat with him. But he won't be leaving custody. Not for a long time.'

The phone rang again. Abernethy looked at it impatiently and then answered it. He listened and then said, 'Thank you, thank you very much. We'll attend directly.' He replaced the receiver. 'That was—'

'Mrs Marjerison,' said Donoghue. 'What did she have to say?'

'How did—?'

'I just did, I just did. I have an inner voice which I have honed over the years and I have learned to listen to it. Of all the things that stick in my mind about the Marjerison household, it's the garden shed, with the door swinging in the wind, and Mrs Marjerison saying that her husband didn't normally leave it like that. All the way back to Glasgow I knew we should have checked the interior of the shed, but for some reason I just didn't turn round... So what has she found? A pile of bloodstained clothes and some computer discs?'

'No, sir, machete. Buried in her garden, wrapped in a plastic bin liner,' said Abernethy. 'She's not seen it before. She says it appears to be bloodstained. Heavily so.'

'Good enough.' Donoghue leaned backwards and drew lovingly on his pipe. 'That's quite good enough.' Then he stood and walked to the window of the CID room and glanced out across the Charing Cross Interchange and watched an elderly man in a flat cap walk underneath the graceful curve of Charing Cross Mansions. Donoghue watched as the man stopped suddenly as if remembering something and then turn and hurriedly retrace his steps.

In Bearsden a woman in damp clothing replaced her phone and stood by it for a minute, perhaps two, and then returned to her living room where she knelt by her infant son and said, 'I don't know what's happening but I think it's just you and me now.' And in the east end of

the sprawling premier city a young man sat mesmerized by the hissing flames of a gas fire, and his mind
dwelt upon the image of a gracefully slim, olive-skinned
girl in a green bathing costume.

...A DANGEROUS THING
BILL CRIDER
A Carl Burns Mystery

First Time In Paperback

PAINFUL CORRECTNESS

The new dean of Hartley Gorman College arrives with an agenda of political correctness that hits Professor Carl Burns where it hurts: Shakespeare, Milton, Homer, Wordsworth—all of his DWEMs (Dead White European Males) must go.

True, the new curriculum at HGC has wrought some controversy, but when a popular professor takes a fatal flying leap out a window, it's death by anybody's definition.

Between grading papers and vying for the affection of the librarian, Burns discovers a sordid tangle of lust, scandal and secrets that draw him into a chase for an elusive and unlikely killer.

"An amusingly self-effacing...mystery series."
—*New York Times Book Review*

Available in October at your favorite retail stores.

To order your copy, please send your name, address, zip or postal code along with a check or money order (please do not send cash) for $4.99 for each book ordered ($5.99 in Canada), plus 75¢ postage and handling ($1.00 in Canada), payable to Worldwide Mystery, to:

In the U.S.	In Canada
Worldwide Mystery	Worldwide Mystery
3010 Walden Avenue	P.O. Box 609
P.O. Box 1325	Fort Erie, Ontario
Buffalo, NY 14269-1325	L2A 5X3

Please specify book title with your order.
Canadian residents add applicable federal and provincial taxes.

 **WORLDWIDE LIBRARY**®

THING

THE JULIUS HOUSE
CHARLAINE
HARRIS

First Time in Paperback

An Aurora Teagarden Mystery

AS LONG AS YOU BOTH SHALL LIVE

Aurora "Roe" Teagarden is busy planning her wedding to Martin Bartell, a successful businessman with a past he hasn't completely shared. His gift to her is a storybook house shrouded in mystery: its owners, the Julius family, disappeared six years earlier.

Roe begins decorating and digging into the puzzle of the Julius house. But when Martin installs a couple in the garage apartment, she gets the feeling they're more than just tenants....

As Aurora discovers the truth about the Julius family, she realizes their fate may well be her own.

"Best of the series to date..."   —*Publishers Weekly*

Available in October at your favorite retail stores.

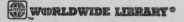

CRIMINALS ALWAYS HAVE SOMETHING TO HIDE—BUT THE ENJOYMENT YOU'LL GET OUT OF A WORLDWIDE MYSTERY NOVEL IS NO SECRET....

With Worldwide Mystery on the case, we've taken the mystery out of finding something good to read every month.

Worldwide Mystery is guaranteed to have suspense buffs and chill seekers of all persuasions in eager pursuit of each new exciting title!

Worldwide Mystery novels—crimes worth investigating...

HARLEQUIN®

I N T R I G U E®

THAT'S INTRIGUE—DYNAMIC ROMANCE AT ITS BEST!

Harlequin Intrigue is now bringing you more—more men and mystery, more desire and danger. If you've been looking for thrilling tales of contemporary passion and sensuous love stories with taut, edge-of-the-seat suspense—then you'll *love* Harlequin Intrigue!

Every month, you'll meet four new heroes who are guaranteed to make your spine tingle and your pulse pound. With them you'll enter into the exciting world of Harlequin Intrigue—where your life is on the line and so is your heart!

Harlequin Intrigue—we'll leave you breathless!